P9-EJP-834

As they walked into the hall, a light, clear voice called out from the head of the stairs, "As I live and breathe, if my dear father has not taken unto himself a bride—or is it the usual liaison, dear parent?"

There was no mistaking the malice in the voice. Then down the stairs came the speaker, a tall, slender young man of about Mellie's own age. He was *en négligé*, a long green retiring robe of brocaded silk trailing on the stairs. Frills of lace draped over his hands, which he waved languidly at his father. Mellie could see that he was painted white with lead, and his cheeks and lips were red, the way a woman might be made up.

This was Lord Henning's son! Mellie was aghast that such a virile man could have fathered an effeminate offspring. Somehow it came as a shock that he had a son, for there'd been no mention of family. Was there also a wife? If Henning meant to take her for a mistress, why did her new wardrobe contain a wedding gown?

"A bit young for you, isn't she, Father?" the son asked with ill-concealed spite. "You're rather long in the tooth to bed such youth."

With an edge that she'd never heard before in his voice, Henning replied, "I know that. I have not brought her here for my pleasure—but for your own.

***YOU AND MELLIE WILL BE MARRIED
BY SPECIAL LICENSE AT THE END
OF THIS WEEK . . ."***

WE HOPE YOU ENJOY THIS BOOK

If you'd like a free list of other paperbacks
available from PLAYBOY PRESS,
just send your request to:

Marilyn Adams
PLAYBOY PRESS
919 North Michigan Avenue
Chicago, Illinois 60611

(Please enclose 25¢ to help pay for postage and handling.)

MOMENT of DESIRE

Rachel Cosgrove Payes

PLAYBOY PRESS
PAPERBACKS

MOMENT OF DESIRE

Copyright© 1978 by Rachel Cosgrove Payes.

Cover illustration by Gino D'Achille: Copyright© 1978 by Playboy

All rights reserved. No part of this book may be reproduced, stored in a retrieval system or transmitted in any form by an electronic, mechanical, photocopying, recording
means or otherwise without prior written permission of the author.

Published simultaneously in the United States and Canada by Playboy Press,
Chicago, Illinois. Printed in the United States of America. Library of Congress
Catalog Card Number: 78-58394. First edition.

This book is available at quantity discounts for promotional and industrial use. For
further information, write our sales-promotion agency: Ventura Associates, 40 East
49th Street, New York, New York 10017

ISBN: 0-872-16481-0

For Norman, Ruth, and Rob
from your very own
Playboy Bunny

Published by arrangement... [illegible]
Avon Books, New York, New York 10019

ISBN 0-87216-481-9

CHAPTER ONE

Melusina Wilton hurried from St. James's Palace to where the palace sedan chairs were waiting. Unless she hurried, she'd be late, Hockley-in-the-Hole would be jammed, and she'd never see young Lord Densbury. It was all Helga's fault for not having her gown mended. Mellie could have worn another dress, but the deep blue velvet of this one set off her golden hair and bright blue eyes to perfection. She didn't know which of the younger ladies-in-waiting would be with Alistair Lord Densbury today; but as they all were older than Mellie's fourteen—almost fifteen!—years, she knew she was at a disadvantage. Rushing up to the first sedan chair in line, a fine affair of gilt with maroon velvet curtains to shut out the ugly sights, sounds, and even some of the smells of London on this fine April day in the year of our Lord, 1715, she rapped sharply to attract the bearers.

The front chair bearer bobbed, tricorne in hand, and asked, "Where to, milady?"

"Hockley-in-the-Hole. And, oh, I'm in the most awful rush." Mellie consulted the program that she'd filched from the pocket in Lady Breckinridge's cloak when she hadn't been looking. "The baiting starts at three sharp."

The bearer, a middle-aged man with powerful shoulders, gave her a sharp look from under bushy black eyebrows. "You ain't goin' alone, milady? Not a fit place for a young lady to go without an escort."

Fluttering her long eyelashes, practicing her coquetry on him, Mellie said, all wide-eyed innocence, "Oh, I'm with a group of ladies-in-waiting to Ehrengard Melusina von Schulenberg. But I forgot my money, and had to run back for it. Please do hurry. They're baiting both a bear and a bull today. I don't want to miss any of the program."

"You want us to wait for you, milady?"

Mellie nodded imperiously, getting into the chair and wrapping her best maroon cloak around her to try to keep her skirts from getting dusty. "I scarcely can walk back all the way from Clerkenwell," she said.

"Then whistle up a linkboy," the front bearer told his younger helper. "It'll be fair dark when we leave Ray Street, if they're baiting two animals. We'll need a torch."

Then the little procession started off, the bearers going at a trot, along the Mall toward Charing Cross. Once they were in motion, Mellie pulled her satin pocket from under one of the flounces on her full skirt, and took from it the tiny silk purse in which she kept her meager supply of coins. She'd heard Densbury mention that it cost four shillings to get into the baiting, and she'd have to give the bearers at least a ha'penny each. Oh, drat! The linkboy, too. Well, she'd have enough, but if she wanted any refreshment, she would have to find Densbury, or one of the other young blades who hung around the court of King George, and use her budding womanly wiles to coax a sweet or a glass of ale from them.

Mellie peered out of the chair's window anxiously. If her men hurried, she might catch up with Densbury and his friends. They could scarcely ignore her once she was there. And, anyway, Mellie'd noticed lately that when she managed to insinuate herself into the group of young courtiers, Densbury's eyes always strayed to her swelling breasts. There was something in the young marquis's hot hazel eyes that made Mellie feel stark naked when he ogled her bosom.

That was one reason she'd chosen this gown and insisted that Helga lace her tighter than usual. It was quite low-cut, and the cinched-in stays pushed her bosom so high that Helga had insisted on tucking a bit of lace into the décolletage.

"Your mother wouldn't allow you out the door without a modesty bit, Miss Mellie."

Mellie had learned not to argue with the abigail who'd tattle to Mama; but once outside, she had removed the lace so that her cleavage showed. Mama wasn't going to bother with her today. Lady Anna Wilton had better things to do than to worry about a nearly grown daughter. The Duchess of Seybrook was in Kent; but the duke was at the court, and Mellie knew her mother would be entertaining the handsome lord in her bed this afternoon. Which suited Mellie just fine. She could go off to the bearbaiting without consulting Mama who might just refuse to allow her to go alone.

Once past Charing Cross, the traffic became so congested that Mellie despaired of getting to Hockley before the program started.

Poking her head out of the sedan chair window, she asked, "Why are we going so slowly?"

The younger bearer in the back said, "Big wreck ahead, milady. A coach and six blocking the road, all leaned over, it is, must have lost a wheel."

Just then he stepped on a slippery rounded stone and nearly fell, making the chair lurch so hard that Mellie shrieked, and clutched at the window frame to keep from being thrown headfirst into the muck.

"Do watch where you're going," she admonished, petulant. "And isn't there some way to go around that coach? I'm in a hurry! I told you that."

"Well, milady," the front bearer called back, "if we go up on the pavement, someone'll object. And I've no wish to be beaten."

"I'll make sure nothing happens," she promised airily. "Maybe you can turn down a side street off the Strand. It's not always so crowded there."

"We'll try; but some of them streets ain't so safe."

Just then another chair hit theirs, jolting Mellie so hard that she bumped her head on the window frame and gave her tongue a painful bite.

Insolent fellows! They just didn't want to have to hurry. When she married well—and Lord Densbury was heir to a dukedom in Kent—she'd have all her own bearers and wouldn't have to put up with such coarse fellows as these. However, Mellie knew all too well that if she said too much to them, or complained too loudly, they'd only go more slowly, always with an excuse that the mud was slippery, or the cobbles too rough for undue haste. Then she'd be unconscionably late to the baiting! She just had to get there in time to sit with darling Alistair. She wished now that she'd coaxed Helga to powder her hair, for so many of the ladies at court were now using powder; but old stick-in-the-mud Helga would have insisted on asking Mama, and Mama didn't appreciate being interrupted when she was entertaining the Duke of Seybrook. Mellie still cringed when she thought of that time about a month ago when she'd gone bursting into Mama's bedroom without knocking: Mama and her current lover had been making the four-poster bed sway until the curtains that had mercifully hid them bellied out around the bedclothes.

Mellie had retreated as rapidly as she'd entered, and luckily her mother had been too busy with her lusty partner to hear the door; but it had been a close call. Mama would have been furious if she'd realized Mellie was there. And the worst part was Mama's utter indiscretion with this latest in her long string of lovers. Her mother's behavior had been occurring for as long as Mellie could remember, while they were still in Hanover and her poor, unlucky papa was still alive. He'd turned his back on Mama's goings-on, preferring to be cuckolded rather than take Mama to task. Mama had a tongue as sharp as an Italian dagger when she was angered.

But if Mama had locked the door, none of this would have happened. One of these days someone else would walk in and find Mama in bed with a man who had a wife, and there'd be a real scandal. Scandals could be fun, and exciting. It was all that kept life interesting at court. But Mellie knew that if Mama was involved in a scandal, some of the nastiness might well rub off on her. If she were to get a rich husband, she'd best not be involved in anything naughty.

Once onto Fleet Street, her bearers did turn off the main thoroughfare into a maze of crooked, foul-smelling little lanes that twisted and turned until Mellie was quite lost.

"Are you sure this is the way to Hockley-in-the-Hole?" she demanded, pulling aside the curtains so that the bearers could hear her, but keeping her head inside for safety. A few blocks past, some woman had emptied a chamber pot out of an upper window, and the contents had just missed Mellie's chair, splattering the rear bearer, and bringing on a torrent of language that startled her. Some of the words she'd never heard before, even at court where the coarsest of talk was commonplace. Mellie stored them up in her quick mind. There might be times when she could use them, perhaps amaze a certain young nobleman with her sophistication.

The younger bearer assured her, "Gets us to the baitin' pit straight away, milady. Never fear. You'll not be late. Me and old Tad, there, will go in and watch, too, long's we must wait to carry you back to the palace."

Mellie wrinkled her nose in distaste. How presumptuous of the fellow to make it sound as if he'd mingle with his betters at the baiting.

A long, shrill whistle was heard up ahead, and her bearers stopped so abruptly that Mellie almost slid off the seat.

This time she did risk putting her head out of the sedan chair window. "Now what? We'll never get there. The bear will be dead and the bull dying before I arrive."

"Shh, milady," the older bearer hissed. "Did ye no hear the whistle? Some linkboy up ahead is signalin' the footpads."

As Tad said this, the younger bearer reached out and caught their own linkboy, a scruffy lad in ragged coat and breeches, by the front of his homespun shirt. "You in with 'em, lad? 'Twas you that said this was a quick way to the Hole." He shook the youngster as a terrier would shake a rat, until his face nearly turned purple.

"N-no, no," he gasped. Seeing Mellie's inquisitive face peering from the chair, he pleaded, "Save me, milady. I'm not in with the footpads."

"Oh, put him down," she scolded. "But get us out of this foul place." She had pulled her vinaigrette from her pocket and was sniffing daintily, not so much to ward off faintness, but just to counter the stench. It had been bad enough along the Strand, with the combination of horse droppings, garbage, and stale water in the ditches alongside the street. But here, in the heart of the London slums, the odor was almost overpowering. "Footpads needn't bother with us," she added bitterly. "The little money my mother gives me wouldn't be enough to tempt them."

"Shh!" Tad warned again. "Don't even say the word of money. Them's fierce men, the robbers. Take a penny off a dead man's eye, they would."

She shuddered. "Then let's get out of this district. You should never have brought me this way."

The younger one started to mutter something about, "*You* was in such a hur——" but Tad gave him a quick shake of the head and a warning glare. It didn't do to antagonize young ladies from the palace, or they'd not be allowed to keep their chair there.

Finally they moved onto Clerkenwell Road, and although it was very crowded, the people moving on it were of a better class than the drabs she'd just been watching in the slum section. How could those women bear to wear such dull gowns? Mellie wondered. She'd be mortified if she must wear such gowns of stuff or coarse wool. How dreary it must be to be poor. Mellie never could stand to exist in such a slum warren as they'd passed through. She pulled a tiny, jeweled mirror from her pocket and inspected her flawless skin to make sure that she'd not picked up some horrid skin disease by passing through that dreadful section.

"Ray Street just ahead, miss," Tad called back to her. "The crowd's still gatherin' for the baitin'. We'll get you close to the door so's not to soil your slippers."

"Oh, I mustn't ruin these," she exclaimed artlessly. "They're made from the finest Belgian kid. They do dye the leathers so expertly, don't you think?'' she asked. But Tad didn't answer.

Mellie was in luck—for once she'd paid her four shillings for a seat, she saw Lord Densbury almost immediately. With a most unladylike haste, she wormed her way through the crush of people, tipping her hoops and showing a lot more leg than was considered proper, in order to ''happen'' on Densbury and his crowd by accident.

By now she had a little silk and ivory fan out, using it to slyly poke at people who were in the way. When she had maneuvered herself into an advantageous position, she opened the fan and half shielded her face with it until she caught Densbury's eye. Then she lowered the fan, smiling the same provocative smile she'd seen her mother smile at the Duke of Seybrook.

Although Densbury couldn't make a proper leg in the crush of people surging toward the railing around the pit, he nodded his head, smiled, and then said something to one of his friends, a rather horse-faced young man, a viscount or baron, Mellie had seen at court on occasion.

Then Densbury worked his way toward her. He looked very elegant today, clad in a satin coat of a rich plum color, with a contrasting waistcoat of gold with self embroidery. He was wearing a full periwig, curled and flowing about his elegantly broad shoulders. Peering at Mellie through his quizzing glass, Densbury said, ''By my life, if it isn't little Mellie Wilton.'' He glanced about perfunctorily. ''Is your mother, Lady Wilton, here to enjoy the baiting?''

''No, she was otherwise occupied, milord. I—I came alone, being so bored with nothing to do at court.''

''I'm sure your mother has no trouble keeping occupied.'' He guffawed, and leered suggestively. ''The—uh—Duchess of Seybrook—have you seen her recently?''

Mellie was mortified. Mama was so indiscreet! But she fluttered her fan and said, in what she hoped was the properly insouciant manner, ''I do believe that the duchess is in Kent—attending to the milking, perhaps.''

Densbury whooped with laughter. By this time his friend had joined them. ''Miss Melusina Wilton, may I present Bertie, the Baron Breckinridge.''

''Your servant, ma'am.'' He bobbed his long head at Mellie. ''And where did you find this choice bit?'' he murmured to Densbury in a stage whisper that could have been heard clear across the arena.

"Oh, she's at court. Just out of the nursery."

"Milord, I'd scarcely be here alone if I were that young," Mellie protested.

"Well, don't faint on us when the bear claws one of the dogs and spills its entrails," Bertie warned.

"If you do," Densbury added, his hot hazel eyes straying to her delectable bosom, "we'll have to unlace you to give you more air," and his hand strayed to the lacings under her full breasts, tugging playfully at the ribbons. In the midst of this horseplay, he managed to caress her bosom, sending a sudden flame of sensation through Mellie which started where his hot fingers touched, but which spread with a suddenness that made her gasp to her loins. Her impulse was to pull sharply away from his touch; but Mellie remembered that she was now fourteen, a young lady, and if this was what a man's touch did to you, no wonder Mama invited so many men to enjoy her flesh.

"Naughty," she managed to say, although her voice came out with a breathiness that was quite unlike her usual manner. She tapped Densbury's hand playfully with her folded fan.

A shout went up from the crowd just then, and Densbury reluctantly said, "They must be bringing in the bear. We'd better hurry or all the good seats will be taken."

It was an exciting afternoon. Mellie had been to only one bear-baiting previously, and in truth it had made her feel quite ill. But she was determined not to show any such infantile emotion today, not with Alistair crowded up against her on one side, and Bertie on the other. Bertie had tried to feel her bosom, too; but Densbury had seen his straying hand, and had warned him off with a fierce look.

"I'm treating myself today," Mellie confided. "Tomorrow is my birthday."

Densbury's eyes peered down her cleavage. "I won't ask how old you'll be. You're obviously old enough."

Bertie guffawed so loudly that people sitting near them turned to stare, and Mellie hid her face behind her fan in confusion.

Then the keeper led in a muzzled brown bear, its fur dirty and matted, its little eyes red and wicked. He fastened a fifteen-foot chain to the bear's collar, then made sure that the chain was secured by a staple on the wall of the pit. With the dexterity and speed of long practice, he slipped off the muzzle and scampered out of the range of the bear's snapping jaws and slashing claws. Then he disappeared through a stout door. Once the keeper was safely out of the way, the dogs—short, bowlegged short-hairs with heavy jaws and sharp teeth—were released into the pit.

A roar went up from the crowd as the bear, maddened by the scent of the six dogs, reared up on his hind feet, growling horrendously.

Mellie and her companions were in the second tier of seats, about twenty feet above the pit, with an excellent view of the tormented animal.

"Look at that little spotted dog go for the bear!" Alistair yelled. "A guinea that he draws first blood, Bertie."

"My money says the bear will kill that one," Bertie countered.

Mellie wished she could wager, too. That was the whole point of going to the baitings. Gambling was the main amusement of the nobility, and of the common people, too. Unfortunately her father, Sir Horace Wilton, had been an inveterate and excessively unlucky gambler until his death of consumption. He gambled away his small legacy as well as the salary he earned as a minor attaché sent by England to the court of the Elector of Hanover. There he'd met and married the earthy Anna, already a lady-in-waiting to Ehrengard Melusina von Schulenberg, one of George's favorites. The only legacy her papa had left Mellie was the excellent English he'd taught her to speak, which now served her in good stead at the Court of St. James.

"Care to make a small wager, Mellie?" Densbury asked, watching the fierce dogs move in on the bear. It was now down on all fours, ranging about the thirty-foot circle the chain allowed him, snarling, snapping, and swatting at the dogs as they dashed in to try to fasten their teeth in his flesh.

"I—frankly, I just can't afford to gamble today," she said prettily. "Mama hasn't given me my allowance yet."

Densbury put a proprietary arm about her, his busy fingers caressing her shoulder, slipping the gown down off her soft flesh as if by accident. "Wager me kisses, Mellie."

"Oh, milord, then you can't lose, can you?" she flirted. "For if my dog gets the first nip, you owe me a kiss—and if your dog wins, then I must give you a kiss."

"Which I'll collect right now!" he said with enthusiasm as the dog he'd chosen made a lunge, leaped for the bear's neck, and fastened his teeth into the flesh, hanging on tenaciously as the huge brute roared and shook his head from side to side trying to dislodge the beast.

Mellie quickly opened her fan to hide her face; but Densbury was quite as adept at the use of a fan as she was. He firmly but gently moved her hand away from her face, then bent to kiss her rosy lips, hiding both of them discreetly behind her fan. His lips were hot, and Mellie felt weak with emotion as they moved on hers, parting her lips so that his tongue could dart into her mouth like a flicking flame.

The roar of the crowd cut short the embrace, and Bertie was on his feet shouting, "Got him! Got him!" as some of the dogs now began tearing bloody hunks of fur from the bear's flanks, while one caught at its throat. The bear fought valiantly, catching a brown spotted dog with a massive paw, disemboweling it with one slash.

Densbury leaped up, too, caught up in the blood lust of the crowd howling with glee as the poor bear was finally brought down. The animal bled from a dozen wounds while the dogs yapped and snapped, ripping the bear's throat open so he died in a great gush of blood. Mellie felt distinctly queasy, so she fixed her eyes on Densbury's eager lips rather than watch the keepers who drove the snarling dogs away from the dead beast with staves, then unchained the bear and dragged the carcass from the pit, leaving a trail of blood behind.

"You owe me a guinea, Bertie," Densbury reminded his companion. "Pay up." He reached across Mellie for the gold piece, brushing against her bare bosom as he did so, casually, as if it were quite accidental. But Mellie saw him look at her from the corner of his eye as if to judge just how far he could go before she scolded him.

"Why is it you always win?" Bertie grumbled, fishing his Moroccan leather purse from his waistcoat pocket where he'd concealed it to foil pickpockets. He took out a gold piece and handed it to Densbury, who promptly fumbled it so that it dropped down the inviting cleft in the décolletage of Mellie's gown.

"Oops! Butterfingers," he chortled. "Mustn't lose the gold Bertie paid me, now, must I?" and before Mellie realized what he was up to, he was reaching down the front of her dress to rescue the coin.

She gave him a quick crack on the knuckles with her folded fan. "Naughty! Mustn't touch! I'll get your gold for you, Alistair."

He sucked his knuckles ruefully. "I was only trying. . . ."

Deftly she recovered the coin while his avid eyes devoured its hiding place between her firm young breasts.

"Ah, would that I were a gold guinea," he murmured in her ear. Then he kissed her ear, sending a warm wave of sensation through her so that her breath quickened, making her bosom heave invitingly. "I'll never spend this coin, dear Mellie," he went on extravagantly, "but shall carry it next to my heart always."

"Milord, how you do go on!" she said, but her voice wouldn't obey her, being breathy and low.

During the baiting of the bull, Densbury paid more attention to her than he did to the show in the pit, although the bull had his horns supplemented by longer oxen horns which were glued to the stumps of his own with pitch. One luckless bulldog was caught on the point of one of these vicious horns; and when the bull tossed his mighty head, roaring with pain and rage, the luckless dog flew through the air to land in the lap of a woman sitting only a few seats from Mellie and her companions.

The woman shrieked with terror and fainted, causing much excitement in the gallery.

Mellie shuddered. "Oh, look, she has blood all over the front of her gown. How dreadful!"

"If any blood should splash on you, I'd gladly wipe it off like this," and Densbury whipped a dainty lace kerchief from the cuff of his coat and proceeded to pat at her bosom until she playfully slapped his face in reprimand.

When the baiting was over, the two young noblemen had their chairs carried alongside Mellie's on the way back to the palace.

"Be sure to come to my special dinner tomorrow," Mellie invited. "The Maypole is giving it for me. I'm her namesake, you know."

"Luckily the only sameness is your name," Densbury said. "If you live to be sixty, you'll never look like the Maypole."

Bertie snickered. "Our gracious majesty likes 'em ugly."

"But with variety, Bertie. The Elephant is as fat as the Maypole is tall and skinny. And you, dear Mellie, are just right," he added, leaning through the window of his chair to talk to her.

Her pulse raced, even though he was no longer pressed close against her as he'd been at the bear pit. Mellie couldn't wait for tomorrow! Her fifteenth birthday was going to be spectacular, now that she'd finally caught the eye of her idol, Alistair Lord Densbury. He was considered the catch of all the younger men at court, and Mellie was sure he was hers. If Mama would consent to an early marriage, Mellie would soon be rich, and a marchioness to boot.

CHAPTER TWO

Mellie had just left her chair and was walking with Alistair and Bertie into the palace when a coach and four clattered up, stopping just ahead of them.

"Isn't that . . ." Bertie started, only to be silenced with a sharp elbow in his ribs from Densbury.

Mellie, seeing the byplay, took a good look at the landau. On the door of the gleaming yellow coach, picked out in brilliant color, was a familiar coat of arms: a griffin rampant on a field of blue. The coat of arms of the Duke of Seybrook. He must be leaving her mother's bed now, to return—then she got the shock of her young life; for the liveried footman leaped to place a stool for alighting as he swung open the door. From inside the landau there came a billowing of taffeta skirts, a dainty foot shod in white kid, and then the duchess herself, obviously in a hurry.

She'd catch Seybrook with her mother, if Mellie didn't get inside to warn them immediately.

"Milords, I fear I am frightfully late. Mama will be in a rage," she said breathlessly, picking up her skirts preparatory to running into the palace ahead of the duchess.

"What's another minute or two, Mellie?" Alistair asked, giving a quick look of recognition to the Duchess of Seybrook, and winking broadly at Bertie. "You must give me a farewell kiss, Mellie, or I shall think you were only toying with my affections."

Before she could escape, Densbury caught her in an embrace so tight that she could scarcely breathe, and his mouth found hers in a hot, passionate kiss that drove all thoughts of her mother's danger from her mind. Her untutored body responded to the nearness of this vital, male animal who demanded all her attention. The kiss left her shaking and gasping, with the blood rushing so tumultuously through her veins that it nearly deafened her.

From what seemed a mile away, she heard Bertie's sniggering, "Let the poor girl come up for air, Alistair!"

17

Bosom heaving, Mellie withdrew from his embrace reluctantly. Only then, when the landau came back into focus, did she remember her mother's possible predicament.

This time she fled precipitately, leaving the two young lords there on the broad steps in front of the palace. Their hoots of laughter followed her as she raced up the steps to try to get to their apartment before the Duchess of Seybrook began looking for her straying spouse.

Mellie fled along the wide corridors, but she was too late. Obviously the duchess had known exactly where to go to find her erring duke. As Mellie ran down the final long passageway, catching at the marble pilaster on the corner to swing her around the corner, she saw the duchess rapping imperiously at the paneled oak door to their private suite.

Hoping desperately that she still might somehow prevent the confrontation between the duchess, her cheating husband, and Mellie's mother, the girl hurried down the corridor, arriving breathless at the duchess's side just as Helga opened the door to the urgent summons.

Dropping a curtsy, Mellie said, quite out of breath, "Your Grace, were you calling on dear Mama?" She could see the vixenish cast of the Duchess of Seybrook's face. It was a sharp little visage, dead white with cosmetic, except for bright red spots of rouge on either cheek, and an elaborate black beauty spot shaped like a coach and four which ran from the corner of her slash of carmined mouth almost to the angle of her jaw. Her eyes were topaz, her powdered wig tight under a round cap of finest India lawn, lace-trimmed.

Flicking an annoyed glance at Mellie, the duchess chose not to answer. Instead, she said to Helga, "Let me pass this instant, you stupid German dolt."

The middle-aged abigail, gray hair in tiny neat sausages, gulped and paled, but stayed firmly planted in the doorway, blocking entrance.

"Milady," Mellie insisted, "Your Grace, Mama is quite ill— with a—a headache. Isn't that so, Helga?" she added in rapid German.

"Tail, not head!" spat the irate duchess coarsely. "I know my husband is in here. Do you think I'm blind? Let me pass." She shoved open the door, her temper more than compensating for her tiny stature. The duchess swept across the expanse of Turkey carpet to the door leading into Lady Anna Wilton's boudoir.

Acutely aware of the sounds coming from behind that closed door, Mellie stood in terror for one long moment. She hoped Mama had locked the door today; but remembering all too vividly how she'd walked in on them recently, Mellie feared that the doorknob would turn easily under the duchess's irate hand.

At the last moment, Mellie flung herself across the room, trying to slide between the duchess and the protecting panel of oak; but the two hoopskirts were much too bulky to allow such a maneuver.

Still trying, though, Mellie begged, "Please allow me to enter Mama's bedchamber, Your Grace, to make sure she isn't sleeping. Sometimes when she has these headaches, she drinks a draught prescribed by Dr. Pemmley. It puts her to sleep immed——"

"I'll put her to sleep," stormed the duchess, flinging open the door and allowing the scene within to fill her hot, angry cat eyes.

As Mellie had feared, the four-poster bed was again swaying, the curtains billowing. Her mother and her bed partner were making so much noise in their mutual enjoyment of each other's physical delights that they had heard none of the commotion that came with the duchess's arrival. She strode across the bedchamber in most unladylike determination and, to Mellie's horror, seized the concealing drapes which fluttered about the on-stage drama, flung them to one side with a ferocity that ripped the ends loose from the rod, and exposed Lady Anna and her paramour, caught in *flagrante delicto*.

Mellie, frozen with shock and shame, unable to cry out to warn her mother of imminent disaster, saw the two nude bodies writhing and bouncing on the mattress.

With a shrill screech that made Mellie cringe, the duchess reached out, seized her husband's hair by the greasy, flowing locks, and yanked him mightily. He took one horrified look at his lady wife, then wrenched free of her clutching fingers and slithered off the high bed onto the other side, snatching at the drapes to cover his nakedness.

Deprived so suddenly of her pleasure, Mellie's mother opened her eyes, took one look at the irate duchess, and promptly swooned, leaving all her uncorseted amplitude uncovered. Helga scurried into the room, pushed past the Duchess of Seybrook, and caught up the coverlet, pulling it over her exposed mistress.

"Smelling salts!" the duchess ordered, her voice trembling with rage. "I want this miserable whore to hear exactly what I'm saying." When Helga cowered there, not understanding all of the English, but knowing that the situation was international in recognition, the duchess roared, "Smelling salts, you imbecile!"

Mellie moved forward and said in a shaking voice, in German, "Sal volatile, Helga, for Mama."

While the abigail waved a vinaigrette of amber under the unlucky Anna's nose, the duchess turned on her husband.

"Get out of here! Cover up that obscene body of yours, and get back to our suite at once. And if you ever come near this German whore again, I'll—I'll—" She nearly choked from anger, and Mellie thought she might have an apoplectic seizure then and there.

The disheveled duke caught up his scattered clothing and hid behind the huge walnut wardrobe until he had on enough of his apparel to hide his nakedness. Then, carrying his silk hose, his white lawn neck cloth, and his pink satin coat and embroidered waistcoat, he fled ignominiously.

Lady Anna, aroused by the pungent aromatic smelling salts, opened her eyes, took one look at the virago hovering over her, and moaned, threatening to faint again. The duchess would have none of such foolishness. Reaching out with a hand that closely resembled a claw, she pinched Lady Anna's ample flesh unmercifully until she howled with pain.

"Ah, you are with us again!" she hissed. "So! You lure my husband into your bed and think that I don't know? You are completely, utterly brazen, and you suppose that no one notices? That I haven't heard what is going on behind my back? My poor, dear husband—seduced by a licentious wench from another country. And I'm supposed to turn my back on it . . . have a blind eye? Oh, no, my darling whore! If you think I shall let it pass, shall ignore it, you are mistaken. You don't know me very well, if you assume that you shall sleep with my husband and escape scot-free. I intend to make sure that you don't have a chance to seduce other innocent husbands here at court. Perhaps you did this in the Hanoverian court and no one minded—but it won't happen here in England!"

Lady Anna Wilton, finally recovering from the sudden shock of being found in bed, in the act, with this shrew's husband, sat up in bed, letting the covers fall so that her heavy breasts were exposed. "Can you not keep your husband interested, Your Grace?" she asked, in tones of honey laced with the sourest of wines. "If you weren't so busy warming other men's beds, you might have time to take care of your own lusty husband, and he wouldn't look for gratification elsewhere." She let her angry blue eyes slide over the duchess. "But you're such a scrawny excuse for a woman, he probably can't get any satisfaction from you, even if you do deign to let him into your bed when you have no other man there.'' She reached out a scornful hand, flicked the duchess's scant bosom. ''What comfort can a man find there? And I'm sure that the private parts you keep hidden under your skirts are equally skimpy.''

That was the final straw. The Duchess of Seybrook turned brick red, then shockingly white, so that her paint looked artificial.

Mellie stood there, appalled at her mother's outburst. The Duchess of Seybrook was a very influential woman in court. Some said she even had the ear of Ehrengard Melusina von Schulenberg, her mother's mistress. Mellie's eyes strayed to the walnut stand beside the canopied bed. As she suspected, the decanter of Madeira was almost empty. It was the wine talking, not her clever Mama. Mellie knew that her mother couldn't resist a handsome man—any more than she could stay away from wine. She only prayed that this time Mama had not gone too far. Behind the duchess's back, she made cautioning motions, trying to get her mother to watch her tongue; but to no avail.

''So!'' the duchess said, her voice low and dangerous. ''You flaunt your lardy, overfed German charms in front of me, you whore! You'll rue this, you blowsy tart,'' she promised, her voice trembling with rage. ''You'll be sorry you ever laid eyes on me or my husband. I'll make you regret every time he lay with you, every time he desecrated our marriage with the likes of you.''

In utter disdain, Mellie's mother flung back the covers that Helga had so carefully arranged to hide her nakedness.

''Leave my boudoir this instant,'' she said, displaying her ample haunches, her rounded belly and full hips, her woman's triangle that the duke found so enticing. ''I'm tired of you, my dear.'' And she dismissed the duchess with a negligent flick of one plump hand. ''Helga!'' she called. ''Where is my robe?''

The little abigail scurried to her, and quickly swathed the ample curves in a robe of emerald green brocade.

''Wine!'' Lady Anna ordered. ''Well, what are you waiting for?'' she demanded, standing so that she was taller than the duchess. ''Get out of my apartment. You aren't wanted here. Go comfort your poor husband—if you can. Although he'll find you dull, pallid flesh after me,'' she boasted.

The Duchess of Seybrook gave her one last, venomous look, picked up her skirts, and flounced out of the suite.

It was now that Lady Anna finally noticed that Mellie was standing there in a state of shock. ''Melusina Anna Hildreth Wilton!''

she scolded. "What are you doing here in my boudoir? All this is for adults, not children. Go to your own room at once. Haven't you learned to knock before entering private rooms? You'll be fifteen years old tomorrow, quite old enough to begin showing some sensitivity."

"But Mama, I was trying to warn you. . . ."

Her mother frowned blackly. "Warn me? What are you talking about, child?"

"I saw the Duchess of Seybrook arrive in her coach, and I. . . ."

"What were you doing outside at this hour?" her mother demanded, brushing aside Mellie's explanation. "And in that gown? Where have you been?" She advanced on her luckless daughter, eyes riveted to the décolletage of her blue gown. "Helga!" and her voice was dangerous, "why have you let Mellie go out in that immodest gown? It's cut so low you can almost see her navel! Where is her modesty bit?"

Quickly, before the abigail could answer, Mellie said, "I must have lost it when I ran inside to tell you that the duchess was back early from Kent! Mama, I only wanted to help you!"

"Well, you didn't get here in time." Then, airily, "But why worry? Who will listen to her? I'm lady-in-waiting to the von Schulenberg—and *she* has the king's ear." She sniggered. "And other more important parts of him, too. Although as old as she is, I'm not sure that she sees to his physical needs the way she once did."

"Milady!" Helga exclaimed, aghast, looking at Mellie.

"Oh, Helga, after today, what secrets do I have from my daughter? And she's now a young lady. Children don't have such bosoms bulging from the tops of their gowns! But do show a bit more modesty in public, Mellie. The young noblemen about the court have only one thing in mind. Save yourself for a good marriage. You'll catch a better husband if you're a virgin, my dear. Wait until after the bishop says the words over you before you entice too many men with your charms." She stood there, giving Mellie a calculating look. Then she nodded. "You've ripened quite nicely, Mellie. I've not noticed—and I should have. We'll have to begin maneuvering to get you well married. I'm sure that the von Schulenberg can arrange something suitable."

Mellie wanted to tell her mother that the only man she'd consider was young Lord Densbury, but she wasn't given the chance.

Her mother shooed her out of the room as if she were a young duckling.

"And do remember to knock, after this, Mellie," she scolded. "Some things need privacy."

As Mellie walked away, she heard Helga, with the familiarity of long association, protesting, "But milady, it was so foolish to antagonize the Duchess of Seybrook. Court gossip has it that she is very close to the von Schulenberg."

"Oh, Helga, stop worrying. I'm her lady-in-waiting! My daughter is named for her. What influence can that bag of skin and bones have with my mistress?"

CHAPTER THREE

May Day dawned bright and fair, although Mellie slept later than usual, and missed the cool, crisp morning air. When she rang for Helga, she was surprised at the grim look on the abigail's face.

Pouting, Mellie said, "You've not even wished me a happy birthday, Helga. I'm fifteen! A woman!"

Deftly, the maid put the tray over Mellie's lap as she lounged back in bed, pillows piled high. As she sipped her chocolate and eagerly spread strawberry marmalade on the stack of toast, Mellie insisted, "What's wrong? Why so gloomy?"

"His Majesty sent for your mother an hour ago. At that early hour, it can only be bad news."

Mellie wasn't going to have this gray little bird spoiling her birthday. "Probably he wants to try out some younger flesh, Helga. Mama's reputation has spread, I daresay."

"Miss Mellie!" The middle-aged woman was stiff-faced with disapproval. "You mustn't talk about your mother that way. It's indecent."

Mellie grinned, stuffing the last bit of toast into her mouth. "What Mama does is indecent, too. But Helga, if Mama hasn't sense enough to lock her door when she's entertaining, you should do it for her—or stand guard like a dragon at the gates, protecting the fair princess." She snickered. "If she'd had her door shut last evening, the duchess wouldn't have been able to catch them in bed together."

Helga clucked in despair. "Oh, don't joke about it, miss. It could be a disaster."

"Why? You know that the Maypole has always liked me."

"Spoiled you rotten," Helga muttered. "But just because you're a pretty little child, with those Delft blue eyes and hair the color of ripe wheat, that doesn't mean much when palace politics are involved."

24

"Pooh! What do you know of palace politics, Helga?" Mellie asked disparagingly.

"I have ears," Helga said, stubborn to the end. "I may not speak this horrid English, but I've learned to understand it. Your mother's gone too far this time, my dear girl."

"Stop worrying, Helga. Get rid of my tray, and get out my new gown. I want to try it on before dinner."

Grim-faced, Helga obeyed, bending over the bed and exposing almost as much wrinkled white bosom as did the king's other mistress, Charlotte Sophia Kielmansegge, who was obese to the point of incredulity.

Mellie had just donned her gown when her mother swept in, her face a mixture of anger, fear, and bewilderment.

"Our cases, Helga," Lady Anna ordered. At Helga's questioning look, she added sharply, "I have been ordered to leave the court."

Mellie heard the words, but they scarcely penetrated her haze of good humor. She stood before the tall, freestanding, full-length mirror and admired the new gown that was a birthday gift from her mother. It was a gown of watered silk, in a blue to match her eyes exactly. Her mother had promised that she could have her hair powdered for the special birthday dinner today, and Mellie was sure that young Lord Densbury, heir to the dukedom of Amberton, would come. For months her heart had thudded so loudly when he was near her that she was sure he could hear the sound; but until yesterday, he had treated her as he might treat a dear, younger sister. At fifteen, convinced she was now a woman, Mellie wanted no sisterly regard from him, but a continuation of yesterday's awareness. She'd show off her blossoming figure to delicious advantage with the extreme décolletage of this new gown. Slyly, she removed the lace kerchief which her mother had insisted she tuck into the bosom of her dress to conceal her cleavage. Densbury had eyed her nearly bare breasts avidly at the bearbaiting, his eyes lingering on the swell of bosom, just as his hands had strayed to caress her high, firm breasts. Her figure had blossomed so that she could put anyone at court to shame. Wise in the ways of court, Mellie had no intention of hiding her assets. No "bosom friend" for her to mask the exciting young flesh!

"Mellie!" Her mother's voice was harsh, pained. "Didn't you hear me? We're leaving—booted out onto the London streets, all because that miserable bitch, the eternal icicle, the Duchess of Seybrook, returned from her estate in Kent a day early."

Still with a bemused look on her face, Mellie turned away from the lovely image in the mirror. "I know she returned early—I was here! But what has that to do with us?"

Her mother flushed, the ugly red rising from her still smooth bosom and flooding her cheeks, the dark stain showing through the white lead paint with which she whitened her complexion. "Little fool. You were there yesterday. You knew I'd been entertaining the duke for months."

Mellie's smooth young shoulders raised in a shrug that threatened to free her proud young breasts from the restraining gown. "I knew. The whole court knew. Is it any wonder that the duchess knew, too, Mother dear?"

Angrily her mother said, "As long as she didn't actually see it with her own eyes, she pretended it wasn't happening." Then she turned on the hapless maid who stood gawking, taking it all in. "I said get my cases, Helga," she snapped. "And pack our things. Everything." Bitterly she lashed out at her faithful abigail.

"But we can't leave now," Mellie argued with sweet obstinacy. "It's my birthday, Mother. Have you forgotten?" She pouted prettily. "Today is my special birthday dinner."

Her mother turned on her, slapping her face smartly. Stunned, Mellie stood there, a hand to her burning cheek, while her mother railed at her.

"Silly ninny! It's all over. Everything! Can't you get it through your head? I thought that the von Schulenberg would protect me; but she had only herself and her comfort in mind. You'd think after all the years I've served her, that she would intercede with His Majesty on my behalf. Would you believe that she called me a whore? Me? She's the biggest whore in all of England!"

Mellie, almost hysterical from the sudden attack by her mother, couldn't control the nervous giggle at this description of the maypole-tall favorite of King George.

Her mother caught her bare shoulders, her fingers biting into the tender young flesh, and shook the girl until her hair fell down about her face.

"She wants to be Duchess of Kendal!" her mother shrieked. "Miserable old whore, now that she's no longer interested in the king as a man, she demands more than she did when she worked for her position in his bed. And she thinks that the Duchess of Seybrook can be of use to her. Even as the king's mistress, the old bag of bones is the laughingstock of London. They all call her the Maypole, and she knows it. But now that she wants respectability in her old age, wants a title, she calls me a whore! And lets me be thrown into the streets penniless.''

''We won't be living at court?'' Mellie couldn't remember ever living elsewhere, either at the Hanoverian court, or more recently, here in London at the Court of St. James. It was the only life she had ever known. ''Where will we live, then?'' She pictured some of the lovelier mansions she'd visited here in the city, with their sumptuous rooms, their many servants, the mark of graceful living. ''Will we have our own town house?''

''I don't know,'' her mother screamed. ''I don't know.''

Anna Wilton paced the floor of their private sitting room, her maroon velvet overskirt sweeping the floor behind her. ''If your father hadn't been such a gambler. . . .'' She glared at Mellie as if it were her fault that Sir Horace Wilton had squandered all of his pay and his meager inheritance at the gaming tables so popular with the *ton*.

''Milady,'' Helga said quietly, puffing slightly as she hauled their cases down from the shelf of the carved oak wardrobe, ''I have a bit of money put by.''

''Helga, I couldn't. . . .'' But there was a sudden flare of hope in her eyes, and Mellie was sure that their problems would all be solved.

The little German abigail was firm. ''You must live, milady. And Miss Mellie must live. You cannot manage without me. And what would become of me if I did not go with you?'' She spoke in German, never having mastered English.

Anna clasped her head in her hands and rocked back and forth as she stood in the middle of the room. ''I don't know what to say—what to do! I'm at my wit's end, with this terrible blow that's been dealt me, a blow I don't deserve.''

Mellie, inured to her mother's dramatics, said with little sympathy, ''Helga's right, Mother. We couldn't possibly manage without her. Who would dress us?'' It had never occurred to Mellie, accustomed to the constant attendance of servants, that it might be possible to put on her own clothes without help.

''But how will we live?'' Anna Wilton wailed.

''First we move, then we worry,'' the efficient Helga insisted. ''Have you friends here in this foreign city of London to whom you can go?''

''Friends?'' Anna said the word as if it were in a language that she was just learning. ''Friends in London?''

''Yes, milady. Friends with whom you could stay until . . .''

Helga let the sentence drift. Then, when she got no response from her distraught mistress, she suggested, "Or are there relatives here in this country, kin of your late husband, Sir Horace?"

Anna, ignoring her abigail's pertinent questions, swept across the expanse of Turkey carpet and threw herself onto an upholstered settee, not forgetting to arrange her skirts so that they fanned gracefully from her small, laced-in waist. "Madeira," she ordered, opening her ivory fan and fanning herself languidly.

Disgusted with her mother's performance, Mellie told the abigail, "Get on with the packing, Helga. I'll pour the wine." She took the glass stopper from a decanter of German cut crystal and poured the golden wine into a matching wineglass. "Here, Mother. Now, do try to think." She pouted prettily. "Can't we even go to dinner?" Mellie glanced at the ormolu clock ticking away on the pink marble chimneypiece. "It's after two. And it's my birthday. Surely the cook has prepared something special for me."

For one dreadful minute, Mellie thought her mother would throw the Madeira in her face. "You little fool. I dare not show my face in the dining room today or any day from now on."

"Well, the Duchess of Seybrook isn't angry with me, Mother. It wasn't I she caught in her husband's bed."

"You little . . ." Anna gulped down the wine, choking on it. Mellie obligingly pounded her on the back until she stopped gasping. "I do not like vulgarity in my daughter," she said, fixing Mellie with a cold, unpleasant stare.

Mellie, realizing that she'd gone too far, murmured, "I'm sorry, Mother."

Helga stepped into the breach to prevent further flare-ups between mother and daughter. With their lives in a crisis, it was no time for bickering. Going back to her earlier, unanswered question, Helga stood in front of her mistress insisting, "Anyone, milady? Is there anyone, friend or kin, with whom you can stay for a time until we get our new lives settled?"

"I—I can think of no one. Who would take me in when I am out of favor at court? No one would be such a fool." She held out the glass for more wine which she drank down as if it were fresh spring water.

"I may be able to arrange something," the abigail said quietly. "Rest here, compose yourself, milady. I shall see what I can do." Then, almost as an afterthought, "Have you any jewels to pawn?"

"Most of them are paste," Anna said bitterly. "The real ones were pawned long since to pay Horace's gambling debts. I have only my diamond eardrops.'' She raised a delicate hand to touch her jewels. ''Surely I mustn't. . . .'' Her distress was there, lining her face, a preview of what she'd look like in years to come.

Helga sighed. ''No, we'll not pawn the earrings at the moment, milady. Let us call them a reserve.'' She bustled out, promising to return as soon as she could.

As Anna reached for the wine decanter to fill her glass again, Mellie made a bold decision. She'd seen her mother drink wine before. While Anna got quietly drunk, Mellie intended to try to maneuver Lord Densbury so that they could be alone. If she could charm him, as she had yesterday at the bear pit, he might offer for her hand. Then she would be protected; for his father, the Duke of Amberton, was as powerful as the Seybrooks. He might even be able to protect her mother; but Mellie knew that if she had a chance to save herself, she'd desert her mother rather than be dragged down by her. In her fifteen-year-old mind, she rationalized it nicely. *If I can marry, even if dear Alistair cannot accept Mother, I will be off her hands, and she will not have to worry about providing for me. After all, she'll not be alone. She has Helga.*

She made sure that her mother was not watching her, then she slipped from the room. Not quite certain how to arrange a meeting with Densbury, she moved from the residential wing of the palace toward the audience rooms, hoping to find the young lord alone.

Entering the red drawing room, she saw Densbury almost immediately. He stood off to one side, chatting with some other young men of the court and several of the younger ladies-in-waiting. She started to edge her way around the wall toward Densbury, hoping to attract his attention when she got close to the group.

As luck would have it, she almost collided with Ehrengard Melusina von Schulenberg herself, done up in a gown of unbecoming plum satin, her sagging bosom propped up with stiff corsets, her skin brown and wrinkled. Her hair, dressed high on her head, was graying and unpowdered, topped by a pompon of curiously wrought silk roses.

''Out!'' screamed the king's mistress, pointing a long, bony witch finger at Mellie, waggling it under the young woman's pert little nose. ''How dare you show your face, you offspring of that infamous whore Anna Wilton?''

The silence was deafening after the Maypole's outburst.

Mellie saw young Densbury turn, and he looked right at her—

just what she'd hoped for. But instead of smiling at her, or showing indignation at the unfair attack on her by the king's favorite,
Densbury turned and muttered something to his friends, grinning
maliciously. Even across the room, Mellie could hear one of the
ladies-in-waiting snicker.

"What are you waiting for, daughter of that Wilton cow?"
raged von Schulenberg. "Get out of my sight and out of my
palace. This instant!"

Hot anger replaced Mellie's careful scheming and she spat back,
"The palace belongs to King George, not to you, you old hag!"

Then someone grasped her arm, not too gently, and Mellie saw
that one of the liveried footmen had moved up behind her.

"Come along, miss," he murmured. "Don't cause a fuss."

He practically dragged her from the room, and Mellie felt tears
of shame and rage flood her eyes. They'd be sorry, all of them.
The time would come when she'd be a person of such consequence
that everyone at court would come begging favors—even—
even—the tears spilled over and burned down her cheeks. *Oh,
Alistair, how could you be so cruel?* That was the cruelest hurt of
all, that Lord Densbury should have witnessed her humiliation,
and that he had made a jest of it to his wicked, snobbish friends.

"Now, miss, no sniveling," the footman warned. "Where's
your mother, Lady Wilton? What's she thinking of, allowing you
to come into the public rooms? The whole palace is buzzing about
her fall from favor."

"But it's my birthday," Mellie wailed. "I was to have a special
dinner party to celebrate it."

"Too bad, miss." His voice had no sympathy whatsoever. In
fact, Mellie detected a certain satisfaction in his tone which infuriated her. Everyone was pleased that her mother had fallen from
grace. Mellie, schooled in the ways of court, knew that this delight
wasn't particularly personal. Most people there liked her mother
well enough. She had no real enemies at St. James's Palace. But
the court thrived on scandal and petty intrigue. None of the courtiers had enough to do to keep busy, boredom was the disease of
the highborn, and any little tempest, any morsel of gossip, however small, was blown up out of all proportion for the amusement
of the court.

Back in their suite, Mellie was dealt the final blow of a disastrous day when she found her mother, head lolled back on the settee
cushions, snoring drunkenly. The empty Madeira decanter told the
whole story and was an ominous sign of things to come. . . .

CHAPTER FOUR

"We're to live here?" The horror and consternation in Lady Anna Wilton's voice were reflected on Mellie's face.

"Mama, it's so—so grubby!" she cried. Then, looking with annoyance at Helga, who was already opening the door of the rented coach which was piled high with their belongings, "Badger Lane," Mellie went on bitterly. "I think it would be better named Badger Den." She looked with loathing at the narrow, malodorous street with rickety three- and four-story narrow houses leaning drunkenly, shutting out the air and sky. The street itself was a mire of mud, for it had rained hard that morning. Mellie knew she'd get her slippers covered with muck, and she'd have to hold her skirts up to her knees to keep the hems out of the garbage that was thrown down underfoot. Even as she thought this, there was a harsh cry from somewhere above them, and a pot of turnip tops and rotting apples was thrown from an upper window to splatter beside the coach.

"Watch what yer doin' " the coachey yelled in wrath, flicking a bit of apple from the multicaped greatcoat which was the badge of his profession.

"Helga," Mellie's mother said firmly, "there must be some mistake. The coachman has brought us to the wrong address. Speak to him sharply."

Sullenly the abigail muttered, "This is it, milady. I found it myself. If you'd had any friends or kin to take us in, we'd not have had to stay here. Once both you, Miss Mellie, and I find suitable employment, we may be able to afford better quarters. But until we have more money, we must stay where it is cheap."

Lady Anna recognized an ultimatum when she heard it. Although she'd already been drinking heavily, she still was sober enough to realize that Helga was right. She'd already spent her wages, the only jewels she had that could be pawned were her diamond eardrops, and life was suddenly desperate.

The coachey was untying their cases and trunks, grumbling all the while about how heavy they were. "You don't expect me to lug 'em upstairs?"

"We'll manage," Helga said shortly, "we'll manage." Occasionally she did use her meager English, when she was confronted by urgent need.

"Helga, who'll carry the cases into the house for us?" Lady Anna asked, looking at the mountain of luggage in dismay. "Why won't the coachey do it?"

"Oh, he will, milady, for a price. But we can't afford to waste our little hoard of money on the likes of him. We're three healthy souls. We'll manage."

And manage they did, with much complaining from both Mellie and her mother when they found that everything had to go up to a poky little room under the sloping roof. Mellie looked about her in dismay. The furnishings consisted of one sagging old bed, one lumpy trundle bed pushed under it, two plain wooden chairs with no padding and no paint, a filthy chamber pot tucked in one corner, and a rickety table against the wall. There were a few pegs on the wall for clothes, and one little window, the glass flawed and dirty, in a tiny dormer that looked out over Badger Lane.

Their boxes filled most of the floor space, and Lady Anna flung herself down on one trunk and began to sob.

"That I'd come to this! Everyone at court had a lover—why banish me? It isn't fair! I cannot live like this." Then, in almost the same breath, "Isn't there some wine?"

Tight-lipped, the abigail went to a wooden box and brought out a bottle of cheap claret and an earthenware mug. "You must not get drunk, milady. Even today we must all try to find work." She brought the *Gazette* out from under her embroidered white apron. "Miss Mellie, you read this difficult language. They tell me that positions available are listed. Read to me."

Recognizing something indomitable in the abigail, Mellie leafed through the newspaper until she came to the advertisements for open positions. Only then did she voice her doubts. "But Helga, what can we do?" She glanced over at her mother who was surreptitiously pouring another tot of claret into the rude cup. "And Mama? Can she be a lady-in-waiting for anyone?"

Lady Anna took a long drink of the claret, frowned at its poor quality, then said with that precision which Mellie recognized as incipient drunkenness, "Ladies-in-waiting are only at court, Mellie."

"Then you can be a companion to some wealthy lady who wishes not to be alone," Helga said distinctly. "We cannot live on the little I can earn. I cannot go as an abigail to someone else, for I must look after you. So I must take employment in a shop, perhaps."

"A shop?" Mellie said with distaste. Then she looked sharply at Helga. "That isn't what you expect me to do, is it? Work in some dreary little shop?"

"No, Miss Mellie. I thought you could be a governess."

Mellie's laugh pealed out, high and tinkling. "Me? A governess? Oh, Helga, how quaint!"

"You can read and write in this dreadful English tongue, miss, and speak it properly. And you also speak German, the language of His Majesty, King George. And some French, too. You could surely teach children to do the same."

"Well, it's better than working in a shop," Mellie grumbled. "Let me see . . . ah, yes, governess wanted, Number Ten, Lamb's Conduit. I think that is a very fashionable section," she added, cheering up. Perhaps it wouldn't be too bad. She might meet some handsome, wealthy young man in that area.

Lady Anna, acting as if this all were a game, cried gaily, "See if anyone wants a companion. I'd prefer a wealthy gentleman, of course, preferably handsome and not too terribly old." She sipped daintily but steadily at the wine.

Helga frowned. "It is a serious business, milady."

"Of course, Helga, of course. But let us not be so gloomy about it. Here, pour me more claret."

Mellie marked several possibilities for her mother and copied out the address on Lamb's Conduit for herself. Next day she presented herself at Number Ten for her first interview. A maid in black dress and white apron and mobcap showed her into the reception room. The maid had buck teeth and a definite cast in one eye, and Mellie wondered how the mistress of the house could bear having such a homely creature around her. Then that good lady swept into the room, her cap with a starched frill that stood up six inches from her tightly dressed hair, her ample figure corseted until she might have been wearing armor rather than the soft wool gown with its rich trim of gold lace.

Mellie curtsied, even though the woman was obviously a commoner—rich but vulgar. "Melusina Wilton, madam. To enquire about the post of governess that was listed in yesterday's *Gazette*. I speak and read German, French, and. . . ."

The woman interrupted her before she could further catalog her virtues. "No, no, you won't do at all. I didn't come all the way from Exeter to get Mr. Bartlet away from those trulls in his woolen factory to hire such a pretty face here! No, you'll not do at all." She rang for the ugly maid. "I should put such temptation in Oswald's way? Not likely."

"But madam, I need the work," Mellie pleaded, suddenly seeing that a milky skin, golden hair, and bright blue eyes might work against, not for, her.

"And to be dressed so shamelessly," the woman went on as if Mellie hadn't even spoken. "Gown cut so low that your bosom might escape momentarily. Modesty, my girl, modesty!"

The maid showed Mellie out. On the street, she stood for a long time, wondering what to do next. She'd not even bothered to write down any other possible openings, so sure she was that she would get this job. Mellie had always lived at court; and because she was a pretty little thing, and the namesake of one of the king's favorites, she'd been cosseted and humored until she was quite spoiled. Adversity did not sit well with Mellie. And the fact that Helga had refused to give her money to hire a chair was still galling Mellie as she trudged back to the misery of Cheapside. A gang of young hoodlums chased her until she fled into St. Paul's Cathedral to escape them; and they were highborn bloods, she could tell from the fine fabrics they wore, the cut of their clothes. Then when she finally crept out of the church's sanctuary she was accosted by a beggar with no legs who caught at her skirt.

"Penny, milady! Lost me legs in th' war with France."

Plucking her skirt away from his filthy hand, Mellie hurried toward Cheapside, and her own miserable lodgings. It was so unfair. If only she could have stayed at the court a few weeks more, Mellie was sure she'd have had an offer from Lord Densbury. She knew he was attracted to her. She also was clever enough to know that what the young marquis wanted most was to bed her. She hadn't lived near her mother for nothing. Lady Anna was a living lesson in carnal passions! But Mellie had no intention of allowing Densbury to steal her virginity. Morals might be lax to the point of nonexistence at court; but there still was some value placed on undamaged goods in the marriage market. She'd learned at Hockley-in-the-Hole when Alistair's hands had caressed her bosom how easy it would be to succumb to the blandishments of a handsome man; but she'd had a taste of life without money and position. Today was enough to teach Mellie for all time that she wanted a noble marriage, with all the amenities that came with it.

She tried to turn off her senses as she got farther away from St. Paul's, and nearer her grubby lodgings. The streets were even narrower and filthier than the main thoroughfares of the city, the humanity of a degree so low that Mellie couldn't understand it at all.

At the end of Badger Lane, two filthy children dressed in rags and tatters were digging—with their bare hands—through the garbage thrown into the street. To Mellie's horror, the little boy, who couldn't have been more than five or six, popped something he'd found into his mouth.

With two quick steps, she was standing over him. Loath to touch him, for his scalp was covered with oozing sores and his face with scabs, Mellie felt impelled to make him spit out whatever filth he'd put in his mouth.

"Spit that out at once!" she commanded, rapping him sharply on the cheek with her folded fan so that her hands wouldn't come in contact with his diseased flesh.

To her astonishment, the other child, a girl with matted hair and rotten teeth, sprang at her like a hunting dog, screeching, "Ours! Don't you steal it!" The child spat on her and clawed at her hands until Mellie backed away in consternation, then turned and fled. Glancing back over her shoulder, she saw the two urchins once again in the garbage, eating bits and pieces. Gagging, she fumbled her vinaigrette from her pocket and sniffed deeply to kill the sickening odor of the street.

Still shuddering, she climbed the creaking stairs to their garret room, only to find that both her mother and Helga were gone. She longed to change into a loose Watteau sacque, but Helga wasn't there to help her disrobe. Never having dressed or undressed herself in her fifteen years, Mellie sat, uncomfortable, for several hours until she finally heard welcome steps climbing to their pinched little room.

It was both her mother and Helga. One look at their pleased faces, and Mellie knew they'd had better luck than she had. "Oh, Helga, I'm so hot and tired," she complained even before they could tell her their news. "Do unlace me."

For one moment Mellie thought the abigail was going to refuse. Then she bustled over to Mellie and with rough hands undid her gown.

"You must learn to do this for yourself, miss."

"Myself! But why should I? You are our abigail."

"I shall be working from early to late in a milliner's, and happy to get the position, with no experience in making bonnets," Helga said. "I was lucky. The shopkeeper is from Saxony. She can speak German. When I told her I'd worked at court, she took me on—for prestige, she said."

"And I am to be companion to an incredibly old and tiresome lady who lives on Grosvenor Square," Lady Anna said smugly. "She's a demanding old bitch; but I shall have a room there which, although it is not large, is better than this." She looked around, her lip curled in disgust.

"When can we move, Mama?" Mellie asked eagerly. "Today?"

"The room is only for me," her mother said coldly.

"But—but where will I live?" Mellie cried.

"You and I will stay on here, Miss Mellie, until we can afford better. But now you'll have the whole bed to yourself," the abigail said, cajolingly. "I'll take the trundle." Then, remembering, "But if you were hired today on Lamb's Conduit, you will be living there."

"Oh, Mellie, you didn't get the position," Lady Anna said, suddenly perceptive.

"I'm too pretty," Mellie exclaimed bitterly. Mimicking, "You'd tempt my Oswald!" She trembled with remembered anger so that Helga had trouble helping her into the sacque of palest lavender silk. "My looks aren't an asset. I might corrupt her merchant husband."

"Never mind," Helga soothed. "There are others who will want a wellborn lady to teach their daughters. You'll try again tomorrow."

"And my slippers are ruined from walking," Mellie went on, kicking off the offending shoes. "How can I hope to impress a prospective employer if my slippers are muddy? I should have a chair."

"Not for short distances, Miss Mellie. We can't afford it. You'll just have to brush off your shoes as best you can before you ring the doorbell. Now, here is today's, *Gazette*. See what other positions are available. With milady settled, you must try even harder to find a place as a governess."

Realizing now that her only escape from this horrid garret was to find a position in a better neighborhood, a live-in job, Mellie marked several prospects in the paper, determined that she'd not come back tomorrow without first finding employment.

Her mother, relaxing with the inevitable glass of wine, said, "It was nice to get back to civilization today. Grosvenor Square is quite the place with the *ton*. There is a huge mansion in the Palladian style going up beside Countess Marchant's home. The countess is my new employer. Ancient, she can't be a day under sixty, she's a real hag. But I think she's impressed by the fact that I've been at court."

"What did she say when you told her you'd been banished?"

Anna looked at her daughter as if she'd suddenly developed a bad case of the pox. "I didn't mention that, ninny. I said that the German courtiers were too vulgar." She snickered. "She never guessed that I'm German myself. Horace did do that much for both of us—our English is impeccable. How the old witch laughed and cackled when I told her I was trying to get away from the court!"

"That's quite clever of you, Mama. Now if only I could uglify myself until I get a position. . . ." She picked up her tortoiseshell hand mirror and peered into it as if she might find some hideous monster hiding inside the glass. "Silly cow of a woman. No doubt her husband beds every woman in sight. And no wonder, after seeing her!"

Lady Anna moved out bag and baggage, leaving a bit more room for Mellie and Helga. The abigail had arranged for them to take their meals with the landlady, a blowsy, obese individual who ate heartily of her own poor cooking and glared at Mellie when she only picked at the plain fare. Mellie went to bed even more determined to find a position tomorrow.

Luck was with her, or so she thought, when she was hired by the first woman who interviewed her, a youngish, harassed mother who lived within easy walking distance of Mellie's lodging. There were six children, the oldest a boy of seven, the youngest a nursing babe.

"They're lively," the woman, a Mrs. Inglewood, said. "But such little dears. Even the younger ones are so bright, I'm sure you can teach them their numbers and letters quite quickly." She went on to explain, "Mr. Inglewood is a clerk with a well-known solicitor with chambers in the Inner Temple."

But Mellie learned quickly that the little Inglewoods were little terrors, not little dears. Robin, the eldest, delighted in pinching her until she was black and blue, while Miranda, his sister, would creep up behind her and shriek in her ears. She wasn't a governess but a nanny, paid poorly to take care of five spoiled brats—and sometimes the babe, too. Lessons were a farce. The children had no interest in learning their letters, only in tormenting their betters.

A crisis was precipitated when Robin pushed Miranda down the stairs, and her ankle was badly sprained. Their mother came running at the shrieks of her eldest daughter, and innocent little Robin insisted, "Miss Wilton pushed her!" His glare at his howling sister warned her that worse would be in store for her if she told the truth, so Miranda, gulping and sobbing, agreed, "Yes, naughty governess pushed me."

No matter that Mellie protested her innocence.

Stiff-lipped, eyes icy, Mrs. Inglewood asked, "Are you saying that my darlings would lie, Miss Wilton?"

She was dismissed. Luckily she was given, surreptitiously, a letter of reference by Mr. Inglewood who knew that his children were little hellions—and who had cast many an appreciative eye at Mellie's charms. "Don't tell Mrs. Inglewood," he cautioned as he slipped the letter to her. "I'm sorry, my dear. I hope you get another position soon."

To add to the burden, when Mellie arrived back at the ugly surroundings of Badger Lane, she found her mother getting out of a public coach, with all her baggage. Together they wrestled their boxes up to the garret, commiserating with each other.

"The mansion being built next door to Countess Marchant—it belongs to the Maypole! She and her daughter are both building on Grosvenor Square. And when that old biddy of a countess found out that I'd been banished from the court, she let me go. Said it would be too embarrassing for her if the Duchess of Kendal—that bitch von Schulenberg got her title from the king—should call."

Mellie then told *her* tale of woe, adding, "But the master did give me a reference. Did you get a letter from the countess?"

Lady Anna laughed raucously. "A letter? I doubt if she can write. Where's the wine? I shall miss her Madeira."

When Helga got home from her job in the milliner's, she found her two ladies sipping away at the claret.

"We must find you other positions, immediately."

But things went from bad to worse. Mellie lost two more jobs as governess, one because the son was almost as old as she, and thought Mellie should teach him more than books. The other because the family decided to leave London for the clear air of Sussex, and chose not to take the governess along with them.

Lady Anna's second position lasted only until her mistress, a veritable termagant, found that her companion was sipping the wine, gin, and brandy. She sacked her without a reference, calling her a drunken bawd.

It was soon after this, while Mellie was out trying to find another position, that she saw her mother going into The Cock and Bull, a tavern with a most unsavory reputation, catering to the dregs of their slum area. When Anna staggered out an hour later, she had a man with her, and she took him back to Badger Lane. Mellie, coming back from an interview some time later, found the door to their room locked, and the sounds coming from behind the barrier were unmistakable.

She didn't tell Helga, although the abigail must have wondered where Lady Anna had gotten money for a bottle of tolerable Madeira. . . .

CHAPTER FIVE

From that time on, it was all downhill. Lady Anna no longer pretended that she would attempt to find gainful employment. She began frequenting the local taverns which were tawdry, full of the scum of society. Her two main interests in life were alcohol—she had gradually taken to gin rather than wine, for gin was cheap and plentiful—and men. She wasn't particular about her male company. All she asked was that they provide her with money for gin, and she slept with any and all who had coppers to jingle in their pockets.

All too many times Mellie would come home to find poor Helga huddled at the top of the garret stairs, asleep, kept out of the room she paid for with her paltry wages by a drunken mistress who was "entertaining."

Mellie had no compunction about interrupting her mother's sex life. She had managed to get a temporary position in a school for young ladies, not one of the fashionable schools, but a lesser one which better-class tradespeople patronized. Although she hated every minute of the time she spent in the classroom, and was the poorest excuse for a teacher on the staff, the Miss Hazlett who ran the school put up with her because of Mellie's court background. "If they learn nothing from you except how to speak, it is something," she'd say grudgingly as she paid Mellie the pittance she'd earned at the end of each week.

Mellie hated the job because she had no room with it, and she had to go back to living in the garret with her sot of a mother and the long-suffering Helga. This meant that she had to walk the London streets alone, often after dark, coming back from her chores at the school. She often delayed her walk until the watchman came by, hoping that if she followed him, she'd have a bit of protection, although most of the watchmen were old, feeble, and ineffective, armed only with their long staffs.

Then Lady Anna began coming to the school to call Mellie out and beg for gin money. After this happened several times, Miss Hazlett called Mellie into her crowded little office.

"Miss Wilton, several of our students' mothers have seen you talking with a disreputable bawd on our doorstep. This is giving my school a very bad name. If it happens again, I shall have to dismiss you."

Mellie was terrified the headmistress would learn that this bawd was her mother, now so far gone in drink that she'd ceased keeping herself clean. Even Helga's efforts were to little avail.

"I'll make sure it doesn't happen again," Mellie said, knowing even as she said it that there was no way she could prevent her mother's coming to the school.

The next day it happened again and Mellie was instantly dismissed, so she was back to looking for other employment.

She was hired briefly at one of the houses near Lincoln's Inn Fields; but there, what her first prospective employer had feared did take place. Mellie's charges, two lumpish half-grown girls of few brains and fewer graces, were finally put to bed; and she climbed her weary way to the tiny chamber tucked under the roof, with one small window overlooking Chancery Lane. Too weary to bother with views from attic windows, Mellie stripped to her chemise and fell into bed, asleep almost immediately. She was wakened when someone fumbled about with her bedclothes, trying to crawl into her bed.

Terrified, Mellie let out a terrible shriek, only to have a man's hard hand clamp down on her mouth, smothering the sound and almost smothering Mellie.

"Be quiet, you little trollop," he hissed. "Don't play the innocent maiden with me. I've seen how you flaunt that lush bosom, inviting me to touch. Well, I've come now to accept your invitation. Be a good girl, now, and we'll have a lively romp."

It was the master, and for the first time in her life, Mellie felt real terror. Struggling, she managed to sink her teeth into the heel of his hand which was crushing her tender lips onto her teeth. The master yanked away his hand, swearing mightily.

The minute her mouth was free, Mellie screamed lustily, "Help! Oh, help me! He wants to ravish me!"

For answer she got a hard fist in her face, the blow stunning her, so that she lay sobbing as the man fumbled in the dark, tearing her chemise, pawing her tender flesh.

He was not successful in his attempted rape. The mistress of the house, waking to find her husband not beside her in their high, canopied bed, had lighted a candle and gone looking, suspicious of the new governess who wore fine, low-cut gowns which showed her swelling young bosom all too specifically. She didn't even tuck a modesty bit into the neckline, the budding young strumpet. At the foot of the attic stairs, the mistress heard Mellie's shrieks. So she caught up her long, full nightdress, held the candle high to light the way up the narrow steps, and flew upstairs, bursting into the room in time to save Mellie's virginity, but not her job.

"She enticed me," the husband blustered, scrambling out of Mellie's narrow cot and hastily adjusting his nightshirt. He turned and slapped the now hysterical girl smartly on the cheek, leaving finger marks on her pale flesh.

"Get out!" his wife said softly, venom in her tones.

"He tried . . . he tried . . ." Mellie sobbed incoherently.

Her mistress advanced across the room, ignoring her husband who scuttled out, nightshirt rumpled and nightcap askew. Standing over the terrified girl, she ordered, again, "Get out! Put on your clothes and get out of my house. Now! This instant!"

"But I didn't do anything," Mellie protested. "He came here while I slept and tried. . . ."

"Doesn't matter. You must leave at once. I won't have my lovely daughters exposed to such vulgarity. What if they should have heard your screams and come running? How could I have explained to them why their dear father was in your bed? Get out!"

"A letter. If I can have a letter." Mellie's presence of mind was returning. Without a letter of reference, she'd have trouble finding another position as governess; and although she hated the work, what else could she do? Be a helper in a draper's shop? Sell flowers on the street in Covent Garden? So she swallowed her pride and begged for a letter.

Her mistress stood there, white nightdress flowing, hair carefully tucked up in a lace nightcap tied under her chin, an avenging angel. "A letter? Insolent trollop! Be glad I don't flog you. You expect me to recommend you to my friends? Miss Melusina Wilton, daughter of Lady Wilton, late of the Court of St. James, is admirably suited as a bed warmer!" She spat the words at the cowering girl. "Fifteen minutes. Not a moment more. If you aren't out of this house by then, I shall summon the watchman."

She touched her candle flame to the stub of tallow beside Mellie's hard, lumpy bed, then sailed out of the room.

Furious, Mellie dressed hurriedly, gathering her few things together into a tiny bundle—the silver-backed hairbrush the Maypole had given her on her thirteenth birthday, the tiny enameled patch-box from her father, the mirror her mother had presented to her last year. She added a tortoiseshell comb and a pot of white lead for her face. Then, flinging her cloak of maroon melton around her shoulders, she stumbled down the narrow stairs. Outside their conjugal bedroom, the mistress stood guard, as if afraid Mellie might yet seduce her innocent husband.

"You owe me this week's pay, madam," Mellie said, stopping in front of the irate woman, determined not to lose the few shillings due her.

"I owe you nothing. Get out."

Against such an implacable opponent, Mellie could do nothing. But as she let herself out into the chill damp of a London winter night, she vowed that she'd take her revenge on all brutes of men, although she could do naught to this one, nor to his shrewish wife. There was only one tiny bit of consolation for Mellie. Although her mistress had placed the blame for the whole affair squarely on Mellie's young and shapely shoulders, Mellie felt sure that once she was out of the house, the husband would suffer at his wife's irate hand, and probably continue to smart for days to come.

Mellie had well over a mile to walk to the lodgings where her mother and Helga still lived; but even though the London streets were dangerous at night, Mellie knew she couldn't use the few coins she had for a hackney or a sedan chair. She'd have to go with great caution. Keeping close to the darkened buildings, she hurried along, wishing for a lantern or a torch, as the narrow pavement was uneven and slippery with mud flung from the rutted street by the wheels of the many coaches found during the day on Holborn. The stink of horse droppings, human offal, and garbage was nigh overpowering; but Mellie's nose was used to it. Her fears were that she might be accosted by footpads who roamed the city with impunity.

There were widely spaced flat-pan oil lamps on poles along Holborn, as it was one of the main streets; but the feeble light only accentuated the black shadows between the lamps. Slinking along, she kept peering around, watching for furtive movement. When she reached the turning for Blackfriars Road, Mellie heard a band of rowdies coming along, so she pushed into the entryway of a house and cowered there in the gloom until the young blades, drunk on gin, had staggered past and rounded the corner.

One, however, shouted, "A watchman's box ahead, men!" and with drunken whoops of delight, they came back onto High Holborn and raced forward, elegant knee boots spattered with mud, to topple over the box and harass the poor old man who tried to beat them off with his long staff. Mellie had no concern for the fellow. All of her energies were needed to take care of herself. Any man fool enough to take on the watchman's job asked for what he got, she thought cynically.

Now she was on Newgate, with the dome of St. Paul's visible off to the right, even at night, its mighty shape towering over the city and blotting out the stars. All it meant to Mellie was that she still had nearly half a mile to go to get home. Where Cheapside started, the girl was accosted by a drunken man who clutched at her and blew sour, beery breath in her face as he muttered, "Gimme kiss, girlie, gimme kiss."

Knowing that screams would only bring more villains running, Mellie fought him silently and fiercely, hauling up her voluminous skirts and aiming the pointed toe of her now shabby French leather slipper at his crotch as the ever-practical Helga had taught her. Then she fled down Cheapside, turning toward the Guildhall into the warren of streets where so many other unfortunates lived crowded together in deplorable squalor and poverty.

Breathless from running, she stopped just after she'd turned the corner into her own Badger Lane, and leaned against the door of the draper's shop that stood on the corner. Midblock was a street lamp, and in the circle of feeble light from the smoking oil, she saw played out the next act in her own tragic drama of life. From the other end of Badger Lane, on the opposite side of the entrance to their mean lodgings, a woman staggered into view. There was something familiar about her, even on the poorly lighted, foggy street. As Mellie peered through the smoke and mist of a typical London night, she realized that the woman was her mother. What was Lady Anna Wilton doing alone on the streets at this hour? That she was drunk didn't surprise Mellie, for she'd not seen her mother sober for days. But recently she had a man with her every time she staggered home from The Cock and Bull, or one of the other taverns nearby—a long series of men. For some reason, tonight Lady Anna had been unable to coax one of her low companions to share her bed with her. Perhaps even the drunken sailors of the waterfront were now shying away from this drunken woman with the raddled face, straggly hair, and filthy clothes.

Knowing that her mother might well need help up the narrow, sagging stairs to their attic quarters, Mellie hurried forward. Almost at that instant, she saw faithful Helga, cloak thrown around her to cover her nightdress, gray hair in a neat braid down her back, come out of the doorway where they lived and move in the direction of the drunken Anna.

The abigail started across the muddy, rutted street when from farther down, behind Anna, a coach came careening around the corner and down Badger Lane, the driver whipping the pair so that they galloped through the nearly empty street.

Seemingly oblivious of the clattering coach, Lady Anna walked directly into the path of the horses. Mellie shrieked and made to cover her eyes with her hands. But some dreadful need to see kept her eyes uncovered, as she waited for her mother to be struck down by the team and trampled into the mud and slime underfoot.

Helga didn't hesitate. With a speed incredible for a short, dumpy woman of middle years, she flew out into the street and flung herself at Anna Wilton, knocking her mistress backwards, out of the coach's path. The coachey tried valiantly to rein in his team; but it was too late. Although Anna was thrown clear, falling heavily onto the pavement, Helga slipped and fell directly in the path of the oncoming carriage. There was one ghastly scream, then nothing, as the horses clattered to a halt just opposite where Mellie stood stunned.

The coachman leaped from the box and rushed back, but there was nothing he nor anyone else could do. Helga's mangled body lay there in the circle of light, a pool of blood widening around her crumpled form.

As if in a trance, Mellie moved toward the disaster. She saw her drunken mother pick herself up from the muck of the street and stagger across to their mean abode, not even noticing her abigail's broken remains, nor the coachman who knelt in the mud beside Helga.

Hearing Mellie's footsteps, the man looked up. His face under the shabby black tricorne was rough, with harsh slabs of forehead and cheek. He had a great jutting nose under straggling grizzled hair hacked off just above the shoulder.

"I couldn't stop, miss. Didn't you see? I tried! As God is my witness, miss, I tried. I hauled on the reins, nigh broke my arms tryin'; but it were too late. T'other woman, that one staggerin' in her cups," and he pointed to Anna's retreating back, "she came right out in front of me. And this one—gar! Saved t'other one, and died doin' it. Not my fault, miss."

"No one is blaming you, coachey." Mellie was surprised to hear her voice, steady and calm, for inside she was churning.

Helga dead. How could she and her sot of a mother possibly manage without the indomitable Helga? Bitterly she looked at the last bit of her mother's bedraggled skirt which showed momentarily before disappearing into the doorway where they lived. It was a wonder that Anna could find her way home as drunk as she was.

"Do you know this poor soul?" the coachey was asking. "Her family—someone must tell them. Maybe you, miss. . . ."

"She had no one, no family," Mellie said, suddenly sad. What an epitaph for a good and faithful servant. "I know who she is, though, who her mistress is. I'll notify her."

Not for the world would she have admitted to the man that the drunken whore he'd seen staggering into the path of his coach was the mistress of the dead woman—and her own mother.

It was all too dreadful, a horrid finish to an already unbearable night.

CHAPTER SIX

Mellie shuddered, holding the last of her lace-edged kerchiefs over her nose to shut out the stench of unwashed bodies, urine, and feces. The noises coming from the cells were more animal than human; and the steady parade of fashionable folk strolling through the corridors and peering into the barred cells of the Hospital of St. Mary of Bethlehem gave it all the aspects of the Royal Zoo. Here were the unfortunate insane of the city, chained and caged as though they were animals.

In the few weeks her mother had been confined here, Mellie had learned to hate Sundays, the only time she could get off from her grubby job in the draper's shop at the end of Badger Lane. Her mother was hopelessly insane, a condition brought on by excessive drink plus a case of the French pox contracted from one of her numerous men friends. The death of the faithful Helga was the final push that sent Lady Anna over the brink into madness.

Picking her way through the crowd of upper-class sightseers, Mellie spotted a familiar face in the group, the Duchess of Seybrook, who had caused her mother's dismissal from the Court of St. James. She hung back, not anxious for a confrontation with the elegant duchess and her companions, a group of lords and ladies from court. The duchess, delicately holding back the hooped skirt of her apple green India silk gown, peered avidly into each cage, masking her face behind an imported oriental fan, tittering at the ravings of the bedeviled inmates.

Mellie noticed that the duke was not in attendance, which did not surprise her at all. The marriage between the Duke and Duchess of Seybrook was one of convenience, with neither taking any notice of marriage vows. This was the supreme irony of Lady Anna Wilton's dismissal from court because of her dalliance with the duke; for the duchess was notorious for her succession of lovers.

Now, her only decent gown beginning to show wear, with the

blue silk splitting at the seams, and the lace pulling loose at the cuffs of the elbow-length oversleeves, Mellie would be mortified if the elegant duchess and her equally splendid friends should see her in such a condition.

The group of courtiers moved slowly, with Mellie trailing far behind; for they were in the corridor where Anna's cell was located, and Mellie would have to brush past the group in order to see her mother. To her horror, the duchess and her coterie stopped directly in front of the barred door to the room Lady Anna shared with other insane women, each of them shackled to keep them from attacking the others.

Clear as a morning church bell in a country village, the duchess's voice rang out. "Is that—it has to be! Look, Miranda, isn't that Lady Anna Wilton, my husband's late and unlamented paramour?"

"Which one, which one?" the others cried, crowding up to the bars that protected them from the unfortunates.

"Over there, in the corner. The one with her hair matted down over her face. But I recognize her. I do!" The duchess fluttered her fan through the bars, a slender wrist inching forward from frills of imported ecru lace. "Anna!" she trilled. "Anna Wilton! Lady Anna! Over here at the door. See who's come to visit."

Mellie had spent a year of torment with her drunken mother, and she had little sympathy for the poor demented thing; but this was too much for her. Uttering a little sound of protest deep in her throat, she moved forward in the forlorn hope that she might, somehow, prevent any further degradation of Anna. Too late. She heard the wild shriek that she knew was torn from her mother's throat in her madness. Not once since she'd been confined here in Bedlam had her mother recognized Mellie. But somehow the shrill, piercing taunts of the Duchess of Seybrook cut through the haze of Anna's bedeviled mind and touched off some kind of recognition and acknowledgement.

Pushing now, ignoring the muttered curses as she crowded forward toward the bars behind which her mother lay in filth, Mellie felt a searing rage at these fancy creatures, these silk- and satin-clad courtiers, who came to mock the poor mad unfortunates locked within these gray walls. She must get the duchess and her friends away, somehow.

"Oh, it's too bad that my dear husband isn't here today," the duchess said, laughing maliciously. "Can you imagine his bedding that?" and she flicked her closed fan in Anna's direction.

"See, Anna," she called, "what happens to those who choose to play me for the fool! Do you enjoy your new home, dear, dear Anna? Is your pallet as comfortable as my conjugal bed which you desecrated?"

By now, Mellie had pushed, pulled, and fought her way up to the doorway to stand side by side with the duchess. Mellie saw her mother raise her head, her hair turned gray in the few weeks she'd been incarcerated here, her eyes glazed with madness; but some spark of recognition lighted them as the Duchess of Seybrook called out her name.

With a shriek that sent cold chills down Mellie's spine, her mother lunged forward, only to fall back onto the filthy floor when the chain that fettered her to the wall would reach no further. "I'll kill you, vicious bitch!" she screamed. "Kill! Kill! Kill!"

Again she sprang toward the door with a rattling of chains, her eyes bulging as if they were about to burst from their sockets, blazing, and saliva dribbled from her open mouth. She bared her teeth as a cornered fox would. It was such a terrifying sight that Mellie cringed, and the duchess backed up a step, a little shriek on her lips.

"Oh, she dares threaten me! Warder!" she called loudly. "Warder! I'm being attacked by a mad woman!"

It was too much for Mellie. Turning, she slapped the duchess so hard that some of the whiting on her face rubbed off on Mellie's palm. "Be quiet!" she said, her voice low, shaking with emotion. "Leave her alone. She's mad, poor thing. Isn't that enough for you, wicked woman?"

"How dare you? How dare you touch me, you . . . ." Venom dripped from the duchess's carmined lips; but then she stopped short, recognition in her pale gray eyes. "The daughter! Anna Wilton's precocious brat! And you dare to strike me? I'll have the constables. . . ."

She got no further. As if aware, finally, that her only child was now under attack, Anna Wilton set up such a racket, screaming, shrieking, wailing, and rattling her chains, that it attracted a warder who pushed his way through to the door.

"Eh? What's going on, now? Stop that racket, you mad woman!" he ordered.

Anna shrieked all the more, her face now a brick red, her breast heaving and flushed above the soiled tatters of her gown.

"Warder, this young creature struck me," the duchess accused, pointing a trembling finger in Mellie's face.

It was all the girl could do not to bite down hard on the long, bony pointer. The warder took her arm, shaking her until her teeth rattled.

"Here now, why would you do such a thing to her ladyship?"

"She was tormenting my mother," Mellie gasped.

Then, abruptly, Anna's shrieking stopped. She stood there, silent, her eyes bulging. She seemed to have trouble getting her breath.

"Something's wrong with her," Mellie cried out. "Do something, please, help her."

Then, as if struck a blow with an invisible quarterstaff, Anna Wilton fell forward, her eyes rolling up until only the whites showed.

"Ugh. Disgusting. Let's leave," the Duchess of Seybrook murmured to her friends. "Forget the silly chit of a girl."

Like spring snowflakes, they melted away, leaving Mellie clinging to the bars of the cell, her eyes fastened on her mother's still form with horror.

"Here, move aside, girl," the warder ordered; but his voice was a bit gentler than before. "I think she's dead, I do. Your mother, you say?" Mellie nodded, not trusting her voice to answer. "Well, if she's dead, it's a blessing and that's a fact." He took a huge key from a ring that hung clanking from his belt and opened the cell door. "Can't come in here, miss. These women are dangerous." He approached Anna Wilton's crumpled body with caution, making sure he stayed out of the reach of the other shackled women who now had set up a horrific racket of their own. "Quiet now," he bawled at them. "Be quiet, I say." It only added to the din. Bending over the inert body, he lifted her head and peered at her eyes, then laid his head on her bosom for a moment to listen for a heartbeat.

Standing, he shook his head at Mellie. "Gone, miss."

"My mother is dead?"

The enormity of it was more than Mellie could comprehend. Helga dead. Anna dead. She was all alone in the world. The final horror was that she had to have her mother buried in a pauper's grave, for Mellie's job at the draper's shop paid scarcely enough to feed her. There was no money left. Her mother's diamond earrings had kept them alive; but Anna had drunk up all of their extra funds.

At the end of the week, the final blow fell. At closing time on Saturday, Mrs. Timms peered down her overly long, pointed nose at Mellie and said, "Business is so bad that I have to let you go."

Mellie felt ill from this added shock. "But, Mrs. Timms, how will I live?"

"I can't worry about that, can I?" the woman asked. "You're not a very good helper. You cut off extra inches when you measure dress goods. That's money out of my pocket, miss. I can't afford you, and that's the truth."

"Please, Mrs. Timms, I'll be very careful after this," Mellie pleaded. But Mrs. Timms's face was carved of stone. "When must I stop working?" Mellie whispered.

"When? Now. You're strong and healthy. You'll find work, if you've a mind to." Grudgingly, she counted out the coins she owed Mellie, a meager sum standing between her and starvation.

In a state of shock, Mellie moved slowly out of the door. The tinkle of the little bell that rang to alert Mrs. Timms that a customer had entered might as well have been a bell tolling for the dead. How could she manage, until she found another job? And what could she do? Mellie had learned a lot in this past year. A pretty face and blooming figure might be assets at court; but they were a curse when she wanted work. No woman wanted her in her home, for fear the husband would be attracted to her. And Mellie knew all too well that this happened. If she were ugly, she'd have a better chance to get a job—some kind of job—anything.

As she went into the mean, narrow building where she lived, the watchful landlady popped out and confronted the girl.

"Mrs. Timms give you the sack, didn't she, my girl?"

Mellie nodded. She didn't even ask where this old harridan had heard of her misfortune. No doubt Mrs. Timms had told her over a pot of ale at the nearest tavern.

"And what about my rent, I want to know?"

"I'll look for a position immediately," Mellie promised.

"I must have my money in advance." Harsh, implacable, she held out her hand. "With no job, I can't keep you on. A week in advance, miss."

Mellie clutched her precious wages. If she paid for her room, she'd have nothing left for food.

"I . . . I'll pawn. . . ."

The landlady sneered. "You've naught left to pawn, and you know it. My money, or out you go."

Something snapped in Mellie's mind. "I won't pay you, you old skinflint!" she yelled. "And I won't vacate my room, not until I have a chance to. . . ."

With the speed of a stoat, a speed surprising from a woman as obese as her landlady, that woman moved in front of the sagging staircase to the upper floors. "Not so fast with your sharp tongue, miss. Don't come up these stairs until I have my rent in advance."

"But my things. . . ."

"Not one step."

In despair, Mellie paid for one week, which left her with only a few pence between her and starvation.

"And don't think you can entice gentlemen in and entertain them in my house!" the woman called after her as Mellie wearily climbed the creaking stairs to her attic. "I'll not have my house known as a whorehouse, miss."

Mustering all the dignity she could find, Mellie looked over her shoulder at the blowsy landlady in her greasy striped dress and her spotted, yellowed apron. "I'm not a whore."

"Well, your dead mother was one; and like mother, like daughter, I always say."

It was the truth about Anna Wilton; but Mellie had more sympathy now for her dead mother than she'd ever felt for her when she was alive. Anna had been driven to her fate by circumstances that she couldn't control.

Inside her grim little room, Mellie took stock of her possessions. She might raise a few shillings on the silver-backed hairbrush. The enameled patchbox might also net a bit. But once they were pawned, then what? Well, she'd have to think of that later. Monday she'd go to the pawnshop over on Cheapside, and perhaps she'd be lucky enough to find work somewhere; although Mellie knew all too well that it wouldn't be easy. She'd done nothing that gave her work experience. The governess jobs had been disasters. The draper was right, she was a poor shop assistant. She'd never cut a length of cloth before in her life. Maybe she could get work in a tavern as a barmaid. Yet Mellie knew instinctively that her educated accent would not set well with a tavern keeper nor with his low-class clientele. She didn't want to grub for a living. A great swell of resentment filled her, and she flung the hairbrush onto the lumpy bed with its thin mattress. She was used to the good life. She wasn't cut out for such an existence as this. Mellie longed for palaces and mansions, velvets and silks and laces, jewels and expensive baubles. Now she had nothing, nothing. It was all the fault of the Duchess of Seybrook who couldn't satisfy her odious husband in bed.

"Someday she'll be sorry," Mellie vowed. "I'll make her wish she'd never heard of Melusina Anna Hildreth Wilton."

CHAPTER SEVEN

No one wanted an inexperienced helper. Without a letter from her last position, no one wanted a governess as young and pretty as Mellie. Mellie didn't know enough about working for a living to find one of the many jobs she might have been able to master. The silver-backed hairbrush bought meager meals for that one week. She resolved not to pawn the patchbox. Some survival instinct told Mellie that she must always hold back some little thing, even the minutest of nest eggs, against utter disaster.

She did apply for a position as abigail to a lady who lived on Great Queen Street. But the woman asked Mellie to do her hair before she would hire her, and when Mellie pulled, being inexperienced in hairdressing, the woman rapped her knuckles sharply with the ivory comb and sent her packing.

On Saturday, she went out in the afternoon just to walk through Lincoln's Inn Fields to breathe a bit of fresh air. This, too, was a mistake, for she was accosted by no fewer than four men who assumed she was a prostitute looking for clients. The final one, a foreign sailor who spoke practically no English, was so persistent that she had to threaten to find a constable before he'd finally left her alone. It was disheartening.

When she reluctantly returned to Badger Lane, she found her small trunk set outside the door, with two beggars trying to pry it open.

"Get away from that!" she screamed, running at them, quickly untying her tattered pocket and flailing them with it. "That's mine!"

Frightened by her onslaught, the two beggars melted away. Thoroughly enraged, Mellie pounded on the door to her living quarters.

Her fat landlady finally stuck her mobcapped head out of the partially opened door, demanding, "What's all this racket? This is a respectable house."

53

"Why is my trunk out in the street?" Mellie demanded.

"Because I have let your room to someone else."

"But . . . but . . ." the girl spluttered, too angry to talk.

"I knew you'd no work. No work, no pay. No pay, no rent for me. I do not run an almshouse, miss. Be glad I was kind enough to pack up your rags and tatters and have my man carry them downstairs for you."

She slammed the door in Mellie's face, and no amount of pounding on it with fist, or kicking it with slipper, brought the lady back.

For the first time since Helga's death, Mellie was fully aware of her plight. Always there had been a few pence she could live on. Now, nothing. The patchbox would bring too little to be of any use. In despair, Mellie sank down on the rounded top of her small trunk and let the tears come. They trickled down her cheeks, washing off the bit of paint she'd used that morning in hopes of appearing older and more sophisticated when applying for employment.

Night was almost upon her. In the distance she could hear the watchman crying the hour, and it was the call of doom in her young ears. From the other direction, she saw an elderly lamplighter, glowing pole in his gnarled hands, beginning his rounds to fire the whale oil in the flat pans attached to the lamp poles.

A coach turned into the end of Badger Lane, and Mellie instinctively shrank close to the brick walls of the house, for the lane was narrow and she didn't want to be splattered by mud from the street. The coach went past, then she heard the coachman shouting his horses to a stop. She paid little attention, being sunk in her own private desolation, when a footman who clung to the back of the small landau hopped down and pulled open the door, setting a wooden stool for the occupant to use for alighting from the coach.

It wasn't until she felt a touch on her shoulder that Mellie looked around. A woman stood there, not a young woman, but one in middle years, probably well into her forties. She was expensively dressed, although there was something a bit flamboyant about her gown of peacock blue satin. Perhaps it was the embroidered roses of gold thread which glittered with dewdrops of Austrian brilliants, or it might have been the glossy straw bonnet which framed a face so pitted by smallpox that even heavy paint didn't hide the scars. Or perhaps it was the many rings she wore on hands that looked like they'd done many a day of hard work; or the French slippers with heels so high that she teetered on the rough pavement. Instinctively, Mellie knew that the woman wasn't one of the *ton*.

When she spoke, her accent gave her away completely. It was uncouth; but her voice was pleasant, her manner kind.

"Trouble, miss? Thrown out of your lodgings? Couldn't pay the rent to the miserable old crab who owns the property?"

"How did you guess?" Mellie asked, gulping back sobs.

"Ah, miss, I've known hard times meself, in the past. Now, thank the good Lord, that's all behind me. But a young thing like you, educated I can tell by your way of talking, a lady, what are you doin' here on the pavement in Badger Lane? You'd be ever so much more at home in Grosvenor Square, you would."

The kind tones broke Mellie down completely, and she buried her face in her hands and sobbed, out of control.

She felt an arm around her, and the woman's voice was murmuring, "Come, come, me pretty, this will never do. You'll be ill, your lovely blue eyes will be all red and swollen. I've plenty of room in me own home for you. Come along, Alf will get your trunk up on back of me carriage. Come, child, I'll take you home, give you hot tea and a good supper with a bit of wine to calm your shattered nerves, and we'll sort all this out in the way as is best for you."

Overwhelmed by circumstances, Mellie allowed herself to be led to the coach where the footman helped her into the landau before her benefactress. Facing that lady, Mellie wiped her eyes on her torn lace-edged kerchief and sat, almost in a stupor, while her trunk was loaded onto the back of the coach and then the coachey whipped up the team and they got underway.

"I've a lovely home in Westminster," the lady gabbled, "plenty of room for another lonely young woman. But how rude of me. I'm Mrs. Mudridge. And you, me dear?"

"Melusina Wilton. But everyone calls me Mellie."

"Melusina? Isn't that one of the Maypole's names? Ah, I see I've hit a sore spot. Well, Mellie, pay no heed to me. I'm just a nattering old woman, lived in London all me life, started lowly but I've had some success." She smoothed the expensive satin flounces of her skirt. "But you've come on hard times, I can tell. All the signs, and I can read 'em better than I can read writin', not being much schooled. You wear a lovely gown, but it is tattered. Slippers nearly through the toe. You've come down in the world as I've come up, eh? So we meet at a common level."

Mellie scarcely knew how to take the garrulous Mrs. Mudridge; but she seemed a kind soul and it had been some time since anyone had bothered to be kind to Mellie.

"I—I lost my position today a week," she admitted. "And my mother died, in Bedlam," she added defiantly. No point in pretending anything that wasn't true.

"Could happen to anyone, dearie, with times as they are. A German on the throne of England, can't even speak the King's English. Now, isn't that a joke for you, Mellie, me dear?"

Mellie summoned up a tiny smile; but thinking about King George did little to raise her spirits. In fact, tears slid down over her cheeks again.

"Come, now, no more tears, Mellie," Mrs. Mudridge cried heartily. "I'll not have it, you know. Things are looking up for you, me dear. We'll go to me lovely home and a maid will bring you water for a bath. You'd like that, wouldn't you? A bath in a lovely tin hip tub, with roses painted on the sides. Nothing but the best in me home. And then a nice supper for you, and you can be tucked up in your own cozy little bedchamber."

"How can I ever repay you?" Mellie wailed. "I've scarcely any money. . . ."

"Tut, me dear! Who mentioned money? I've plenty of money for us both. 'Tis me Christian duty to help young ladies in distress. Later, you can help me a bit, perhaps, when you feel livelier. Nothing hard, you understand. We don't want those lovely hands of yours marked with calluses, do we? Must keep them soft and lovely, nice to touch. No, we've plenty of servants. But sometimes you might help me entertain me guests."

"Oh, I'd be glad to, Mrs. Mudridge," Mellie said. What incredible luck! An hour ago, she thought the end of the world had come for her. Now, suddenly, out of the London smoke and fog, she had a wealthy patroness—eccentric, no doubt; of lowly birth, obviously. But although her taste wasn't the best, Mellie recognized money when she saw it; and if she'd learned anything this past horrid year, it was that money was even more important than high birth. If her mother had been in funds, even dismissal from court could have been dealt with. Anna could have opened a salon, collected a coterie of those who hadn't court connections but wanted to be noticed in society. But without money, nothing was possible.

Now, a wealthy woman had chosen her as a protegee, and Mellie intended to be practical about it. She might have wished for someone of the nobility, or at least of the gentry; but Mrs. Mudridge had presented herself, and Mellie didn't intend to let her escape.

Such pleasant thoughts dried up her tears, and she was able to smile for the eccentric lady who sat opposite her.

"I do so enjoy a drive along the Strand, even at night," Mrs. Mudridge was saying. "Alf is well armed, and so is my coachey. Spent time in the army, he did. Knows how to handle the blunderbuss he keeps up in the box. So don't worry your pretty little head about footpads, or even highwaymen. They'll not dare hold up a coach belongin' to Mrs. Mudridge." Then, her eyes narrowing suddenly so that her kindly face seemed almost sly, she asked, "Haven't heard of me, have you, little Mellie Wilton?"

Mellie scarcely knew how to answer. Would the woman be annoyed if she were someone the *ton* knew about, and Mellie failed to recognize her? Temporizing, she told her Good Samaritan the exact truth. "I'm sorry, madam, but I have been in such straitened circumstances this past year that I have been able to buy the newspaper, so I have lost track of all the activities of the *ton*." There, that should do splendidly. She'd made it sound as if she thought Mrs. Mudridge a member of high society. Surely that would set well with her.

It did bring a smile to the lips, such a wide smile that Mellie could see blackened, rotting stumps of teeth behind the paint. "Ah, yes, you've been out of touch, indeed, me dearie. Well, you'll find many highborn coming to Mrs. Mudridge's," she cackled. "Ah, you'll be quite an asset at such gatherings."

It had been so long since anyone had complimented her looks without some ulterior motive that Mellie preened. If this woman's generosity extended to some new gowns, she'd be the belle of any social event Mrs. Mudridge might stage. And she might well receive members of society. Money talked in all walks of life; and although the nobility tended to be snobbish about their high birth, Mellie had seen in court that they all wanted to increase their wealth. Many a lord had married his daughter to a rich merchant, in order to get money into the family, then wheedled at court to have the new son-in-law given a title. Ah, Mellie knew how it all went. She'd learned it the hard way.

When they reached Charing Cross, instead of proceeding along the Mall past the palace, the coachey turned the team into Whitehall, past the Abbey, its gothic spires pointing at heaven, until he neared the bend in the Thames.

"We are delightfully close to Ranelagh Gardens," Mrs. Mudridge told Mellie. "So nice in the summer, a pleasant place for me young ladies to stroll."

Mellie, well acquainted with Ranelagh, was doubly glad that Mrs. Mudridge had happened onto her in mean, grimy Badger Lane. If it crossed her mind to wonder what such a grand, rich woman was doing in that miserable, crowded part of the city, she dismissed the question before it was more than half-formed. Mellie wasn't about to put her hand in this gift horse's mouth to count its teeth. It was enough that her benefactress had seen her outside her lodgings and had stopped.

"Me mansion is Queen Anne, with lovely, warm brickwork," the running commentary went on. "You'll love it. Very large, with fine gardens. Sometimes I think it almost foolish for me young girls to bother to go to Ranelagh, when our own gardens are so enchanting—with a summer house hidden away in back, ever so intimate."

Heavens! The old woman must love men, Mellie thought unkindly. Yet who would be attracted to her, with her coarse manners and speech, her pocked face, and her rotten teeth? Mellie knew, though, that even young men often called on women old enough to be their mothers, usually because they had money or were socially influential. The picture of the flamboyant Mrs. Mudridge in an intimate tête-à-tête in her charming summer house was so hilarious that it took all of Mellie's social training to keep from laughing in the good woman's face.

"Ah, now nice to see you smile, Mellie. You've a lovely face, when you're happy; and at me house, in Westminster, happy you'll be. And popular. Oh, the young gentlemen will swarm about you like bees around clover." Then, again, that sudden transformation, the sly look, which Mellie thought she must be imagining. The light inside the coach was so poor, for the outside lamps cast only a faint glow within, emphasizing the shadows rather than relieving them, that Mellie decided she was seeing things. "You don't have a young lord dangling after you, do you, Mellie? No, of course not, or he'd never have allowed you to fall into such a state as I found you. And how old did you say you were, me dear?"

Mellie didn't remember that her age had come up before; but by now she was so tired, and Mrs. Mudridge was so garrulous, that the question might have been asked and she'd not noticed.

"I'll be sixteen May Day."

"Ah, a lovely age, Mellie. I can remember me own sixteenth birthday—but that's not a lovely story, not lovely at all. Well, we'll have to plan a special party just for you, me dear. And May

Day's just next week. I'll introduce you to me guests on your birthday."

A party. Mellie remembered all too well her fifteenth birthday, and the aborted party. This year she'd make up for it. Obviously Mrs. Mudridge didn't have to look hard for her next tuppence. Mellie did wonder, briefly, why the woman should be so generous to a perfect stranger, but then she decided that perhaps the woman was religious. Religion was very passé with the *ton*. Oh, some made a show of going to St. Paul's, or one of the other fashionable churches in the city, or to the Abbey if they lived in Westminster; but no one Mellie knew was a bit religious. However, Mrs. Mudridge was an original. Maybe she went about London, rescuing young women who had fallen on bad times, as Mellie had.

When they finally turned in between the tall brick gateposts on one of the better streets off Whitehall, Mellie was almost asleep.

"Come, come, me dear, into the house with you. And then a nice bath, a bite of supper, and bed. Tomorrow will be for rest; but come Monday, you'll spend the day with the dressmaker, being fitted for some new gowns. If what you've on your back now is typical of your wardrobe, you won't fit in with me stylish girls at all."

Some small bit of sanity forced Mellie to murmur, "I can't afford new gowns, Mrs. Mudridge."

"Afford! Listen to the silly girl. Why should you afford gowns? I've all the gold we need, me dear. And it's me pleasure to deck you out in new clothes. Such a lovely young woman as you. With a birthday coming up, you see. Call it a gift for your sixteenth, me dearie."

The rest of the evening was a blur. Mellie was whisked upstairs by a middle-aged abigail who saw her into a charming bedchamber, helped her undress, called up a sturdy young maid with pitchers of hot water for the hip bath, and then produced a nightdress of indecently sheer India muslin bedecked with lace which might have been made for Mellie, it fit so well. Over this went a retiring robe of palest blue brocade worked in silver and peacock blue. Mellie reveled in such luxury, even more than she'd known at court; for there her mother had been only a lady-in-waiting, and their personal quarters had been nothing like this for opulence.

After a light supper of cold pheasant and a pasty washed down with a good hock, Mellie crawled into her enormous high bed, the maid dropped the curtains around it, and she was asleep before her head dented the soft down pillows.

CHAPTER EIGHT

There was a tap at her door, and Nell, the middle-aged abigail who'd been dressing her, admitted Mrs. Mudridge who was resplendent in purple, her hoops wide over the hips so that she had to turn sideways to get through the door. Her gray hair was in little sausage curls, topped with a snowy cap with a starched frill that was six inches high. Her décolletage was so deep that her ample bosom, supported by tightly laced corsets, was a white mountain of flesh. She wore an amethyst necklace which must have cost a fortune, but which was altogether too much with the purple gown; and the amethyst drop earrings looked downright gaudy. Her overskirt was looped high in front, showing a cloth-of-gold underskirt embroidered with seed pearls, and her fashionable French slippers had such high heels, set midway on the soles, that the woman tottered along as if she were crippled.

Mellie was still young enough to be unkind, at least in her thoughts, about older women; and Mrs. Mudridge was vulgar, there was no other word to describe her. Yet Mellie had been in a whirl of preparation this week, with no stinting on the guineas that had poured into her sumptuous wardrobe. The little dressmaker had brought the latest fashion plates over from the Continent, and the fabrics she'd produced were mouth-watering in their elegance. Fortunately, Mrs. Mudridge hadn't chosen the styles, leaving this up to Mellie and little Mrs. Gumple, a pouter pigeon of a woman; so the girl had been able to avoid flamboyance in her own attire. Her gown tonight was a soft shade of rose, the silk falling in flounces from her tiny waist. Each flounce was edged with white lace and narrow velvet ribbon in a darker shade of rose. The bodice was fitted, with cunning lacing of ribbon under the bosom. Cuffed sleeves ended just at the elbow, so that her rounded young arms showed from the frills of lace as if they were growing from beautiful flowers.

Nell had dressed her hair very simply, with one long curl falling over her right shoulder. A wider velvet ribbon about her throat only emphasized its elegant length. Her shoes were of white kid, and she was admiring the entire effect when Mrs. Mudridge came sweeping in.

"Oh, lovely, lovely!" that worthy lady cried. "Sixteen. Delicious!" She came up to Mellie and whispered loudly. "Those young bloods will dangle after you tonight, me dear. Such highborn young men. You'll see. They all come to Mrs. Mudridge's routs. And when they see you. . . !" She rolled her eyes in a most comical fashion. "And here's a little gift for you, me dear."

"But you've given me so much already," Mellie cried.

"Just a little fan, to flirt with."

It was a dainty little fan of painted kidskin, and when Mellie opened it, she felt herself blush at the pictures on it; for it was of unclad nymphs enticing handsome, young, equally nude men into explicit sexual encounters.

"Quite sophisticated. All the rage in Paris," Mrs. Mudridge told her, snickering at Mellie's embarrassment. "Do all your blushing here in private. Then use the fan with the young nobles downstairs—you'll know how! Old Mother Mudridge doesn't have to instruct you in coquetry, now, does she?"

For answer, Mellie opened the fan, half hiding her face, and looked coyly at her reflection in the long mirror.

"That's just exactly right," cried her patroness. "Come, now, time for the festivities to begin. Come along. The other girls are already in the drawing room."

Mellie had been kept so busy with the refurbishing of her wardrobe that she'd scarcely gotten to know the other protegées of Mrs. Mudridge. They were all young women of exceptional good looks; but they had not seemed especially friendly to Mellie. Ah, well, no doubt they were shy of someone new. Tonight as they celebrated her birthday, Mellie hoped to get to know them better. She wondered if they, too, had fallen on such hard times as she had. Truly, Mrs. Mudridge was a saint.

Feeling very confident, knowing that she looked quite lovely, Mellie followed Mrs. Mudridge down the winding staircase and into the main drawing room. It was a large, beautifully proportioned room, done in the classical manner. Half pilasters of snowy marble rose to a beautiful ceiling with a large central mural of gods and goddesses in a sylvan setting. Gilt plaster garlands surrounded the picture and were repeated around the ceiling, with intricate festoons at the four corners. The walls were of a soft green, the floor a geometric design of parquetry, highly polished. There were masses of spring flowers, all forced for the occasion by Mrs. Mudridge's gardener, about the room. The furniture was delicate gilt with gold and white brocade upholstery.

There was already quite a gathering of elegant young men, all decked out in their brilliant silks, satins, and velvets. A small orchestra sat on a raised platform in one corner, and they played softly, a charming background to the hum of voices.

As Mrs. Mudridge led Mellie into the room, she made a signal to these musicians, and they played a short, lively fanfare which broke in on the conversations.

All eyes turned to the doorway, and Mellie couldn't help but notice the looks from the young gentlemen. Several gazed at her through their quizzing glasses, nodding approval.

"Tonight I wish to introduce a new young lady to you gentlemen," Mrs. Mudridge brayed. "Our own dear Melusina. If she finds you attractive enough, you may be allowed to call her Mellie."

Mellie dropped a low curtsy to the assembled guests, who bowed in turn to her. It was while she was rising from her curtsy that Mellie realized something very odd. The only other women in the room were Mrs. Mudridge's girls. There was Pamela, jet black hair now powdered to set off flashing dark eyes; Clarissa, a natural redhead who chose to wear her chestnut locks dressed tight to her head, their natural color topped with a delicate pinner of lace which matched the lace of her deep blue velvet Watteau sacque; Prudence, a mischievous minx, with hair a paler gold than Mellie's; Becky, whose background Mellie suspected was not as elegant as she'd like one to believe; and Tamsen, from Scotland, the burr in her soft speech very fetching.

Then everything stopped for Mellie. Moving out in front of the young men assembled in a cluster around the other young women was a familiar figure, Lord Alistair Densbury.

"Upon my soul, if it isn't little Mellie Wilton!" he exclaimed. He turned and murmured something to some of his companions, and Mellie heard a few guffaws. How could he! Still remembering that dreadful scene a year ago at court when the Maypole had banished her.

He was moving toward her, though, an eager smile on his face. Perhaps she wronged him. Her first impulse had been to cut him dead; but he was so dashing, so handsome, wearing a full periwig tonight of a rich brown which went well with his hazel eyes and dark complexion. His coat was beautifully cut of a deep brown velvet laced with gold, and his waistcoat was a pale tan embroidered with brown and gold. His neck cloth was snowy, the frills at his wrist were so long they almost covered his hands, and he was altogether the most elegant young blood there.

Making a leg, he said, "Mellie, how interesting to find you here! And looking lovely, I must add." He turned to Mrs. Mudridge saying, "As always, your taste is impeccable."

Mellie, who thought Mrs. Mudridge's taste appalling, put the remark down to Lord Densbury's good breeding. Most of the men in the *ton* were given to extravagant phrases when complimenting their hostesses.

"You have met? How very interesting," Mrs. Mudridge said, a calculating edge to her tone which didn't escape Mellie. Well, perhaps Mrs. Mudridge was an inveterate matchmaker. Many of the matrons Mellie had met at court were thus inclined.

The tiny orchestra struck up a gavotte, and Lord Densbury asked, "May I have the pleasure, Mellie?"

Using the fan, she nodded ever so slightly, and he led her to the other end of the room where the others were forming a set to dance.

"Have you been well? I've not seen you in—how long, now?" Densbury murmured, taking her hand for the dance.

Not wanting to remind him of that dreadful day just a year ago, Mellie said, "Oh, several months, at least. Time flies, doesn't it, when one is busy?"

"You're no longer at court?"

She was glad that she moved away from him at just that moment. He knew very well that she was no longer at court, and why. When they came back together in the dance, she said, only, "No, I'm not at court." She'd rather die than tell him what had been happening to her these past dreadful months, so she volunteered no information. Let him assume she'd been abroad, if he liked, back in the Hanoverian Electorate, or in Paris.

"Your mother is well?"

He asked it in such a peculiar tone of voice that Mellie knew he remembered Anna's banishment from court all too well. Putting on a sad face, she said, "Mother is dead, milord."

As they moved through the dance, she had other partners, but each time she was with Densbury, he continued the delicate interrogation. "And how long have you been here with Mother Mudridge?"

"Not long."

"She was a friend of your mother?"

What difference did it make? Mellie wondered, feeling a bit cross with Densbury. Why all the chatter about her mother? She had a sudden impulse to shock him. What would he do if she said, "Mother died, mad, in Bedlam, a drunken whore," but of course she said nothing of the kind. She sidestepped the question of how she'd met Mrs. Mudridge.

As the evening progressed, the crowd in the huge drawing room thinned out. Before long, Mellie realized that all of the other girls had disappeared, and many of the men. Wherever could they be? Perhaps they'd made up games of whist or bezique in one of the smaller parlors.

Another young man was making a big play for her, a fellow much too free with his hands, forever fondling her bare shoulders or tweaking the curl that fell so temptingly. Mellie didn't even recall his name; but she wished he'd disappear. She glanced around for Densbury, and saw him talking with Mrs. Mudridge. He saw her look, and smiled and bowed to her.

One of the maids was moving about with a silver tray of glasses of gin, and Mrs. Mudridge took two and moved toward her, with Densbury at her side.

"Mine, Benjie," Densbury said to the bothersome young man who scowled, but then shrugged, made a leg, and moved toward the group of remaining men, leaving Mellie with Densbury.

"I thought you might like a sip of gin, Mellie, to celebrate your birthday," Mrs. Mudridge said rather archly, holding one stemmed glass out to her. But somehow, before Mellie took hold of it, Mrs. Mudridge let go, and the glass fell to the floor, spilling gin down the front of Mellie's lovely new gown.

"Oh, how clumsy of me," Mrs. Mudridge cried, sounding not a bit annoyed with herself. "Run up to your room and have Nell help you change, Mellie. Hurry, now."

Mellie had been dabbing at the stain with a lace kerchief, distressed that her lovely gown was ruined, and fearful that Mrs. Mudridge would think she'd been clumsy; but that charming woman was taking all the blame for the accident. Murmuring, "Excuse me, milord," to Densbury, she hurried out, picking up her skirts and skimming up the stairs to her own bedchamber where she found Nell waiting almost as if she knew Mellie would be needing her.

"Oh, Nell, gin got spilled on my gown."

"Well, not to worry, miss. Here, let me unlace you."

Deftly, the abigail undressed Mellie, handing her a lovely negligee of apricot silk. "Just slip into this for a moment. I might just be able to remove this stain."

Before Mellie could protest, the abigail was gone with her gown. Going to the huge wardrobe, Mellie opened the doors and tried to decide which gown to put on to replace the other one. She knew the abigail couldn't get that gin stain out right away, if at all. How stupid of her to have gone off without helping Mellie into another gown.

Then there was a tap at the door. "Come in." She turned to tell Nell that she'd wear the green taffeta instead; but it wasn't the abigail who came into her chamber. It was Densbury. Stunned, Mellie caught her robe together to hide her chemise and stays.

"Wh——what are you doing here?" she squeaked, not at all liking the look on his lordship's face. It was an avid, hungry, animal look she'd seen men have when they looked at her mother.

"Oh, come now, Mellie, no need to be coy with me." He advanced on her, loosening his neck cloth as he did so. "Worth every penny of it," he murmured, eating her with his hot hazel eyes.

She didn't know what that meant; but Mellie wasn't stupid. She knew exactly what Densbury had in mind.

Summoning up all her courage, she stood her ground and announced, with only the tiniest quaver in her voice, "If you as much as touch me, Alistair Densbury, I shall scream."

"Scream?" He raised one dark eyebrow, giving his face a satanic look, actually quite interesting, Mellie thought. "I say, Mellie, no need for coquetry. Leave that for the younger ladies-in-waiting at George's court. I don't like to play games. Here at Mother Mudridge's, there's no need to dissemble."

By now he had taken off his coat and was rapidly unbuttoning his waistcoat. Mellie clutched her apricot silk about her, as if it were armor; but even as she did so, she knew that it would do little to protect her. And she was right. When Densbury had backed her against the wall, she tried to slip away from him. But he trapped her with one arm as strong as the iron bands on her traveling trunk, then ripped away the concealing silk with one powerful sweep of his other hand. Then she was in his arms, struggling against his superior strength, as he rained hot, wet kisses on her face and throat while his demanding hands moved fiercely over her unwilling flesh.

A year ago, at the bearbaiting, Densbury had aroused her own sexual desires by the subtlest of caresses, fondling her breasts surreptitiously, kissing her ear, sitting crushed against her; but tonight there was nothing subtle in his approach. He had been her ideal, the man she thought she loved, the one she had hoped to marry. His slightest touch had inflamed her—but now, being brutally pawed, knowing that he intended to force her, all Mellie felt was disgust. When he picked her up bodily and threw her upon the bed, she lay there naked, her fair skin already marked by his rough handling, while he quickly finished disrobing.

With bitter eyes she looked at his strong, muscular body, saw that he was ready for the sex she now loathed.

Too late Mellie knew who Mrs. Mudridge was, and what role she played in London society. Her lovely Queen Anne mansion was only a high class brothel. How could she have been so naive as to have thought that such a coarse old woman could be a patroness interested only in helping young women in distress.

With realization, Mellie knew there was no point in further struggling. Screams would avail her nothing. Mrs. Mudridge had arranged this all very cleverly, including the spilled drink, and there was absolutely nothing Mellie could do to save herself.

She submitted to him, humiliated and hurt as Densbury forced himself on a young, inexperienced woman who had not been prepared for the experience. If he had been gentle with her, pretending love, if he had taken time to caress her, to fondle her full young breasts, to bring her slowly to a height of passion which equalled his own, then Mellie might have enjoyed this first taste of sex; but Densbury was neither gentle nor particularly skillful as a lover. His performance was brutal but mercifully short, and once his own passion had been gratified, he had no further interest in his unhappy, unwilling partner.

In fact, when he was finished, while he still lay sprawled on top of her, he said loudly, "I should get that old hag, Ma Mudridge, to give me back my guineas. You aren't worth what I paid for you, Mellie Wilton. A virgin! I should have let Benjie have you first. He likes inexperience, does old Benjie; but when I pay my gold, I expect expertise. Being your mother's daughter, and knowing that she was the most willing whore at court, I thought you'd be something special. Too bad Lady Wilton died before she had you properly trained. Any little flower girl in Covent Garden would have given me a better ride than you did." He rolled off her and flung on his clothes, leaving without a backward glance, slamming the bedchamber door behind him. It was the final humiliation, and Mellie lay there, silently weeping, not even covering her violated body, as the bitterness enveloped her.

If her fifteenth birthday had been disastrous, her sixteenth was an utter catastrophe. It wasn't so much that Mellie prized her virginity so highly. She'd been raised at court where morals were notably loose; and her mother had set her a fine example with her love affairs and her final degradation, as Densbury had been quick to point out. Even with such examples, Mellie had romantic illusions about surrendering herself to some handsome young lord who loved her passionately, even as she adored him. Lord Alistair Densbury had been her ideal, the object of her girlish affection. To have to yield to his carnal desires under such circumstances was degrading; and to think that she had walked, wide-eyed, into the situation was completely mortifying.

Mentally she damned the garrulous, treacherous Mrs. Mudridge who preyed on young women in trouble. And she promised herself that someday, somehow, she would pay back Densbury in the same coin with which he had bought her unwilling body.

But the humiliation was not yet complete. While she lay there, angry and disillusioned, Mrs. Mudridge came sailing into her bedchamber without so much as a tap at the door.

"I'm very displeased with you, Mellie." Gone was the honeyed manner. Instead, the woman stood there implacable and vindictive, brothel keeper written on her every feature. "After all I've done for you—I picked you up out of the gutter, brought you here to me lovely home—outfitted you with expensive gowns, introduced you to the cream of London society—and what do you do in return? Nothing. For the first time in me life, I've had a client complain to me about one of me girls. Inexperienced and unwilling, he announced. A virgin who wanted to stay that way. No cooperation, he complained. Said you lay there like a lump of suet, without so much as a wriggle or a twitch of those luscious hips. Might as well have lain with a china doll, he told me. He demanded his money back! So I lost two gold guineas on you, because if I hadn't given him his money, he'd have gossiped about me in all the gambling halls in London. He'd have told everyone at White's that Mother Mudridge's girls aren't worth the money she charges for their services. I have me reputation to maintain, me girl, and you'll do better in the future, or I'll sell you to one of the cheap houses in the worst slums of London. Badger Lane will look like Pall Mall compared to them! See how you'd like that, me girl.

No lovely clothes, a new client every fifteen minutes. And most of those girls die of the French pox before too many years go by, servicing the rough sailors from the London docks. Is that what you want? If you expect to remain here, you'll have to mend your ways, me girl—or out in the streets for you.''

Mellie lay there, numb. The vista opened by Mrs. Mudridge's vicious words was bleaker than a London day in deep winter.

CHAPTER NINE

"You were a virgin? Until last night? And you're sixteen?" Becky shook her head in amazement, her gypsy locks falling into her face. "My stepfather took care of that for me when I was nine."

"I'm just surprised that Ma didn't give you some instructions, knowing you were inexperienced," Tamsen said in her soft, Scottish brogue. "When I told her it would be the first time for me, she was quite thorough in telling me just what to do to please the customers."

"She didn't know." Mellie was bitterly resentful, for obviously her fiasco as a prostitute was by now the talk of the entire *ton* of London. The other girls here certainly knew all the lurid tales of last night's disaster.

"Well, dearie, you should have just up and told her, same as Tamsen did," Becky said. "Nothing to be ashamed of. But Ma wouldn't expect it of someone of your age, raised at court—is that really true, Mellie? The old hag is such a liar. She thought you'd been bouncing your bed for ages."

Mellie toyed with the toast and marmalade and sipped her coffee. She wasn't about to admit the ultimate stupidity, that she'd had no idea she was living in a brothel. The girls would laugh her out of the house.

When they finally left breakfast, it was noon, the sun high. "Let's go for a stroll in Ranelagh Gardens, Mellie." At Mellie's questioning look, she assured her, "Ma knows we're going strolling. Alf will be there in the background, just to make sure no one molests us."

"Or that we try to run away," Mellie added bitterly.

"Where would we go?" Pamela asked, her voice sensible. "Believe me, it is better here at Ma's than in most other houses in London. Unless you are lucky enough to have some lord set you up in an establishment of your own—and how many women can expect such good fortune as that?—this is the best place to be.''

Mellie quickly dressed in a morning gown of fine India muslin embroidered all over with delicate flowers. She tied a charming, wide-brimmed straw hat over her white lawn round cap to keep the sun from her face, and drew on long gloves to protect her hands. When she joined Pamela downstairs, Mellie found that Tamsen was going with them, too. Both young women had on similarly simple morning gowns, Pam's of a deep green which set off her dark hair well. This morning it was dressed long, without powder. Tamsen, with eyes the blue of mountain tarns and hair black as a raven's wing, wore a tartan shawl over her pale blue gown.

Alf, in his footman's livery, did follow; but far enough behind that they could chat without his hearing them. The gardens were especially lovely at this time of year, with the flower beds vivid with flowers, and the paths bright with fashionable people strolling in the sylvan setting.

''We thought perhaps you'd prefer some suggestions from us, rather than from Ma Mudridge,'' Pamela said in her soft voice, smiling and bowing to various young blades who eyed the three attractive young women appreciatively. Mellie wondered what they'd think, how they'd react, if they knew that the trio of ladies were actually whores. ''You won't last long at Ma's if you don't please the men who come to see us.''

Tamsen, seeing the rebellion on Mellie's face, added, ''Don't fight it, Mellie. What were you doing before Ma brought you home?''

In a flood of bitterness, Mellie poured out her story to them— the banishment from court, the governess jobs, the pawing men, her mother's disintegration and death, everything except Densbury. She couldn't bring herself to tell that.

''So you were down to your last tuppence. Where else could you have gone?'' Tamsen asked. ''Believe me, there are worse places in London than a mansion near these gardens. I came south, thinking the streets of London were paved with gold; but I found the same muck I've waded in on the streets of Edinburgh. I was selling flowers in Covent Garden, and after months of that, of beating off the riffraff who prey on young women, I was glad Ma found me. So I sleep with men for pay. We're necessary in the scheme of things, Mellie.''

''You enjoy it?'' Mellie asked, appalled. Romantic affairs were one thing, but this—sex with strangers, for pay.

''I for one don't enjoy it,'' Pamela said. ''But I've learned to close my mind. I lie there, dreaming of a handsome, rich man who will set me up in my own town house. I go through the motions, but I've learned to detach my mind from my body.''

''We all do it, honey,'' Tamsen assured her. ''Except for Becky, who actually enjoys it. She's been tumbling in the hay with every man she's met since her stepfather seduced her—and I'm not sure but what she seduced him, knowing our Becky.''

''The rest of us, though, are consummate actresses,'' Pamela explained. ''We caress them, we learn to undress seductively, we tell them they're bigger and better than any man we've ever had. We cajole the young ones, and help to arouse the old men who are nearly past it.''

''Ugh. That's what I hate,'' Tamsen said, her mouth twisting with distaste. ''The old ones with their huge bellies, or their skin that's too big for their bodies. The ones with the rotting teeth and foul breath.''

''I hate the ones who want the whips,'' Pamela said. ''I had welts on me for a week, once. Ma wouldn't let me work until they faded.''

''And she allows . . .'' Mellie's mind filled with half-understood horrors. She'd heard whispers of such things. . . .

Pamela shrugged. ''Our business is to please. They pay for that. So, Mellie, you are going to have to work harder at giving the men what they want. It's that—or something a lot worse.''

''Look at it this way,'' Tamsen said matter-of-factly. ''Here we are strolling through Ranelagh Gardens, wearing the latest Parisian fashions. We live in a lovely mansion, we have abigails to wait on us. Very well, we have to give something in return. Most of the girls I knew in Edinburgh married young, to apprentices or at the best, to older tradesmen. Surely you don't think they married for love? They married for security. And when their husbands take them to bed, it is their duty to do whatever is asked of them, whether they want to or not.''

''It's only in romantic novels where the heroine marries the man of her dreams,'' Pamela added drily. ''Sex is a part of life. We provide a service, and for it we are well rewarded.''

''But—but what if you become pregnant? Then what?'' Mellie asked.

''Then Ma Mudridge stews up some molded rye grain for the ergot, and we drink it. And if that doesn't work, she knows a midwife who is more skillful at delivering an unwanted babe at one month than at nine. In that we're luckier than wives who haven't that choice, unless they're very clever, very rich, or extremely discreet.''

"That's why all of us girls like the Baron of Questerly," Pamela said, giggling suddenly.

"Let's walk through the rotunda," Tamsen suggested, "while we tell Mellie all about the baron."

They strolled with the crowds toward the galleried round building in the center of the gardens, passing a group of costumed dancers around a maypole, reminding Mellie again of her sixteenth birthday yesterday, and its misery. And of her namesake, Melusina von Schulenberg, now Duchess of Kendal.

Inside the rotunda an orchestra played from one of the galleries, the flutes and violins blending light melodies for their enjoyment.

"What about this baron?" Mellie reminded them.

"Oh, yes. He had mumps when he was a boy."

"So?" Mellie thought she saw Densbury in a group of elegant bloods across the hall, but then he was lost in the crowd.

"You've heard of mumps? Are you really from Hanover?" Tamsen asked curiously, "Or is that just one of Ma Mudridge's fictions to make us all seem more glamorous? According to her, I'm the daughter of an impoverished laird," and she snorted in an exceedingly undignified, nonladylike manner.

"Yes, I'm from Hanover. And from the Court of St. James," Mellie added defiantly. "But not recently." She didn't enlarge on it, although she could tell that the two women were avidly interested in her history. "What has that to do with a children's disease?"

"So you do know mumps. I thought maybe it was only in England. Well, children get it, of course. But so do adults occasionally, and when a man gets mumps, if he doesn't stay in bed, they drop—you know—to his privates, which swell up. And from then on, he can't father any children on you."

"Then why would he bother to come to a brothel and pay for something he can't do?" Mellie asked, cross with them for this nonsensical conversation.

"No, no, he can still perform like a man. But he just can't get you with child," Pamela explained patiently.

"Now, Pamela, I'm not sure that's exactly true," Tamsen argued. "Becky was telling me about some farmer she knew who'd caught the mumps from his own babe, and then didn't have any more babes until he was an old man of fifty. When suddenly he fathered a child on his dairy maid. His wife wouldn't believe the girl, said she was just trying to get money from him to support her bastard.''

''Probably was,'' Mellie said, properly cynical.

''But the babe looked just like this man who had flaming red hair. And so did the babe. So it's not always safe when the man has had the swelling.''

''We just all hope we don't get pregnant,'' Pamela said. ''Unfortunately all our clients are not like the baron.''

It was a pleasant enough stroll; but Mellie still wished she could run away. Tonight, when the men came, she'd be expected to take one up to her room.

''I can't do it!'' she exclaimed.

''Can't do what, Mellie?'' Tamsen asked.

''What you do every night. I can't.''

Tamsen's beautiful Highland face hardened. ''You can and you will. When we get back, we'll show you some tricks. Pamela has a book with pictures. The thing to remember is that you have to pretend you're enjoying it. Pretend you reach a climax. Remember, sometimes if a gentleman is particularly pleased with your performance, he'll give you a bit of extra money, just for yourself.''

''And don't tell Ma, or she'll claim it,'' Pamela warned. ''Then, when we shop, we can get a bit extra for ourselves. Ma pays our expenses, and gives us pin money. It's better than soliciting on the streets and taking your customers to some grubby little room in the slums.''

When they got back to the house, the young women took Mellie up to her bedroom for instructions. Tamsen demonstrated the sexy way to disrobe. ''If he wants to undress you, then let him, by all means. Sometimes they want you to take your hair down. If so, be sure to ring for Nell before you go back down to the salon. Ma doesn't like us downstairs unless we are perfectly groomed.''

''You mean—I have to entertain more than one man each evening?''

''Of course! Occasionally some man pays for one girl for the entire evening—but then you have to do it with him as often as he wishes. So what's the difference? They're really all alike, Mellie.''

Pamela brought the book of pictures she'd mentioned. Mellie was no prude; but she was stunned at some of the plates. ''I'm expected to do that?''

''You'll get used to it,'' Tamsen assured her. ''Just relax—and think of other things. Pretend you are with the man of your dreams. That he's madly in love with you. Be an actress. They don't all perform at the Drury Lane Theatre."

The nearer it got to the hour for "entertaining," the more nervous Mellie became. "I think I'm sickening for something. My head hurts. I feel hot. Do you think Ma? . . ."

"No she won't. It's nerves, Mellie. Think of it as stage fright. Remember, the finest actresses are completely calm once they are on stage." Pamela smiled encouragingly. "Use that naughty little fan you had last night. Let the men see what's on it. Flirt with them. Pretend it's a rout at some famous salon in Mayfair. You're the belle of the ball, the toast of London and Westminster."

"Now, get on the bed and show us how you move with a man," Tamsen ordered. Seeing the rebellion in Mellie's face, she insisted. "If you don't please your man tonight, Ma might just toss you out into the streets, Mellie. I've known it to happen. So you must learn in a hurry, since you don't know how to please a man."

They had her strip down to her chemise, lie on the bed, and then began the series of lessons on how to move.

"Abandon yourself," Pamela said. "Remember, a man likes a real romp, not a stilted little minuet in bed."

Mellie still went down to the evening's gathering in an emotional state nearer terror than abandon. Nell laced her so tightly that she felt she'd faint; but the abigail insisted, "It makes your bosom stand up more, miss, entices the gentlemen." She wondered what she would do if Alistair were there; but she knew no one in the crowd.

There was one young man who seemed very quiet, although there was much joking around him, and his friends seemed inclined to slap him on the back and laugh a lot. Ma Mudridge took Mellie over to this group and introduced her, whispering to her that she should be extra nice to the shy young gentleman.

"Do you come here often?" Mellie asked him, only to see him blush beet red.

"N-no, miss, I've not been, uh, here, uh, before," he stammered. And his companions roared with delight. Suddenly Mellie realized that this was his first trip to a brothel, and that he was in an agony of embarrassment. Feeling sorry for him, she slipped her arm through his and drew him away from his raucous companions, asking, as they sat down together on a love seat, "Are you from London, sir?"

"Uh, no. I'm from Bath."

"I've never been to Bath, but I understand that it is very fashionable there."

"Oh, very," he assured her as she smiled at him and leaned closer. His eyes strayed to her enticing bosom, then he looked frantically away.

Pretending she'd not noticed, Mellie kept on chatting to him about Bath, and London, hoping his shyness would go away. Finally she said softly,"Would you like to go up to my room with me?" deciding that she could manage him better than his boisterous companions.

For one moment, Mellie thought he might bolt; but then he noticed one of his friends slyly looking his way, and he said, a bit too loudly, "Yes, I'd enjoy that, miss."

Once inside her bedchamber, he stood poised as if he might run away any moment. Trying to put him at his ease, Mellie asked, "Can you help me undress, sir? I have such trouble with the lacings."

Again he blushed a beet red and approached her very hesitantly. For a moment, she was tempted to let him leave. But looking at his embarrassment, remembering her own humiliation last night, aroused a great compassion in Mellie. Obviously it was the first time for him. If he left her now, his friends would never let him forget it. Humiliation could be a vicious weapon in the hands of one's acquaintances. How well she knew! Smiling at him, trying not to be bold, for she knew instinctively that such an approach with a man as shy as this would be disastrous, Mellie coaxed him along, letting him help undress her. As her bosom was bared, she leaned toward him so that her breasts brushed against him, causing him to breathe faster.

"Here," she murmured, "I'll help you disrobe," and she reached up, sliding her hands around his neck to unfasten his neck cloth, pressing herself against him as if accidentally. By the time they were nude, he was fully aroused. Kissing him as Pamela had instructed, darting her tongue in between his suddenly hungry lips, she remembered Densbury's brutal approach last night. Well, she'd erase it from her mind, pretend it hadn't happened.

Whispering in his ear, she begged, "Carry me to the bed, sir."

Shyness gone in his urgent desire, he caught her up and laid her gently on the bed. Then, as if again unsure of what to do next, he stood there, hesitating, until she reached up and drew him down on her, accommodating herself to him, guiding him when he fumbled unskillfully. Then his instincts took over as Mellie moved with him to bring him to climax.

Afterward, lying beside her, he said, "I have a confession to make. It was my first time. Did you guess?"

And Mellie, remembering her instructions, lied gallantly, murmuring, "I don't believe you. You were so . . . so strong—you gave me so much pleasure."

He reached eagerly for her, caressing her breasts, suddenly bold as he kissed them. "Take hold of me," he ordered, gasping as her fingers closed on him. "I want to do it again." This time he needed no guiding. Sex was a lesson easily learned.

CHAPTER TEN

"You seem very young to be in Mrs. Mudridge's care."

He was a strange man, not the type who usually came to the house in Westminster. Older, probably in his late thirties, he called himself only Mr. X; but Mrs. Mudridge, who could smell out a title from a mile away, insisted he was of the nobility.

"Incognito, so to speak. For reasons best known to him. I never question me clientele. He's a gentleman and his gold's as good as the next man's."

The girls were all atwitter about him, because of the air of mystery. The first time he came, he didn't even take one of them up to a bedchamber, although he paid for expensive French champagne for all of the assembled guests.

Mellie, knowing that she was trapped here, at least for now, had learned her lessons well. In a few weeks, she'd become one of the most sought-after girls. She was sure that old Mrs. Mudridge whispered to the men that she'd been raised at court, which was true. And as the young bloods were all such insufferable snobs, it enhanced Mellie's considerable charms in their eyes. In Mellie it produced only more cynicism. If they knew her history, she might be less glamorous to them. In fact, she was a bit surprised that Densbury hadn't gossiped about her; but apparently he'd not mentioned the fiasco to his friends, or there'd have been rumors of it coming to her ears.

Now Mellie smiled her trained courtesan's smile at the mysterious Mr. X, but didn't answer him, nor give her age. Sixteen wasn't that young to be in a London brothel.

"I've asked Mrs. Mudridge if I can take you to the opera this week," Mr. X continued.

This did startle Mellie, who would have thought that nothing ever again could surprise her after life in this beautiful, tarnished mansion in Westminster.

"And what did the worthy Mrs. Mudridge say?"

His smile was as cynical as Mellie's own. "My dear Mellie, anything can be arranged for a price. Will Thursday evening be satisfactory with you?"

"Whatever Mrs. Mudridge agrees to," Mellie said bitterly.

She was surprised, however, when Mr. X did not accompany her to her room, surprised and a little miffed. Wasn't she attractive enough for him? Yet he'd invited her to the Italian Opera House, the King's Theatre, in the Haymarket, something unheard-of in Mrs. Mudridge's establishment.

Next morning, that worthy lady sent for Mellie, interviewing her in the small study that she used for a business office.

"Our Mr. X seems to have taken to you, Mellie."

Not invited to sit down, Mellie stood in front of a massive Kent desk of walnut, the feet carved in the popular lion's paw design. The large matching chair suited Mrs. Mudridge's larger-than-life style perfectly.

"You are to attend him at the opera on Thursday." She scowled mightily, and Mellie quaked inwardly. She'd learned that dear Mother Mudridge's smiles and pleasantries were no deeper than her pox-scarred skin. "I must warn you, me dearie, that there'll be no eloping with the gentleman. I own you. And I pay the local magistrates enough that if one of me young ladies takes it in her pretty, empty head to abscond, then I have her fetched back right smartly, with the aid of the constables."

"I hadn't planned to run away." But Mellie had secretly been planning how to escape the terrible life she now lived. Somehow, soon, she had to get away from this dreadful harridan. Mellie knew that she'd have to disappear completely, leave London, perhaps even go to the Continent where she was not known, if she hoped for any kind of a life. Here she was just one more girl in a London brothel; and no matter how lax morals were in the *ton*, it still would never do for people to know she'd worked for Mother Mudridge.

"I am charging Mr. X a pretty penny for your time, as you will be away for hours and not available for me other gentlemen. And we'll have to see to your wardrobe. He left funds for you to be suitably attired. He's even sending a seamstress in tomorrow to sew a special gown for you." Her mouth was pinched as if she'd bitten a green persimmon. "I assured him that me girls are all well gowned; but he insisted."

The seamstress came with a footman who carried bolts of velvet and satin, and she fashioned a gown for Mellie of the utmost elegance, a pale blue overskirt and basque, with petticoats of cloth-of-silver, decorated with tiny midnight blue rosettes which were repeated around the deep décolletage. The elbow sleeves ended in frills of silver lace. She even fashioned a pinner of the lace, trimming it with the same midnight blue rosettes as on the neckline.

With Thursday still two days away, Mellie was in a torment of anticipation. It was the first time she'd been allowed away from the house since that evil night when Mrs. Mudridge had found her on Badger Lane. Could she, somehow, escape? Would Mr. X help her? She still did not know how to assess him. He'd paid for her favors, but he had not collected them. He'd used none of the other girls, either; although he had spent money on all of them, buying wine and flowers for the entire household.

Mellie, now very wary of all proffers of friendship, suspected that Mr. X had ulterior motives. She'd heard whispers from Pamela and Tamsen of dreadful things some men expected of the girls when they'd paid their gold. Was Mr. X one of these perverts who was playing out his own little game with her? Yet he'd been the perfect gentleman when he had been with her here.

Word quickly went through the establishment that Mellie was to go to the opera with their mystery visitor.

"You are very lucky, Mellie," Clarissa said; but Pru was catty about her good fortune. "He'll make advances in public, mark my words. Or expect you to do really ugly things," she guessed.

Mellie was in a fever of doubt. She still was expected to entertain the young men who presented themselves at Mrs. Mudridge's nightly "routs." She'd learned to turn her mind to other things, so that what happened to her body no longer mattered. Was she expecting too much of Mr. X? Was he going to be like all the rest of Mrs. Mudridge's clients?

She tried to remember what he looked like; but try as she might, she couldn't. If she met him on the street, would she recognize him? He was not handsome, in the classic sense; yet Mr. X was not ugly, either. His features were regular, his eyes a dark, almost velvety brown. His full periwig was brown; so perhaps his own hair was that color, although Mellie couldn't be sure. Many of the men were beginning to powder their wigs; but Mr. X had not adopted this fashion when he came to the house off Whitehall. He was a well set up gentleman, a bit over average height, and Mellie was sure his teeth were his own. The main thing she remembered about him was his air of assurance, as if things never bothered him; or if they did, he was able to deal with them competently. That was it. Mr. X exuded an air of quiet competence which was singularly reassuring.

The opera was at seven; but as Mrs. Mudridge did not keep to high society meal times, Mellie had plenty of time to dress after she'd eaten with the other girls.

"I don't think I'd like opera," Becky declared. "Singing and all that, and often in a foreign language. How will you know what's going on?"

"They have little books with the story in English," Mellie told her; for in her court days, she'd attended the opera several times with her mother.

"But it's dark in the opera house," Becky objected.

"The ladies light little candles so they can read the words, Becky."

Fanny, who was serving them, said with the familiarity of a family servant, "Don't drip candle wax on your new gown, or Mrs. M will have your hide, Mellie."

Mellie, who'd fallen in love with the new dress, assured Fanny that she'd sit quietly in the dark to protect her velvet skirt.

Then Mrs. Mudridge, who had been working on accounts in her office, came in to eat. "Hurry along there, Mellie. Maybe ladies at court can keep their men waiting; but we working women can't indulge in such nonsense. And mind your manners. This Mr. X may be a gold mine for us, if he likes you." Then her shrewd eyes raked over Mellie. "Although I do wonder what he's up to. Hasn't had you to bed yet, has he?"

"You know he hasn't." Suddenly Mellie's saffron cake was dry and tasteless in her mouth. The coming evening, which loomed as an enormous adventure, now took on sordid overtones with Mrs. Mudridge's coarse question.

"Let me make one thing very clear to you, me girl. No bedding him elsewhere. If that's what he has in mind, tell him he has to pay me extra in advance. I prefer to keep control of my business properties."

"I'll tell him, if the occasion arises," Mellie promised, curbing the impulse to scream at the old hag with her painted face and her crepy neck, her blowsy figure and her flamboyant gown of jade brocade.

She wouldn't put it past the old witch to send Alf along to spy on them. Well, once Mr. X came to collect her and she was out of this house, Mellie would put her dreary life out of her mind as if it had never existed. She'd pretend that her escort was madly in love with her, about to offer for her hand in honorable matrimony. So what if he was twice her age or more? Marriages of convenience, marriages of young women to old men, were common. If he did indeed have a title, and for once Mellie trusted old Mother M's instincts, and if he were wealthy, Mellie would marry him tomorrow if he could arrange a special license that quickly. Or she'd elope with him to Gretna Green in Scotland without a second thought. Anything to escape being a body-for-pay in Mrs. Mudridge's brothel.

Mellie was dressed ahead of time. She agreed with Mother Mudridge on this, too. She had no intention of keeping Mr X waiting. The sooner she got out of this house, the better. It was the long twilight of June, with that shimmering quality to the air that comes so seldom in London. A light breeze off the Thames had wafted away the smoke, and trees in nearby St. James's Park were in full leaf.

Promptly at six thirty, the appointed hour, Mrs. Mudridge herself came tapping on the door to Mellie's bedchamber to announce that her gentleman had arrived and was awaiting her pleasure in the small red salon on the ground floor. Mrs. M carried a soft white shawl of Scottish lamb's wool picked out with silver threads. "In case the night air is cool, me dearie." She motioned with a revolving finger, and Mellie turned about slowly, showing off the gown to perfection. White kid slippers with high red heels peeped from beneath the hoops that formed a bell from Mellie's tiny waist, and the swell of white bosom above the low neckline was exquisite "You'll do, me girl. And remember, you've me reputation to uphold. Mr. X is a lord, I know it. Conduct yourself like a lady."

What irony, that this creature from the seamier side of London should tell her that! Mellie, born a lady, would never lose that indefinable something that good breeding provided. And Mrs. Mudridge, though she died rolling in gold, would never be a lady, never.

Mrs. M preceded Mellie down the winding staircase and ushered her into the red salon as if she were a majordomo. "Sir, Miss Wilton is ready to attend you."

Mr. X had been standing at a window that overlooked the side garden of the mansion. He turned, a wineglass held in one hand, and stared at Mellie. He had a quizzing glass hanging on a ribbon about his neck, and he raised it and peered at her as if examining some rare and lovely botanical specimen.

Then, as if remembering his manners, he set the wineglass down on a tripod table of walnut which stood on short cabriole legs. The top was carved to mimic a silver salver with a gadrooned edge. The wineglass safely out of his hand, Mr. X dropped the quizzing glass onto its ribbon and made a sweeping bow.

This was the first time Mellie had seen him in fine dress. His coat was of a rich green velvet with a trim of self colored braid. Down the front were set at least three dozen buttons of hammered gold, and there were more of the gold buttons on the wide cuffs and on the deep pockets of the long-skirted coat. His waistcoat was lime green completely covered with gold-thread embroidery of birds and flowers. The white neck cloth was edged with fine lace, and the frills of his lawn shirt were of a matching pattern. His trousers were of a fawn so pale as to be almost white, and the green stockings matched the lime green of the waistcoat. His shoes were highly polished brown calf, with fashionable high heels and gold buckles. The quizzing glass was set in gold and hung on a gold ribbon. His wig was much smaller than the full periwig he'd worn previously, carefully powdered and curled—the hair tied back at his neck with a dark green velvet ribbon.

"Miss Wilton, your servant, madam."

She dropped a low curtsy. It was as if she were going out with an entirely different man from the one she'd met. The other man was as unobtrusive as his garb. This man was exciting, and if he was not exactly handsome, he was striking in appearance, with that tremendous presence he'd exhibited earlier. Mellie felt her pulse race as he solicitously helped her with her shawl, the casual touch of a hand on her bare shoulder sending an unexpected thrill through her. Mellie had looked forward to this outing, only because it would get her out of the hated Queen Anne mansion that housed her shame and degradation; but suddenly, with one touch, this was all changed. Mr. X had become interesting in his own right.

"Take good care of me little girl," Mrs. Mudridge cooed, sending a cold chill down Mellie's spine. The look that the brothel keeper gave her was explicit. Mellie knew that this evening would furnish her with no opportunity to escape Mother M's clutches, unless she were very clever, indeed.

A small closed coach was waiting outside the door, with a footman to hand her inside. With Mr. X beside her, Mellie heard the crack of the coachey's whip, and the team of matched bays set off down the driveway. Whitehall was crowded with all manner of carriages and sedan chairs, but as it was still light, there was no

need for the myriad linkboys with their smoky torches to light the
way. As they neared Charing Cross, a watchman, rattle shaking,
called, "Quarter to seven on a still summer's eve."

"You look ravishing, Miss Wilton," her companion said. But
there was only approval in his voice, not desire, and Mellie found
herself wondering what was wrong that he found her only attractive in appearance.

"Thank you, sir." She called him nothing. It seemed ridiculous
to refer to him as Mr. X when she talked to him. "Milord" would
be natural to use, but she dared not, for fear he might think someone had spied out his identity.

"Mrs. Mudridge has given me a bit of your personal history,"
he continued. Then, with a wicked twinkle in his eyes, he added,
"But I'm not sure I can swear to her accuracy."

Drily, Mellie agreed. "It would be interesting to know my own
life, as told by Moth——Mrs. Mudridge."

"After the opera, we'll have supper, and I'll tell you all about
yourself," he said, laughing. "You do enjoy opera, I hope? I
should have asked sooner."

There was something about him that made Mellie want to be
completely candid. "As a matter of fact, I do, sir; but it has been a
year or more since I've had the pleasure of attending."

"Tonight it is not Italian opera, I fear, but Purcell's *Dido and
Aeneas*."

"Oh, I love that one," she cried, forgetting her sophistication
for a moment, which brought a brilliant smile to Mr. X's face.

Now they moved into Haymarket, where the crowds were almost overwhelming. Chairs jostled for position, and coachmen
shouted imprecations at each other as they fought to deposit their
passengers at the Opera House. Their coachey was skilled in maneuvering in traffic, and they soon drew up to the entrance.

To her delight, Mellie discovered that they had a private box, to
which Mr. X had escorted her immediately, not trying to mingle
with the operagoers in the lobby. In fact, she realized that he'd
been sneezing, or pretending to sneeze, for the entire trip from
coach to box, with his face well concealed behind a handsome
lace-edged kerchief. Now, instead of sitting up beside her, he had
his chair back so that his face was in shadow.

This worried Mellie. Who was this man? He seemed the perfect
gentleman; yet he wanted not to be noticed or recognized. This
was obvious from his actions. Could he be one of the gentleman
rogues who prowled the highways, robbing innocent travelers?

I couldn't stand it if he were a highwayman. The thought made Mellie feel faint, and she fumbled in her pocket tied under the overskirt of blue velvet for her vinaigrette, daintily sniffing the smelling salts.

"Do you feel faint?" Mr. X inquired solicitously.

"It's just the excitement," Mellie assured him. "And Nell laced me very tight," she said, boldly, then could have cut out her tongue. What if she shocked him? But then, how could she? He had found her in a brothel.

He only smiled at her, his eyes straying to her tiny waistline, just as she'd hoped when she mentioned her lacing.

After the opera! Mellie didn't know what her escort had in mind for her; but if he wished to take her to bed in some room other than her own at Mrs. Mudridge's, Mellie had no intention of saying no to him. She'd been interested in no man who'd paid for her at the brothel, even though they were almost exclusively members of the *ton*; but for the first time in her sixteen years, Mellie was in love. She'd thought she had loved that miserable young Densbury. Now, with this exciting older man, she had fallen desperately and deeply in love, and she didn't even know his name. It didn't matter. All that mattered to Mellie was that he found her attractive enough to bring her to the opera, and that he had further plans for her later that night.

CHAPTER ELEVEN

"Would you be willing to leave Mrs. Mudridge's house for mine?" Mr. X asked her over the supper of cold pheasant and wine.

It hadn't gone at all as Mellie expected. Her escort had made no advances. He had been polite, attentive, and impersonal. Now the question was a stunning eye-opener. Mellie looked down long vistas into the future, a future beside this exciting man. She'd teach him to love her. She was sure enough of her powers of attraction to know she could win him.

She did not ask in what capacity he intended her to be introduced into his establishment. It was enough that he wanted her; yet how could she escape from Mother M?

If Mellie had learned anything in sixteen years, it was that there was a time to be coy and a time to be direct. This was the latter. "I would be willing never to see dear Mrs. Mudridge again, and that includes her precious Queen Anne house in Westminster."

"Excellent. Then it's settled. Could you leave there tomorrow?"

"Sir, I am not sure I can leave there at all." It nearly broke her heart to say those words.

"Why not?" He frowned, and Mellie shook inwardly. It was the first time she'd seen Mr. X show displeasure, and she saw that he could be as implacable in his anger as he could be gallant in his pleasure.

"Sir, Mrs. Mudridge owns me."

"My dear Miss Wilton, that is utter nonsense. We don't have slaves in England."

Mellie sighed. She'd not expected him to be so imperceptive. "Mrs. M took me in when I was locked out of my dreary little room in Badger Lane because I had no rent money. I'd lost my equally dreary position as a shop girl in a draper's on the corner. I had pawned the few trinkets I had left after Mother drank us to the door of debtor's prison.''

''I know all this,'' he said impatiently, pouring more wine and gulping it down. ''I've made inquiries into your upbringing, Mellie. I do not issue my invitation lightly. I know exactly who you are and how you came to where you now live. But Mrs. Mudridge does not own you.''

''She—warned me,'' Mellie murmured. Perhaps it was unwise of her to tell him what Mrs. Mudridge had threatened; but suddenly she felt reckless. This gentleman had offered to take her into his home. Having fallen in love with him, she had no thought now but to accept by some means, Mrs. M or no Mrs. M. As he seemed to be capable of anything and everything, Mellie decided to throw herself on his mercy. If he could extricate her from the sticky web that the brothel keeper had spun around her, she would give him all her love and loyalty.

''And what kind of warning did that old harridan give?''

''She said I mustn't plan to go off with you. She'd have the bailiffs after me, if I did. I think she bribes the local magistrates.''

''No doubt. And perhaps with more than guineas. But money fights money, lovely Mellie; and money is something I've plenty of and to spare. I'm perfectly willing to pay her to release you from your bondage.''

''She'll overcharge you, sir!''

''Probably. It doesn't matter. I've decided that you are the woman to fill my special need. If you are willing to go home with me, then trust me. I'll arrange it with that she-dragon.''

Then, emboldened by his straightforward announcement that she was the woman he wanted, Mellie whispered, ''She—she also offered another admonition. I mustn't go to bed with you anyplace but at her house in Westminster. But,'' defiantly, ''if you want me, sir, she need never know.''

He reached over, then, and laid a large, warm hand over hers. ''Sweet little Mellie. We'll not cheat her, though. I shall arrange it all in a business-like manner, so that she'll have no legal recourse later. You need never fear that you'll be forced back into the sordid life she makes you live, Mellie. From now on, I shall be your protector.''

His touch was thrilling; but he removed his hand from hers almost as if he regretted touching her. Mellie could have wished for a more impassioned speech. She did not know what role she was to play in Mr. X's household, nor did she care. It was enough that he was taking her with him. Nothing could be worse than her present life.

When he left her at Mrs. Mudridge's, it was after midnight. He bowed over her hand, not even kissing it, and promised, "I shall arrive tomorrow with my solicitor. He'll draw up binding articles which Mrs. Mudridge will sign and which will release you from bondage here."

"Oh, sir, what if she refuses?"

"She'll not refuse. Gold is a great persuader, Mellie."

Mellie crept past the drawing room where Mrs. Mudridge was entertaining late comers, and slipped up to her room. Nell came when she rang and helped her undress.

"You had an enjoyable evening out?"

"Very enjoyable, Nell."

"And the opera?"

"Well sung."

"I've never been to an opera," Nell confided. "But I did once go to the theater in Drury Lane." Then, as if sensing Mellie's great excitement, she warned in a low voice as if she thought Mother M's ears were everywhere. "They all come here for only one thing—don't forget that. Don't expect anything from this man, Miss Mellie."

It was on the tip of her tongue to tell the abigail that Mr. X was not like the other patrons of the house in Westminster; but in time, she realized that Nell might well tattle to Mrs. Mudridge. Perhaps that old hag set her maids to quiz the girls who went out with the gentlemen clients.

"I know why the men come here," Mellie said, suddenly bitter. Why couldn't she have met Mr. X on her sixteenth birthday, instead of that pawing, demanding Alistair Lord Densbury?

Mellie was so excited by the prospects of a life with her Mr. X that she had trouble getting to sleep in her huge high-curtained bed. It was nearly dawn before she dozed off, and the birds in the garden woke her early. She rang for chocolate, surprising the little maid, Fanny, who carried breakfast trays to the girls.

"Up early, miss."

"I couldn't sleep," Mellie told her, trying to contain her excitement.

Dressing in a Watteau sacque of watered rose silk, Mellie whiled away the morning hours by brushing her golden hair and reading the latest naughty French novel to improve her French. Or so she told herself.

It was gone eleven, and the whole house was stirring, when the maid tapped on her door and told her that Mrs. Mudridge wished to see her in the study.

This had to be it! Now that the actual hour had arrived, Mellie was frightened. Her heart beat like a hammer, and she felt momentarily faint, resorting to her smelling salts before she started down the ornate spiral staircase to the lower floor. It wouldn't do to swoon on the stairs and fall down them. With such lovely prospects in sight, Mellie didn't need a broken neck.

Before going into the study, she peeked outside. A carriage stood before the door; but whether it was the same one she'd ridden in last evening or not, she couldn't be sure.

Taking a deep breath to compose herself, she rapped on the oak door to the study.

"Come in," Mrs. M called.

Inside she found that redoubtable lady ensconced behind her great desk, with Mr. X and another gentleman in chairs ranged along to one side. Both men rose and made legs when she entered, and Mrs. M nodded to a small chair off to one side, where Mellie sank before her knees gave way and let her topple to the Turkey rug in a heap of rose silk.

"Mr. X you know," Mrs. Mudridge said with a trace of asperity in her voice. "And this other gentleman is Sir Homer Stackpole, Mr. X's solicitor."

"Miss Wilton." He was rotund and rosy, his full periwig curled and powdered, the long locks flowing over the shoulders of his black velvet coat. His waistcoat, too, was sober, as befitted his profession, although it had lovely silver buttons. He was sleek and well fed, Mellie decided.

"Mellie, you are very fortunate," Mrs. Mudridge said, with that same undercurrent of annoyance in her voice. "Mr. X, who chooses not to divulge his identity, at least to me," and she shot Mellie a venomous look that seemed to say that she thought Mellie knew his true name, "has taken a liking to you, finding you most decorative and accomplished." Mrs. Mudridge then smiled at the solicitor, showing her bad teeth. "All of my young women are of the highest quality. I won't have any other kind working for me."

Mellie felt as if she were a prize mare on display to prospective buyers at the Southwark Fair, which, in a way, she was.

Sir Homer smiled genially and said, "Your establishment has the highest reputation, madam."

"Indeed. I shall hope to see you here at one of my routs," she replied, causing momentary consternation to that worthy gentleman, and quickly hidden hilarity to Mr. X.

"Yes. Hrrmph! As to the matter at hand, madam, the disposition of this charming young lady, Miss Melusina Anna Hildreth Wilton, daughter of the late Sir Horace and Lady Anna Wilton. For the sum discussed and agreed upon, you relinquish all claims to her, ah, services." Then he said to Mellie, "If this is satisfactory with you, Miss Wilton. My client has assured me that you are not averse to a change in status."

Again the venomous look from Mother M.

Mellie found her voice was almost gone, but she managed to whisper, "It is agreeable to me, sir."

Sir Homer flourished the document at Mrs. Mudridge and said, "If you will sign here, madam."

She dipped the quill in an ornate German crystal and silver inkstand and signed, almost breaking the quill in her barely suppressed anger. Then she held out her hand.

"And the agreed sum, madam." He put a small leather bag that clinked in her hand, and her greedy fingers curled around it.

"How soon can you be ready to leave, Mellie?" Mr. X asked. "I shall wait for you, if you can go immediately."

Before she could answer, Mrs. Mudridge rose and said, her voice icy, "She'll need to change. I have invested a large sum in her wardrobe, and under the circumstances, it must stay here." She walked to the embroidered bellpull and gave it such a vicious tug that Mellie expected it to pull loose from the wall. "I shall have Nell find her old clothing in which she came here."

"I shan't be long," Mellie promised Mr. X. Then she fled from the irate mistress who had lured her into this sordid life of shame. Mellie was glad to wear her old, shabby gown, anything, just to escape.

But she'd reckoned without Mr. X. "Just a moment, madam," he said, his voice as cold with anger as her own. "I paid for a blue velvet gown which Mellie wore last evening when she accompanied me to the Italian Opera House. That gown goes with her."

There was nothing Mrs. Mudridge could say, for Mellie's new protector had indeed paid his gold for the dress. "Of course," the old harridan muttered between clenched, rotting teeth. "Although it is scarcely suitable attire for this hour."

"I'll wear my old dress and pack the new one in my trunk," Mellie said, eager to get out of the study and away from such bickering over her.

Nell had come by then, and Mrs. Mudridge gave orders for her to pack up Mellie's things and see that the footman brought the trunk down straightaway.

There was no leave taking. The other girls were still asleep, and Mellie had made no fast friends in the weeks she had been here. She walked out past Mrs. Mudridge without a glance in the procuress's direction, followed closely by Mr. X and his solicitor.

"I shall drop you at your chambers, Sir Homer," Mr. X said as they clattered along the Strand, headed for the Temple Bar.

"Kind of you, mil——Mr. X." Sir Homer darted a quick look at Mellie to see if she'd noticed his slip of the tongue.

She pretended deafness. Mellie was sure that her new protector was a lord, just as she was sure that in his good time he'd tell her who he was and why he traveled incognito. And his reasons for buying her from Mrs. Mudridge.

The city was alive with hustle and bustle, with produce wagons lumbering along the streets, their wide wheels acting as rollers to help smooth the roads. Numerous carriages of all sorts, from light gigs driven by dashing young blades to large berlins complete with coachey, guard, and footmen clinging behind, crowded the narrow road which led directly from Westminster to London.

As they passed through the Temple Bar, Mellie shuddered at the heads displayed on spikes, one a woman's head. What terrible crime had that poor female done to deserve such an awful fate?

Mr. X, who was sitting beside her, noticed her shudder.

"They were all low criminals," he said, realizing the cause of her distress with his usual perception. "Don't trouble yourself about them, Mellie. Unquestionably they deserved their fate. The judges know what they are doing. Unless criminals receive swift justice for the crimes they commit, our country will revert to barbarism."

"But one was a woman," she protested.

"You think women don't break the law, miss?" Sir Homer rumbled. "They're up before the magistrates as often as men, Miss Wilton. Some are hardened, vicious criminals. That one," and he jerked his head toward the archway through which they had just driven, "was Petula Scraggs, a notorious highwaywoman, as cruel and as nasty as Frenchy Claude Duval, madam. Murdered her victims, as like as not, after she'd relieved them of their purses and their gold and jewels." Then, glancing out of the coach window, "Drop me here at Ye Olde Cock Tavern please, sir. I'll have a dram and then walk around the corner to my chambers."

Mr. X obligingly rapped on the coach roof and called out directions to the coachman who pulled up to let the solicitor off.

Once out of the coach, he bowed to Mellie. "A pleasure, madam, to help rescue you from that old harridan. Not sure but what her head should decorate Temple Bar."

Mellie's eyes narrowed. "That head I shouldn't mind to see hanging there," she declared. "In fact, I'd cheer as we drove beneath it."

Then they clattered along Fleet Street toward Ludgate Circus. Fleet Street was very fashionable, and the members of the *ton* were beginning to appear, strolling along to pass the time with their friends in gossip, and hurrying into the more popular coffeehouses to sip coffee or chocolate and try to find someone willing to play cards and gamble.

"I've taken a room for you at the Oxford Arms in Warwick Lane," Mr. X said as they started down Ludgate Hill. "You need to have at least a semblance of a new wardrobe before we travel to Kent, where I live. There are no doubt dressmakers in Canterbury; but London has the latest fashions just over from Paris. We'll spend a week here, before going home." Then, as if realizing that he'd been giving orders, he added, "If that is satisfactory with you, Mellie."

"Oh, quite, sir," she assured him. A new wardrobe! And Kent. She'd never been to Kent, except when they came from Hanover and landed at Dover.

"So your home is in Kent," she said, ingenuously.

"Yes, beyond Canterbury."

He offered no further information, and Mellie decided not to push her luck with this man who had rescued her from Mother M. Life with him could not possibly be worse than it had been the past year. She would hold her tongue and count her blessings.

The Oxford Arms was a typical London inn, the gateway leading into the courtyard with galleries on the inn side and the back, and stables to the right. They were expected, for Mr. X led Mellie immediately to the staircase and they mounted to the first gallery, where a diminutive maid in a green striped stuff dress, white apron and mobcap, curtsied them into a spacious room, well-furnished with canopied bed, wardrobe, two chests and several chairs, one well-upholstered in blue damask. A screen closed off the corner where the washstand stood, with pitcher and basin ready, and towels hanging on the bar.

"The dressmaker and her assistant will come within the hour,"

Mr. X told her. "Shall we plan to dine at six?"

"Whatever you say, sir."

"And perhaps I can get tickets to 'The Fatal Marriage' at the Drury Lane Theatre. If you'd like to see the play."

The opera last night, the theater tonight! Heaven! Mellie wanted to clap her hands in glee; but she must preserve her dignity. Mr. X was no callow young blade, but a mature man who might not care for such childish enthusiasm. Quietly she said, "That would be quite enjoyable, sir"; but she could not keep the sparkle of excitement out of her eyes.

Then her sponsor made a leg and bade her good day.

Incredible. The little maid had discreetly disappeared, and Mellie had assumed that now Mr. X would take his payment for all he'd done for her. And she was quite prepared to pay—eager, in fact. It was not to be. Perhaps he expected that the dressmaker might interrupt them. Well, time enough for love later, after the theatrical performance tonight.

It was within the hour that there was a tap at her chamber door, and Mellie opened to a bustling little woman with her gray hair in tight sausage curls, her pigeon-body in serviceable black. She was trailed by a youthful apprentice, her eyes already weak looking from too much fine stitching in poor light. This was not the seamstress Mr. X had sent to Mrs. Mudridge's. Perhaps he chose that this woman not know Mellie had been working in a brothel.

"Miss Wilton, please disrobe. We must measure you."

The dressmaker was Mrs. Hawkins, and the assistant was called Tabby; although whether because her Christian name was Tabitha, or because she had a pointed face, and the weak eyes were cat-amber, Mellie never knew. Mellie thought that Tabby was a poor advertisement for Mrs. Hawkins's wares, for the young woman was clad in a gray wool, very plain, over petticoats, not hoops. Her drab brown hair was covered with a white lawn round cap with lappets that stood out, as her ears protruded under the flaps of lawn, even though she had tied down the lappets under her chin.

It was like a repeat performance of Mrs. Gumple at the Queen Anne house in Westminster, with Mrs. Hawkins strewing Parisian fashion plates all over the bed so that Mellie could choose the styles she wanted.

"The gentleman said to spare no expense," she murmured discreetly. "He suggested a riding habit—scarlet would be very striking with your fair hair, miss. And a wide variety of morning gowns, dinner dresses, and at least two ball gowns. We'll be hard pressed to get everything finished in time. I've called in extra seamstresses to my shop to do the sewing. If he'd not offered me a bonus. . . .''

Mellie, though young, was very fashion conscious; and she knew what was most becoming to her. She and Mrs. Hawkins agreed in principle on almost every article of clothing, even to the most intimate undergarments. ''Finest silk, he ordered, miss. Oh, you are very lucky to be marrying such a fine gentleman. Some young girls won't marry an older man, more fool they.''

Marry him! Mellie didn't bother to set Mrs. Hawkins right about the relationship between Mr. X and herself—or at least the intended relationship. Perhaps the little seamstress would be shocked to find that Mellie was to be the gentleman's mistress, not his wife.

Therefore, Mellie almost fainted from shock when the pigeon-breasted little woman snapped her fingers at her poor assistant, crying, ''The bridal gowns, Tabby. That's all we have to settle on, now.''

Tammy drew three fashion plates from the portfolio she carried, and presented them to Mellie as if they were votive offerings to some alien goddess.

''The gentleman was very particular about the wedding gown, miss,'' the garrulous Mrs. Hawkins explained. ''He looked at more than two dozen of the very latest plates from the Continent before he narrowed the choice down to these three. He said for you to choose the one you like best.

Mellie's hands trembled as she held the pictures. He meant to marry her! In her wildest dreams, she hadn't expected this—and she didn't even know his name! The rest of the afternoon passed in a rosy haze. Marriage! In a lovely gown of white brocade overlaid with silver net, the simplest of the three gowns shown to her, yet the most beautiful.

''Ah, miss, you do have a good eye for fashion,'' Mrs. Hawkins complimented. ''Chose the one I'd have picked for you had you been my own daughter. Now, miss, you'll be very busy the rest of the week. We'll have to come early and work all day to finish the trousseau in time.''

''I'll be available,'' Mellie promised. Oh, indeed she would. A trousseau! The very word sent shivers of delight down her spine, set her heart to thudding, her pulse pounding.

To be married to her handsome, mysterious love, Mellie would stand for hours upon hours of fittings. Everything must be perfect, so that he'd approve of her looks; for her appearance would reflect credit upon him, for choosing such a beautiful, fashionable bride. Strange. Mellie had dreamed, as all young women do, of being swept off her feet by a young, tall, handsome man with a title and a fortune. But the reality was far more thrilling than the girlish daydream. Perhaps he loved her so deeply that, even though he knew she'd been working in a brothel, he intended to wait until their wedding night to make her truly his. If this were so, then Mellie hoped that the wedding would not be long delayed; for she longed to feel his arms about her, to know his kisses and caresses, as she truly became his wife.

CHAPTER TWELVE

It was Sunday, and the bells of St. Paul's were ringing as their post chaise clattered down Cheapside and Poultry en route to London Bridge. Mellie's new trousseau was in trunks and boxes in the basket of the chaise, and she traveled in a lovely suit of light brown velvet trimmed with dark brown braid. A perky brown felt tricorne perched atop her golden locks which were dressed high and close to her head for the journey to Kent. They had delayed a day or two so that Mrs. Hawkins could finish the entire sumptuous wardrobe.

"Sir," Mellie said as they rattled across London Bridge, their view of the Thames completely obscured by the houses and shops built the length of the span, "sir, would it be impertinent of me to know your name, now that we are en route to your home?"

He smiled that winsome smile that took years from his rugged good looks. "Be patient just a little longer, Mellie," he begged. "We're making a change of carriages in Southwark, at The Elephant and Castle. Then, when we're in my own coach, I shall satisfy your natural curiosity."

"As you wish, sir."

"It has been good of you not to pry, Mellie," he added. Then he continued, "We may not make my estate by nightfall. I had thought of a very early start; but I hated to disturb such a lovely young thing as you at three in the morning, when the stages start off. It is possible to make my house in Kent in a day of hard travel, when the weather is good. In winter, of course, when the roads are bad, I usually break the trip at Rochester. Have you ever been to Rochester?"

"When we came to England, on the trip from Dover, we were in Rochester."

"Ah, yes, of course. Your English is so excellent that I sometimes forget you were born on the Continent. How did you like Rochester, then?"

"We only passed through. And I was younger. I remember only

that the journey seemed interminable. The Maypole complained every inch of the way.'' Then she clapped a neatly gloved hand over her mouth, aghast at her indiscretion. What if he were well known at court? He might resent hearing Ehrengard Melusina von Schulenberg called the Maypole.

He only grinned. "She needs long ribbons dangling from her pinner,'' he said. "And a circle of dancers twining them about her, of course.''

They now approached the famous inn, The Elephant and Castle, which stood about a mile south of London Bridge in Southwark. It was an old building, tall and narrow, with a steep pitched roof and tiny attic dormers to the front. The sign hanging out over the front entrance showed a huge elephant with a castle howdah on its back. The inn stood at a crossroads, with the signpost in the middle, and flat lamps mounted under the four pointers.

Mr. X escorted Mellie inside and ordered a glass of claret for her. "I must see to the luggage. My coach is not due here for a bit. I prefer to have it arrive after the hired post chaise has returned to London.'' More mystery!

It was nearly an hour before her escort came for her. Meanwhile, large numbers of travelers had been in and out of The Elephant and Castle, stopping to refresh themselves before continuing their journeys.

"Our coach is ready, Mellie,'' Mr. X said, offering his arm to escort her out of the inn.

It was no surprise when she saw a shiny berlin with a coat of arms blazoned on the door. Mrs. Mudridge had an unerring instinct about such things. Mr. X was, indeed, a lord.

Seeing where her eyes rested, that gentleman assured her, "As soon as we drive off, I shall solve the mystery. Patience, Mellie, for a little while longer.''

Two liveried footmen perched behind, and they carried both coachman and guard of their own. As they clattered along the road to Dover, Mellie finally found out who her benefactor was.

"I am Ritchie Jamison, Sixth Earl of Henning. And we travel to Henning Hall, just the other side of Canterbury. The house has been in the family for generations, built by the first earl in the early fifteen hundreds. It has been much remodeled, fortunately. Living was quite primitive in the days of Good Queen Bess. I prefer life under Good Queen Anne, God rest her soul, and King George, thank you.''

An earl. She'd be a countess! How she'd come up in the world in the past two weeks. Mellie felt she should pinch herself to make sure that she wasn't dreaming. In this short time she'd met this virile, exciting older man who had literally bought her for himself. It was a situation right out of the pages of the most racy French novel. But she had a beautiful wedding dress in the boxes behind the coach as proof that the earl meant to make her his lawful wedded wife.

"Milord, now I can thank you properly for rescuing me," Mellie dimpled. "I was tricked into Mrs. Mudridge's establishment. I should have known better—but I was so disheartened; our abigail had been killed by a coach, mother had died in Bedlam, I had been dismissed as a shopgirl. And when Mrs. Mudridge invited me to live with her, I saw only the light at the end of the long tunnel, and was blind to the terrors that lay along its dark length."

"Try to forget this past year, Mellie. As I told you, I investigated you thoroughly, to make sure you were just the woman I needed."

Her heart pounded so wildly that Mellie thought surely this personable man, the Earl of Henning, could hear its thuddings. He needed her. After the disastrous turn her life had taken, the man she loved wanted her, chose her particularly, and her cup overflowed with joy. Yet even as she sat there, ecstatic, in the elegantly appointed berlin pulled by four matched chestnuts, attended by men dressed in Henning's dark blue and silver livery, Mellie had one horrid moment of doubt. She'd been so sure that Mrs. Mudridge meant only good toward her; and see how wrong she'd been. What if she had been hoodwinked again? What would she do if she discovered that she'd been duped, that the Earl of Henning had motives for rescuing her of which she had no inkling? Then she scolded herself mentally. He was a perfect gentleman. He'd scarcely touched her, although she had tried to convey to him, subtly, of course, that she would not rebuff his advances. He knew that she had worked in a brothel, that his attentions would not shock her. It wasn't as if she were a sheltered maiden, with no knowledge of men. Far from it. Mrs. Mudridge had seen to her education in that respect! Yet even though he must know that she would welcome his love, he had been absurdly distant with her.

Mellie longed to ask about the wedding. It seemed ridiculous to be marrying this man, and know only that she had a suitable wedding gown in her wardrobe. She could not, though, bring up the subject when he gave no opening in his conversation.

The road to Dover was very busy, for Dover was the most important port in the area. Most of the ships coming from the Continent put in there, and travelers to England landed there every day. Because they were so heavily traveled, the roads were rutted and rough. Luckily, there'd been little rain, so they were well dried out; but Mellie knew that it would take only a shower to turn the dust to slippery, treacherous mud. But it didn't rain. The sun shone down on them, and she loosened the fitted basque jacket of her traveling suit, unbuttoning it to show the delicately embroidered bodice that she wore underneath. She was proud of the full swell of her firm young breasts, and smiled when the earl's eyes strayed to her cleavage. Well, he'd paid for her. He was entitled to look, or to touch, if he so desired.

Tonight, she thought. *There's nothing now to stand in the way. He knows I am no simpering virgin. So tonight, away from the prying eyes of London, he'll make me his own.* She longed for the day to end, for the journey to be broken at Rochester, or perhaps at Sittingbourne or Faversham, depending on what kind of time they made in the berlin.

I'll pretend to be tired, Mellie promised herself. *Then he'll stop before Canterbury. If we go that far in one day, we'll both be much too tired to enjoy our love tonight.*

She looked at him out of the corner of her eye. He'd taken off his tricorne, for it was exceedingly warm for June. June, the month for lovers. His profile was strong, his nose straight, his jaw firm. Today he had his own hair dressed into a style for traveling, the dark brown locks which were touched with silver at the temples, pulled back and tied, the ends tucked neatly into a black silk bag in the new fashion. She liked it better than the full periwig he'd worn the first time she'd met him. Yet Mellie realized she'd be attracted to Ritchie Jamison, Lord Henning, if he were dressed in the coarse linen smock of the shepherd they were passing just then, his hair cut as if he'd put a bowl over his head and hacked the locks off in the shape of the container. For the first time, Mellie realized that there was more to a gentleman than fine clothes and fashionable wigs, clever conversation and *ton* gossip. Life at court had not prepared her for this insight, nor had her experiences at Mrs. Mudridge's.

The long, weary miles flew by, for Lord Henning was an interesting conversationalist, chatting about affairs at the court of King George, as well as informing her about some of the politics of the times. He also pointed out places of interest on their journey. They stopped for a hearty meal at The George in Rochester.

"Are we breaking our journey here?" she asked ingenuously.

"No, we'll press on," Lord Henning told her. Then he changed the subject by explaining to her that this inn dated from the fifteenth century, "although I'm sure that little save the crypt under us is from that time."

Rochester Cathedral towered high over the town, but Mellie was interested in neither its gray stone walls, nor in the duplicate of the White Tower of London which stood nearby. Her only concern was with her aloof traveling companion. Not once had he taken her hand, although they certainly had a great deal of privacy in the coach. Nor did he try to flirt with her or steal a kiss. Somewhat piqued, she tried to use her womanly wiles to attract his attention; but he seemed amused by her efforts, which quickly put a stop to them. What could be wrong with the man? Surely he wasn't one of those nonmasculine men of whom she'd known about for years. She couldn't be attracted to one of them. And there was the wedding gown, the trousseau, riding along in the basket behind them. No man not interested in a woman would go to all this trouble for a marriage—would he? She remembered, then, whispered stories about such men who married for political, social, or financial reasons, who even fathered children.

Mellie cast sidelong glances at his lordship. No, it couldn't be true about him. He was all man, of this she was certain. When they arrived at Henning Hall, when the knot was officially tied, then he would prove his virility to her in their marriage bed.

Rochester lay far behind, as the long summer twilight cast its glow over them. Mellie now was bone tired, for the coach jolted along over execrable roads. Even though this was the main highway from the port of Dover to London, it was rutted and rocky, with mud baked stone hard in places, slippery in others where small streams crossed the highway, turning the earth to mud. Their staging stops were fairly frequent, for Henning told her he didn't like to run a team to death.

They stopped for refreshment at a half-timbered inn, The Owl and Raven, in Sittingbourne, and had a light supper at Faversham. But still Lord Henning did not suggest that they stop for the night, although by now Mellie was so tired that her only concern was a bed, not necessarily one shared with his lordship.

"You're tired, aren't you, Mellie?"

"It's a long journey, milord," she admitted.

"We're taking advantage of the long twilight to get home," he said. "I've been away from Henning Hall too long." A shadow crossed his face, but was gone almost immediately. "Tomorrow you can rest. You'll have your own abigail, and you can lie in bed all day if you wish. But I want to make the Hall tonight if it is possible."

She sighed wearily, but tried not to let him see how disappointed she was.

"I am anxious to see the Hall," she said, not dishonestly.

"It's a lovely estate," he promised. "Portions of it date back to Tudor times, but I assure you that it is most modern in its appointments. I believe in living according to one's station in life."

"So do I," she agreed fervently, and this brought a shout of laughter from Lord Henning.

The cottages were closer together along the road now, and even though the hour was late, there were still many coaches and wagons on the road.

"We're coming into Canterbury. Another hour and we'll be home," he assured her. "My estate lies just beyond the town on the Dover Road. Handy for traveling to the Continent. Perhaps we can have a trip to Paris soon."

"Paris!" All fatigue left as Mellie thought of this delicious prospect. She'd never been to Paris, and it was one of her fondest ambitions.

The lovely cathedral towered over the town, but Mellie paid it little heed, even though its silhouette bulked dark against the waning light of the summer sky. Her mind was on Henning Hall. Cathedrals had never been a part of her life.

As if knowing they were near the end of their journey, the horses clopped along at a fair pace, and Mellie was tossed about on the carriage seat, falling against Lord Henning at times. He politely supported her, helping her keep her seat; but as usual, he took no liberties. By now Mellie was so bone weary that she didn't care. Time enough for that in the days to come.

They made their way through the narrow, crowded streets and out on the other side of the town, still on the Dover Road. It wasn't much farther. A little more than a mile, and the carriage slowed and swung off to the left, through a centuries-old brick gate arch with the gate house attached to it. The guard had blown on a trumpet, and the gatekeeper hurried out of his snug little house to swing open the ornate iron gates.

The driveway was through a tunnel of lime trees backed by ancient elms which loomed black against the sky. Then the driveway curved, and Mellie saw for the first time Henning Hall's massive bulk, sitting atop a knoll in a park that might have been natural, but was more likely a carefully contrived garden planned by one of the more famous gardeners of the time.

With a flourish, the driver pulled up in front of Henning Hall. Mellie could see by the light of torches that flared brightly in the courtyard that the house was built in an E shape, with a two-storied porch in the center, and encircling wings closing them in. The courtyard was cobbled, and everything about the place spelled wealth. Indeed, her husband-to-be was everything her young heart could desire. How many young ladies not yet seventeen, girls with such checkered histories as her own, could claim such good fortune?

The footman hopped down from behind, set the stool, and assisted Mellie to alight. It had been such a long, tiresome trip that she felt her knees buckle as she tried to stand; but Henning was immediately behind her, and his strong arm was about her waist in support so that she did not fall. His very touch was inflaming, and she wondered if he could feel the thudding of her heart at his nearness? If proximity to her was as exciting to Henning, he carefully masked his feelings, no doubt so that the servants would notice nothing.

"Welcome to Henning Hall, Mellie," he said quietly. "I hope that you can be happy here. I feel that you are admirably suited to the life I plan for you."

"Oh, milord, it is magnificent," she said, voice tremulous with excitement underlaid with fatigue. "I am most fortunate."

Then his lordship said something very strange. "I hope that you'll still feel the same way this time next week." Or that is what she thought he said, for he muttered it almost as if he were speaking to himself.

Then the great carved oak doors of the porch were thrown open, and a liveried butler was ushering them inside.

"Parkins, this is your new mistress, Miss Wilton."

The butler bowed. "At your service, miss."

They were led into a great hall, probably part of the original Tudor edifice, with a minstrel gallery and carved mahogany screen at one end, an enormous fireplace at the other. Even on this summer evening, a small fire burned in it to fight the damp of the plastered brick walls. They moved through the hall into a long gallery leading to a second, smaller room although it, too, was massive. Here, an ornate staircase of carved oak led up to a second story.

As they walked into the hall, a light, clear voice called out from the head of the stairs, "As I live and breathe, if my dear father has not taken unto himself a bride—or is it the usual liaison, dear parent?"

There was no mistaking the malice in the voice. Then down the stairs came the speaker, a tall, slender young man of about Mellie's own age. He was *en négligé*, a long green retiring robe of brocaded silk trailing on the stairs. Long frills of lace draped over his hands which he waved languidly at his father. His hair was dressed in carefully contrived ringlets which hung in powdered swirls to his shoulders; and even from where she stood at the foot of the stairs, Mellie could see that he was painted white with lead, and his cheeks and lips were red with carmine. An artfully placed beauty spot was at the corner of his full, girlish lips.

This was Lord Henning's son! She was aghast that such a man as her beloved should have fathered such an effeminate offspring. Somehow it came as a shock that he had a son, for there'd been no mention of family. Now Mellie had a sudden terrible thought. Was there also a wife? Was she wrong? Had she been brought here for the usual purpose—but that did not explain the wedding gown in her wardrobe.

The languid fellow finally drifted to the foot of the stairs and looked at Mellie with ill-concealed spite.

"A bit young for you, isn't she, Father? I'd think you were getting rather long in the tooth to bed such youth as this one has."

With an edge that she'd never before heard in his voice, Henning said, "Miss Melusina Wilton, may I present my son, Jamie, the Viscount Triller."

Jamie bowed and Mellie dropped a perfunctory curtsy.

Then Henning went on, "And don't worry that Mellie is too young for me, Jamie. I know it as well as you. I have not brought her here for my pleasure, but for your own. You and Mellie will be married by special license at the end of this week."

CHAPTER THIRTEEN

Mellie woke with a headache. She had slept poorly, after the terrible shock dealt to her on arrival here at Henning Hall. Nightmares of a wedding plagued her sleep when she finally drifted off, dreams in which she was standing in a great cathedral, with Lord Henning at her side, ready to marry him. A bishop said the words over them, pronouncing them man and wife; but when she turned for her lover's kiss, it was Jamie who stood there, a Jamie wearing her own lovely wedding gown.

It was a temptation to dissolve in tears; but Mellie had learned a lot in this past year since she'd been banished from the Court of St. James. She had learned to fight for herself. No one else was going to do it for her. For a few glorious days, she had thought that Ritchie Jamison, Earl of Henning, was to be her protector. Now in one horrid moment she'd learned that her fate had not improved. Married to that—that effeminate popinjay, Jamie Jamison, the Viscount Triller. Well, she'd be a viscountess; but at what a cost!

She reached for the bell that stood on the marble-topped walnut table beside her beautifully canopied walnut four-poster. Last night she'd been too exhausted, both physically and emotionally, to properly examine her bedchamber. Now she saw that it was a well-proportioned room, with wall coverings of the same turquoise and emerald green oriental floral design that draped her bed. The rug was blue, the furniture upholstered in a rich green which set off the highly polished dark furniture to perfection. A simple chimneypiece of white lacquer, and white woodwork and dropped ceiling lightened the room. Under other circumstances, Mellie would have delighted in such a charming bedchamber. Now it was all ashes in her heart.

Oh, Ritchie, she mourned, *how could you have played me so false?* Yet even as she blamed him for her unbearable predicament, Mellie had to admit that it was she who had misunderstood. Never once had Lord Henning suggested by word or action that he had a personal interest in her, that he loved her—or even that he desired her young body. It was she who had built up the fantasy of marriage, or at least romantic liaison, with the mysterious Mr. X, now known to be the Sixth Earl of Henning.

Her bitter reflections were interrupted by a tap on the door, and then a rosy-cheeked, chubby young woman, probably about Mellie's own age, came in, her face happy and bright. Dropping the slightest of curtsies, she inquired, "Did you have a good night, miss?"

"Dreadful," Mellie grumbled.

"Oh, I'm sorry, miss. Probably it is sleeping in a strange bed that does it. I have trouble dropping off unless I'm in my own little cot. But a cup of tea will put it right for you. I have it just outside."

She brought in a silver tray with a lovely china teapot and matching cup and saucer. Mellie did feel a bit more perky after the tea and a wash behind a screen paneled with the same fabric as the wall covering.

"Here, miss, let me do your hair. His ladyship—" Her hand flew to her mouth, and she turned a bright red. "Oh, miss, I'm ever so sorry. They call him that in the servants' quarters, and it just slipped out."

"You don't have to tell me who 'his' ladyship is," Mellie said drily. "I met him last night."

"You won't tell, will you? His lordship, the earl, would send me packing."

"Don't worry, I'll keep your secret." Then, "What is your name? I was so exhausted last night after the trip from London that I just plain didn't hear it."

"I'm Dora, miss. Your abigail, if you think I do all right." In a rush of girlish confidence, she added, "I've never been an abigail before. But I'm willing to learn."

"You'll do fine, Dora," Mellie assured her. "Ouch!" she cried almost immediately as Dora brushed her hair. "That is, if you don't pull out my hair by the roots."

"Oh, miss, I'm ever so sorry," Dora moaned. "It's so tangled from the trip. You didn't want it brushed out last night."

"I was too weary then. Now, tell me all about his ladyship, as you call him."

"The viscount, miss. He wants to see you ever so urgently. Said he'd have breakfast here with you, if it was all right with you, of course."

The last person Mellie wanted to see was the young person of the "third sex," as it was delicately called by the *ton;* but she was trapped again in a situation not of her making. Having accepted the aid of Lord Henning in escaping from Mother Mudridge's brothel, she now found herself being sold into something only slightly more genteel than the prostitution of recent months. Married to such a one as Jamie! And with his virile father as a constant contrast. How could she bear it? Yet what other choice did she have? She now knew all too well what happened to a penniless young lady in London.

So, with what good grace she could muster, she told Dora, "Of course the viscount may have breakfast with me."

"I'll unpack your cases later then, miss. I did only enough to find your night robe, last night." She finished brushing Mellie's hair into long, golden ringlets which lay on her shoulders bared by the sacque she wore *en négligé*. "Do you wish a morning dress, or will you receive him *en déshabillé?*"

If she were being forced to marry this popinjay, she needn't pretend modesty. "I'll receive him as I am, Dora."

The little abigail scurried out with the tea tray, and Mellie prowled about the room, fingering the silver appointments on the dressing table, and peering out of the windows at the lovely gardens below. Her room faced the back gardens, laid out in intricate geometric patterns of bright flowers. Everything about Henning Hall spelled money, and Mellie was so tired of grubby living, of less than genteel poverty. This was even more luxurious than the old days at court. She didn't want to give it up. Very well, if marriage to Jamie Jamison was the price she had to pay for the kind of life this house offered, then she'd pay for it. At least Mellie was sure of one thing. With his obvious proclivities, she'd not have the ignominy of sharing a connubial bed with him. And as most ladies closed their eyes at their wandering husbands' lady loves, Mellie could ignore Jamie's boys, she supposed.

Then there was a bustle at the door, two footmen brought in breakfast on trays, and the viscount presented himself. He, too, was *en négligé*, this time wearing a printed robe of soft China silk with a matching turban. Pointed harem slippers peeped out from the bottom of the robe which swept the emerald green carpet with its train.

He bowed. "Good morning, dear Miss Wilton."

"Your lordship."

"Shall we dispense with formality, under the circumstances?"

"I'm Mellie."

"And my friends call me Jamie. You may, too." It was said insolently, with a tone that made it quite plain to Mellie that her betrothed did not consider her a member of his circle of friends. Well, she didn't like him, either. At least she had normal instincts in her dislike of him.

"Do get on with the serving," he said to the liveried footmen. Then, as if they were part of the furniture, he asked, "How did you get to be cast as the bride in this coming farce?"

Mellie hesitated, covering her confusion at the directness of his question by sipping the chocolate that one footman poured for her.

"Shall I be honest, Jamie?"

His disconcerting habit of a penetrating gaze, which seemed to see through all artifice, was her only answer.

"Very well, I don't know exactly why I'm the bride. According to his lordship, I have certain attributes that he finds suitable." There! Let him decipher that.

"Indeed." Jamie lounged back in the pretty Queen Anne chair which suited his feminine looks admirably. "You must be well born, knowing what great store my dear father sets in blood lines, and such." He laughed, then, a high-pitched sound which grated on her nerves. "Ah, Mellie, you don't understand that joke, do you?"

"No." She was short with him, because being with him was completely distasteful to her. How could she possibly endure marriage with this creature?

"Some day I may tell you the joke, so you, too, can laugh. Well, what are your antecedents?"

"My father was Sir Horace Wilton, an attaché to the court of the Electorate of Hanover. He met and married my mother there. She was Lady Anna, lady-in-waiting to Ehrengard Melusina von Schulenberg."

"The Maypole! My, my, court connections. Dear Father pretends that he finds the court tedious surroundings, but I see he chooses my bride from just such a background. Perhaps he wishes me to be bored by matrimony." Then he asked, with a casualness that didn't fool Mellie for a minute, "Are you rich?"

"I haven't a farthing."

"What a bother. He keeps me on a very slim purse, you know. But he's been hinting, of late, that with marriage I'll get a much more generous allowance. After all, it is only fair. I'm his only son and heir—his lone chick," and again he neighed that high whinny.

How different he was from his father. He must take after his mother's side of the family. There'd been no mention of his female parent, and Mellie hesitated to ask, although she was dying to know if the earl had a living countess. She couldn't bear it, if his wife were to be here underfoot constantly, even though she knew that Henning had eyes for her only as a daughter-in-law, a bought bride for his foppish son.

"You are willing to go through with this marriage, Jamie?"

He shrugged, a precious gesture. "I have no choice. As I said, dear Father keeps tight hold of the purse strings. Once married, he'll give me more to spend."

"And you don't resent his arriving here with me this way— unannounced?"

"One woman is of as little interest to me as another." He gave her one of those sharp glances from his dark eyes that were like glass, hard and glittery. They made Mellie shudder. "I'm sure that if you've been raised in court, you understand about me. I don't have to explain, I hope."

"No." She let her disgust show. "I understand."

"Good. It would be such a bore to have to tell all." Through all this he'd consumed quite a breakfast of toast and butter with his chocolate, never seeming to stop talking even while he ate. "So, dear Mellie, soon to be my blushing bride, I hope you do not expect to see much of your loving husband after the knot is tied. My affections are elsewhere. And, of course, I shall turn a blind eye on any diversions you might seek. In fact, I shall welcome them." He snickered, quite disgusting Mellie.

Then Jamie took his leave, much to her delight, and the footmen cleared away the breakfast. Now Mellie was left with nothing to do. She was not accustomed to the country, having spent the formative years of her life in London. Although Henning Hall was obviously a showplace, she wondered what she'd do to fill in all the endless hours looming ahead of her. Suddenly marriage to the Viscount Triller terrified her. She'd be tied for life to this creature who preferred men to women. What kind of life did that leave for her? He'd already told her he hoped she took lovers. Where were they to be found, in such a remote place? In court, lovers were *de rigueur;* but here in the Kentish downs? Mellie had had enough of men who paid for her body. She was young and pretty and she longed romantically for one great, true love even though she was worldly enough to know that life was a series of compromises, and that true love was easily as ephemeral as fairy gold.

Ah, Ritchie, Ritchie, she thought. *Why did you have to bring me here to this travesty of a marriage?* She'd have been willing to be his mistress, if it were not possible to be Countess of Henning. He was the first man she'd truly loved. Mellie had thought she loved Lord Densbury. But after that dreadful, humiliating episode at Mother Mudridge's, she'd known that she had been infatuated with him because he was young and handsome, and she was a silly young chit. Well, she was little more than a year older in actual age, now; but Mellie felt as old as the fabled Sphinx of Egypt. There was nothing quite like a few months in a London brothel to make you grow up fast.

Dora came in then to help Mellie dress. She chose a morning gown of sprigged India muslin over a small bell hoop. The fichu was of the daintiest lawn, and there was a beautifully embroidered apron, all the rage now in London, with a pair of satin pockets tied under it.

"Although I have little to put in my pockets," Mellie said wistfully. His lordship had seen to a complete new wardrobe, but had not thought of the little niceties such as patchboxes, vinaigrettes, and the like to complete her outfits.

"There's a peddler who comes once a week, with pins and combs and other elegant things which we can't afford in the kitchen," Dora told her. "He'll be along today."

But another thing Henning had neglected was money. "I haven't tuppence to rub together." Mrs. Mudridge had provided for their needs, but had given them only pin money to spend. She had pocketed the fees charged the clientele. How Mellie resented that. It was bad enough to give herself for pay; but then not to get the money was galling.

"No doubt his lordship will see to it that you can buy if you like, when the peddler comes," Dora suggested slyly.

Mellie knew that the abigail was dying of curiosity; but she didn't want to gossip about her affairs now. The time might come when she'd want a confidante, but not yet. First, she must feel out the servants' hierarchy, learn where loyalties lay. Were they loyal to Henning, or to his popinjay son, Jamie?

"I shan't worry about the peddler," Mellie told the maid. "I'm sure he'll return. No doubt there is good trade for him at a place like Henning Hall." Then she realized she had a chance to do a bit of questioning on her own. "I assume that Lady Henning buys from him regularly."

"Lady Henning? Oh, miss, she's dead and buried. And she wasn't here when she was alive, you know."

No, I don't know, Mellie wanted to scream; but instead she pasted on a smile and said nothing, hoping Dora would go on chattering until she found out what was what.

"I've not been here long, miss; but of course they gossip about it in the kitchen."

"I'm sure they do." Again a pause, letting Dora talk if she chose, but not giving the little abigail any fuel for talk about her in the kitchen.

"They say she left him when the viscount was born. I never saw her, but there is a picture of her in the gallery, holding the wee babe."

"I assume the viscount looks like his mother."

Oh, what a look she got from Dora. "Well, miss, you'll be able to see for yourself if you choose to walk that length of room that's the gallery. Full of old paintings, it is. There's even one of the earl as a wee babe."

It was something to do, and Mellie was lured by a chance to see the infant Henning. Not used to such inactivity, she found it boring here, excessively so.

"I'm afraid I don't know my way about the Hall, yet. I'm sure I'd get lost."

"Oh, miss, I'd be glad to guide you. It is a huge place. I got lost several times when I first came here to work. I lived with my gran in the village towards Dover. My ma and pa died of the pox when I was a wee girl; but lucky for me, I didn't get it." She touched her rosy, unblemished cheek with pride.

"Oh, all right, we'll look at the portraits. I haven't anything else to do," Mellie said, then recognized the whine in her voice. That would never do. She must be grateful for whatever life brought her, always remembering the ghastly year on Badger Lane, and the time in the brothel.

CHAPTER FOURTEEN

"We're in the east wing," Dora explained as she led Mellie through a maze of corridors. "The gallery is over the great hall. You came in that way last night."

"Yes, and so weary I have only a slight recollection of a huge room."

"The gallery is long, but not so wide, of course."

They turned at right angles, went through an archway, and the gallery stretched out before them, with tall windows at frequent intervals on one side, making the space light and airy. White woodwork and light ceilings also helped. Along the blank wall were portraits, some quite ugly and obviously very old.

"That's the First Earl of Henning," Dora said, pointing out a man in doublet and hose, a stiff white ruff around his neck.

"He looks like! . . ."

"The present earl. Yes, miss. There's a strong family resemblance in many of these. And on the other side," and she indicated a small portrait in a heavy gilt frame, "is his lordship, the present earl, as a wee child."

Even in his long lace gown and fitted lace cap, Mellie could see the Henning looks she so loved today.

"He was darling!" she exclaimed.

Dora giggled. "Best not let him hear you say that, miss. He might be mortified."

They walked the length of the gallery before coming to Jamie's mother. She had been a lovely woman, with olive skin and flashing dark eyes. Her hair was dressed close to her head in the style of twenty years before, and she held an infant who wore the usual long, lace-covered dress and bonnet. There wasn't the slightest resemblance to Jamie in his mother's face, except for the general coloring.

"See, the viscount doesn't look like her, either."

Mellie wasn't stupid. She knew that Dora was hinting that the young lord wasn't the earl's son. But there was always such gossip in the large estates—or in London, for that matter.

"They lived away from here?"

"So I understand, miss. In London. Until about a year ago when her ladyship died and the viscount was brought here to live." Then, with a sly look at Mellie, she added, "His tutor came with him."

"Surely he's ready for university."

"Could be, miss; but he's not ready to discard his tutor."

So he'd brought along his lover. How dreary, Mellie thought. But if she had to be married to him, no doubt he'd be happier if his paramour were in residence. Mellie knew it wasn't the first marriage with his kind. Members of the nobility married for many reasons, most of them family and money, blood lines and influence—seldom for love. Only in romantic novels did young women love the men they married.

Very well, she'd be a part of such a scene; reluctantly, true, but she'd go through with it. What choice did she have? For some reason Henning wanted his son married; but for the life of her, Mellie couldn't imagine why he'd chosen her to be the bride. All right, she was well enough born, even though her consumptive father had gambled away his fortune, and her mother had died in Bedlam after a licentious life. But Henning had chosen her from a brothel. Why? Even with his son's obvious proclivities, surely Henning would want no such taint on a daughter-in-law as Mellie brought to this strange marriage. She hoped that his lordship would enlighten her before the wedding. If she were to have special duties, she needed to know them.

As if thinking of him had conjured up the Earl of Henning, Mellie looked away from the portrait of the late countess to find that the earl had entered the gallery. This morning he wore a coat of pale tan satin laced with brown, and his waistcoat was eggshell embroidered with Arabic designs in brown and green. Eggshell breeches, tan silk hose with brown clocks, and brown calf shoes made for great elegance. He wore no wig today, but had his own brown hair drawn back so that the silver wings at his temples showed. His hair was clubbed and tied with a brown velvet ribbon.

"You may go, Dora," he said, dismissing the abigail who curtsied to him, bobbed again to Mellie, and hied herself out of sight.

"You look charming this morning, Mellie."

Mellie couldn't help it. She dimpled at the compliment, and her heart pounded. Surely he must realize how she felt about him. She searched his face for any sign of passion; but all she saw was his usual kindness.

"I am well rested, milord," she replied.

"Have you breakfasted?"

"Yes, Jamie invited himself to eat with me."

Dark eyebrows raised. "Indeed. I must say that surprises me." He offered a hand, palm down, and Mellie laid her hand on the back of his as he escorted her back the length of the long gallery away from the picture of his dead wife. He made no mention of the portrait, nor of the fact that Mellie had been looking at it. Instead, when they came to the end of the gallery where a little alcove was furnished with two settees of French design, gilt and upholstered in white and gold brocade, he said, "Shall we sit here and talk?"

Instead of sitting on the settee beside her, Henning chose to sit opposite her on the second settee, where he leaned back, one arm stretched along the back of the settee.

"You understand about Jamie?"

There was no need to be coy with Ritchie Jamison where his son was concerned. Yet some perverse feeling, some annoyance with this attractive man who showed no personal interest in her when she found him so devastatingly desirable, made Mellie say, "That he's interested in men, not women? Oh, that's all too obvious. I'm surprised that he has agreed to marry me."

"Don't be bitter." The words were sharp, biting. "Anything is better than life in Mrs. Mudridge's establishment, I should think."

Incensed, Mellie spoke with spark. "Indeed, I'm still being sold, although this time the buyer is most reluctant to sample my wares."

"True. But I have told Jamie that he must marry you." A shadow crossed his face. "I owe it to explain about Jamie. You saw the picture of him with his mother?" She nodded. So he did know she'd been looking at his countess. "When he was just an infant, his mother chose to live apart from me, returning to her home where her widowed mother and two unmarried sisters lived. I can be frank with you, Mellie. My wife did not enjoy the physical side of marriage. She found it distasteful. No, that is not a strong enough word. She found sex with me revolting. Once she learned that she was pregnant, she refused me my marital rights entirely. I—I allowed it, for I wanted so desperately to have a son. The Jamison line is an old and honored one. It was very important to me to have an heir to carry on the name. I was ecstatic when Jamie was born. It seemed to me that my wife, even though she had been disappointing as a bed partner, had given me the supreme gift, and I owed her everything." He sighed, his face somber. "After our son's birth, she became severely depressed, so much so that the doctor feared she might try to take her own life. After a few months, when she told me that she wished to go to her mother's for a while, the doctor and I thought it might be for the best. After a year, when I went to her, begging her to return with our son, she became severely agitated. I was angry. She was my wife, but she gave me no wifely comfort. When I reminded her that legally I could force her to come back here to live, she told me that she would kill our child before she'd ever submit to me again. That she had no intention of returning to Henning Hall."

"How terrible!" She longed to offer him more comfort than mere words, she ached to hold him in her arms. How could his wife have denied him his pleasure? But how could she not have re- veled in the delights his body could give her? Delights denied Mellie.

"I dared not force the issue, Mellie. The doctor even suggested she might have to be locked away; but I would not agree to that at all. If she could live in quiet at her mother's home, then she might be able to finish out her days in a semblance of peace. I even stopped going to see my son, for each time I visited, she became so agitated that I feared for the child's safety."

"That must have been very difficult for you. Could you not have divorced her, milord?"

"She was my wife, the mother of my son. The Jamisons do not petition for divorces," he said coldly.

"So all these years you've had a series of other women," she spat at him. His holier-than-thou attitude didn't fit in with the taunts Jamie had thrown at his father last night.

"I'm a man, with a man's needs. Of course I had women. Jamie would understand this if he'd not been raised in an atmosphere where men were despised. I'm sure his mother whispered to him about what brutes men are, how they do ugly things with women. Oh, Mellie, it's my fault that Jamie's the way he is. I didn't keep close enough watch over him. Now—I hope it isn't too late to rec- tify the wrong. All those formative years, when he needed a man to use for a model, he had only the company of man-hating women. When his mother died, I brought him here, for he is heir to Henning Hall and the earldom. Alas, the damage was already done."

"Yes, I understand that he brought his *tutor* with him."

"Has Dora been gossiping?" he demanded, obviously angry.

Not wishing to get her abigail in trouble, Mellie said ambiguously, "I told you Jamie had breakfast, and a long, informative chat, with me." Let him think that Jamie had told all if he chose. She owed nothing to Jamie. Better for the viscount to be blamed for the gossip than poor Dora.

"Very well, you know the situation. Jamie doesn't want to marry; but I've told him that I control the fortune he inherited from his mother, as well as my own, and will continue to do so until he marries. When he has an heir, he inherits his mother's estate outright, although he does not yet know that the inheritance is thus entailed."

"But why me?" Mellie burst out, unable to control herself any longer, and confused by all this talk of estates. "Why choose me for his wife?" Then, before Henning could reply, she answered her own question. "But I suppose it would be hard to find many young women of gentle birth who'd marry Jamie, even though it would mean becoming Viscountess Triller, with even greater prospects. Me you could buy."

"That's right." His voice was like a whiplash. "You I could buy—and did, paying that old witch an exorbitant sum for you. I know your background, which is suitable. You are very beautiful, and you had no choice in the matter."

"Most girls in brothels don't."

"I came specifically to a brothel. You see, I want the Henning line to continue. I want my son to father a son to be his heir. And I don't need to tell you that his inclinations are elsewhere. I chose a brothel-trained wife hoping that she'd be skillful enough to help him produce an heir. I want to see Jamie's son before I die."

Aghast, Mellie sat there silent. So that was it! Her job was to make sure the marriage was consummated and fruitful.

"And if I don't succeed?"

"I brook no failure." He said it quietly, but there was iron in his voice; and for the first time, Mellie was afraid. What would happen to her if she failed to produce a grandson for this implacable man?

"When you produce my son's male heir, I shall settle a lifetime income on you which will be separate from your share of the estate through my son. I know that when I die, I cannot control what my son does; but at least you will be provided for if he should abandon you for his men."

"That is very generous of you." She tried to keep the loathing out of her voice. He expected too much of her. Her experience at Ma Mudridge's had been with men all too interested in women. Those of Jamie's persuasion didn't patronize brothels that hired women, although she'd heard rumors that there were some tucked away in the great city of London who catered to the Jamies of England.

"The wedding will take place Sunday in our chapel. Have you seen the chapel? No, of course not. You've had no time for much sight-seeing." Then he paused and asked, his voice cold, "How did you happen to be here in the gallery?"

Mellie thought fast, again protecting Dora. "I said I'd like to see the house, and my abigail obliged; for I knew that if I explored on my own, I would get lost. We'd scarcely started our grand tour, though, when you arrived."

He gave her a look that said he didn't strictly believe her, but Henning didn't openly challenge her statement.

"Then perhaps you'll allow me to show you your new home."

The next hour was spent looking over Henning Hall, from minstrel's gallery to the kitchens, from attics to wine cellar. "You'll be mistress here one day soon, so you must know your domain," his lordship told her. He didn't show her his own private suite, although he mentioned that it was in the same wing as her own chamber.

The chapel was gothic, with high arched windows of stained glass which depicted ancient saints and sinners. It was on the ground floor of one of the wings, with light streaming in from both sides, which kept it from being too gloomy.

It struck a chill in Mellie's heart, though; for here was where she would be legally tied to Jamie Jamison. Here, where she'd thought she would marry Lord Henning, she'd be irrevocably tied, instead, to his effeminate son. What a horrid fate!

For one moment, Mellie was tempted to pick up her skirts and flee, to run as fast as she could down the hill to the Dover Road, and keep right on running either to Canterbury or to Dover, anyplace, to escape this fate. The moment passed. Mellie had seen too much of the sordid side of the world this last year to allow herself to be swayed by such a foolish, impractical thought. She'd seen her mother die in Bedlam. She'd worked as a shopgirl in a grubby draper's shop on Badger Lane. She'd sold her body in a London brothel. No, she would not go back to that. She had to stay here and go through with this travesty of a wedding, had to endure it until she became with child—with male child—and then she would be independent, with an income.

But if she left Henning Hall, she'd lose her child. Nothing in Mellie's background had provided her with guidelines for this eventuality. A child. Her child, even though it would be fathered by so repulsive a creature as Jamie Jamison. Mellie was swept with a sudden, shaking wave of possessiveness, so fierce that it frightened her. It would be her child, and she had no intention of allowing it to be taken over by anyone else. If this meant that she would have to stay on here, married to Jamie, then so be it. He had already made it quite plain to her that he would demand nothing from her, that this would be a marriage in name only. He hadn't told her that they must consummate this marriage and produce a child before he could become independent of his father's largesse; but Henning had told her that Jamie didn't know all of the terms of the agreement.

Did Jamie have some ugly plan in mind? Mellie had no illusions about the viscount. He was an unlovely type. It wasn't only his sexual proclivities that she found so distasteful. She sensed in Jamie a streak of malice, which bordered on the sadistic. He would make a formidable enemy. It was to her advantage to maintain at least a semblance of friendly relationship with her all-too-soon-to-be-husband.

"Are the wedding arrangements to your liking?" Henning was asking, and Mellie realized that while her thoughts had been on the child she must produce, Henning had been telling her of the wedding plans. Not wanting him to realize she'd not been paying proper attention, she smiled amiably and assured him that it all sounded very grand.

"It would have been more impressive to have the Archbishop of Canterbury officiate, of course; but he's suffering from the gout and can't make the trip from Lambeth Palace in south London. And I preferred the ceremony to be held here in our own chapel, rather than in the Cathedral."

"I'm sure it will be a lovely wedding, milord."

She wanted to burst into hysterical laughter. Here she stood, making inane answers to Lord Henning's questions about this wedding which would be the most important thing yet to happen in her life. It was as if she were at a tea party, chatting blithely about the latest hangings at Tyburn.

And before her stood the one man she loved, the man who was so hard-heartedly planning this dreadful fate for her.

Oh, Ritchie, Ritchie, how can you not guess my feelings? How can you force me into wedlock with that creature who is your son? It was frightening to think how little we could control how our children grew up. Surely Henning would never have expected any son of his to turn out the way Jamie had.

Mellie wished she knew the full story behind the late Countess of Henning, and the fact that she had lived elsewhere. Perhaps, if she kept her ears open, Dora would tell her all the gossip. Mellie was sure of one thing. Henning had left untold far more than he'd divulged.

CHAPTER FIFTEEN

Mellie was wandering through a very complex boxwood maze in the gardens when she met Gerald Norwood. He was sitting on a bench which was decorated with chubby little cherubs. Her first impression was of power, almost as much power as Henning possessed. This man was tall, broad of shoulder, and his face had a coarse handsomeness which she found strangely repelling. His eyes were an odd green shade, his hair black and unpowdered, pulled back in oily strands into a loose queue. His clothing was not ornate, but his dark blue coat was well cut and trimmed with gold lace, while his waistcoat of a pale blue brocade was exquisitely fitted to his burly physique. Skintight trousers of biscuit color were tucked into knee high boots of the softest Morocco leather.

"I'm sorry, I didn't know anyone was here," she said, feeling impelled to say something.

"I've been waiting for you, Miss Wilton."

Surprised, she said, "But I don't know . . ."

He rose then, almost insolently, and bowed in a perfunctory manner. "Gerald Norwood, madam." He paused expectantly; but Mellie said nothing, for she had no idea who he was. "I'm Lord Triller's tutor," he added, eyeing her intently, his green eyes glittering with something, some emotion, which gave Mellie a most uncomfortable feeling.

"Oh, yes, the viscount mentioned a tutor; but he did not give me your name."

She would have liked to snub Norwood; but she thought it to her advantage not to antagonize Jamie's lover more than necessary. As with her betrothed, Mellie sensed in this man the capacity for malice, or worse. She preferred not to have it directed at her.

"Please sit down," he suggested, although not very graciously. "We must talk, I think."

Piqued by his manner, and curious, Mellie gave a little shrug and sat on the stone bench he had vacated, spreading her full skirts so that he couldn't sit too close to her. She eyed him.

"This marriage," Norwood said abruptly, after settling beside her. "Jamie doesn't want it."

With a haughtiness that she seldom used, Mellie told Norwood, "What Jamie wants doesn't matter. His lordship, the earl, wishes Jamie wed, and has chosen me as the bride. I daresay he didn't feel it necessary to consult his son's *tutor*," and she emphasized the word, "about his plans."

"Do you know about Jamie?"

"That he prefers your attentions to the more natural ones of women? Oh, yes, I know."

"Yet you intend to go through with this travesty of a thing called marriage?"

"I do. The ceremony will be Sunday, in the chapel. Perhaps Jamie will invite you, as a guest. Or," she added cruelly, for this man brought out the very worst in her nature, "maybe he'll ask you to be best man."

An ugly flush darkened Norwood's face. "You jest, but it isn't funny, Miss Wilton. Do you think you'll win over Jamie's affection with your lovely white bosom peeking above the modesty bit you've tucked into the décolletage of your gown? Or with your caresses?"

"No, I don't. Which changes nothing."

Then Norwood's green eyes narrowed. "He's paying you, isn't he? Henning's paying you to marry my Jamie! I should have known."

Incensed that Norwood was so close to the mark, Mellie said, with somewhat feigned indignation, "Sir, I do not intend to sit here and be insulted by a tutor." But when she made to rise, Norwood caught her arm in a grip so harsh that she gasped.

"I'm not finished talking to you, madam. And as I am the one who enjoys Jamie's favors, you might do well to listen."

He loosened her arm, and she rubbed it, fearful that her tender flesh might be bruised.

"Well, what do you want?" Her tone was surly.

"Does Jamie get his full inheritance when he weds you? You do understand that this is only a marriage of convenience, that old Henning thinks to quiet gossip about Jamie by marrying him off to some young woman—and for some reason, he's chosen you. But you can still back out of this situation."

"I don't choose to discuss Lord Henning with you," Mellie said coldly. "I know what your trouble is. You fear that once Jamie is married, you'll lose your influence over him. But you can scarcely expect me to be your ally."

"Henning's paying you to marry Jamie, isn't he? I know it's true, even if you won't admit it. Oh, not necessarily in guineas—but a woman can be paid in other ways than gold coins. You get a title. You become a mistress of Henning Hall. Although you may be no more happy than Jamison's countess was." And he sneered.

"Jamie's mother?"

"Jamie's mother." He was gloating as he added, "Who couldn't stand Jamie's father. She found life so beastly with Lord Henning that, as soon as she'd produced the obligatory heir, she took said heir and fled to her parental home, never again to return, never to see her husband again. Nor to allow him to see his son."

Henning had explained that he'd been unlucky enough to marry a frigid woman. *I'd not be frigid with him*, she thought.

"I find your remarks most offensive, Mr. Norwood."

"Do you, indeed? I find your entire presence here offensive, Miss Wilton. You may wed my Jamie, but he'll never be yours."

She didn't dignify that remark with a reply. If Norwood only knew how close he'd come to the truth, he'd be gloating.

"You'll have a most unusual wedding night," he said slyly. "The groom won't even spend it with you."

"Don't be too sure of that, Mr. Norwood!"

Again the flush stained Norwood's harsh face. Mellie got up, wrenching her arm loose from his grasp, and left as hurriedly as she could without seeming to run. Odious creature! He and Jamie were welcome to each other; but she had been placed in a most unenviable position. Not only must she wed Jamie to achieve security for herself, but she must also produce his male heir. Lord Henning was depending too much on her skills as a courtesan. If she didn't become pregnant soon, if she couldn't lure Jamie into their marriage bed, what would happen to her? Would Henning toss her back into the gutters of London?

She wished she'd become friendlier with the other girls at Mother Mudridge's, listened to their whispers. Perhaps they'd have taught her skills which would now serve her in good stead.

Sunday dawned all too soon. Mellie lay for the last time in her own bed. From now on, she would have to share her bed with Jamie, unpleasant thought. Perhaps, though, once he'd done his duty and gotten her with child, he would desert her for his own true love. She hoped so. Gerald Norwood was welcome to him.

Dora was all atwitter that morning, with coy remarks about brides and wedding nights.

"Ah, miss, you're smiling," she cooed.

Shall I shock her? Mellie thought. *What would she do if I told her I was fresh from a notorious London brothel?* But Mellie couldn't do such a thing to nice, wholesome little Dora with her country-rosy cheeks and guileless manner.

Finally gowned, Mellie gazed sadly at herself in the mirror. Her wedding day. How thrilled she'd been when the little London dressmaker told her a wedding gown was to be part of her wardrobe. Her heart had pounded wildly, for she thought she'd soon thrill to the touch of her new husband, Ritchie Jamison, Earl of Henning. She'd known of no former countess, no effeminate son. All she'd known was a flood tide of love which almost overwhelmed her. Now she must live in this Hall, seeing Henning constantly; yet she'd be separated from him by a gulf that would never be bridged.

Did he suspect how she felt? If so, he was cruel, cruel, marrying her off to his pitiful son when he could have her for the asking himself. Mellie knew she would make him happy. The first Countess of Henning must have been fit for Bedlam to have deserted such a man as her husband.

A tiny worm of doubt crawled through Mellie's mind. Did Henning have a side to his nature that she'd never seen? Was he cruel? Sadistic? She'd not gossiped with Pamela and Clarissa, with Becky and Tamsen—but she'd heard enough to know that some of the perversions men practiced were enough to drive a wife from her husband. *No, not my Ritchie,* she told herself, loyal to her first true love. It was the fault of the countess, herself, a character flaw. She was a man hater, no man could have roused her. Look at the son she'd produced, if he could be called that masculine a word.

There was a knock at the door and Lord Henning himself, resplendent in an outfit of rich blue trimmed heavily with silver thread, was ready to conduct her to the chapel.

"The local bishop will perform the ceremony, and we have prepared a reception afterward for a few of my more intimate friends, as well as some people from London for the occasion." He shrugged. "Some I don't know so well; but I'm sure you understand that at times politics must enter in at weddings. His Majesty cannot attend the wedding in person, but he has sent his personal representatives to wish you well."

Mellie's eyes widened. Never in her dreams had she realized that Lord Henning was this important. Jamie had said his father sneered at the court; but he'd invited the king himself to his son's wedding.

"I'm honored, milord."

"The honor is mine to welcome you into the bosom of my family, Mellie. I have great hopes for you, great faith in your abilities."

She felt as if she might faint; and apparently she paled alarmingly, for Henning called for Dora and the sal volatile.

"Oh, milord, how romantic," Dora gushed, thinking Mellie's faintness was brought on by the emotions of her wedding day. In a way Dora was right. It was an emotion, all right; but the emotion was deadly fear of what would happen to her if she did not fulfill Henning's demands to produce an heir to the earldom.

All through the ceremony, Mellie was in a daze. Jamie looked a most reluctant bridegroom, and she couldn't be glowing as a happy bride, not when she was marrying the wrong man. The chapel was packed with handsomely dressed friends and well-wishers. She heard Jamie make the promises mouthed by the bishop, and she responded when it was her turn; but it was as if it were happening in a dream, where she was out of herself, watching her own marriage being performed.

The gold ring on her finger was not a dream, though; nor the scowl on the face of Norwood, who sat glowering as his lover married her. Finally it was over, she walked up the aisle of the lovely Gothic chapel on Jamie's arm, with all of the faces on either side a blur.

She couldn't escape from the crowd, though. Mellie and Jamie, along with Lord Henning, had to stand in the great Hall, converted into a bower of flowers which the gardeners had worked on all night to get ready, and greet the guests.

To her horror, she found herself confronting the Duke and Duchess of Seybrook, that odious woman who had caused her mother to be ousted from court, and the man who had bedded her poor mother, bringing on the disgrace and degradation that followed. Mellie longed to do something violent, spit in the painted face of the duchess, slap her, insult her; but she just stood there, simpering, while the duke extended the greetings of His Gracious Majesty, George.

"Little Mellie Wilton," the treacherous duchess fluted. "It's been so long since I've seen you. My, you've grown into a lovely woman. You and this dear husband must call on us soon.''

Blessedly, they did finally move on to the groaning tables of food set out for the wedding guests. Jamie, all too perceptive, murmured, ''Not your favorite duchess, eh?''

Mellie gave a tiny shrug. She'd scarcely tell this creature—her husband! Oh God!—about her mother's banishment from court because of the Seybrooks. She hoped he never heard the gossip. Jamie was the type of person who would store up such tidbits to use when it would wound most.

But further horrors were in store for her. Coming along the reception line was Lord Alistair Densbury. Mellie almost panicked. Her heart fluttered wildly, she felt hot and cold in turn, and she was sure she'd faint dead away, disgracing Lord Henning. Then she took several quick breaths. She'd not give the odious Densbury cause for gossip. He'd betrayed her, and she would never forgive him; but she'd stand here today, look him in the eye, smile charmingly, if it killed her.

Densbury's hazel eyes widened at the sight of Mellie, and she realized that he'd not known who it was that the Viscount Triller had married.

''Upon my soul, if it isn't Mellie!'' He looked her up and down, undressing her with his eyes, and then he laughed. ''Where did you find this charming bride, Jamie?'' he asked.

Jamie wasn't stupid. ''So you know Mellie, eh, Densbury?''

Mellie found she was holding her breath. What was Alistair Lord Densbury going to say? Surely he wouldn't—but she remembered that dreadful time at Mrs. Mudridge's, recalled how she'd expected him to rescue her, only to have him force himself on her instead—then complain to Mrs. M, demanding his money back because Mellie was an inexperienced virgin.

''Ah, Densbury. Good of you to come.''

It was Lord Henning, on her other side, taking Densbury's hand and moving him along expertly. She wondered if his lordship realized what was wrong.

There were more guests, though, and no chance to talk to her new father-in-law. She was kept busy accepting the good wishes, as well as the sly glances, of many of the guests. Jamie's proclivities must be widely known in Kent. No doubt they were wondering where she'd come from, and whether she knew what sort of bridegroom she'd acquired.

When all the guests had greeted them, Henning asked her quietly, ''Where did you know Densbury?''

"He was at court when mother and I were banished." Should she tell him more? Mellie sighed. Probably it was best for Henning to know the worst. "And he came to Ma Mudridge's once while I was there."

She could see that Henning was bothered by this bit of information. He'd been so careful, going to the house in Westminster incognito, trying to keep his identity hidden.

"He'll gossip, malicious young pup that he is."

Mellie's temper flared. It had been an exhausting day, both physically and emotionally. "Did you think you could keep my past a secret? Remember, I 'worked' in a rather public place."

Jamie, realizing that something was happening, turned away from some guests, his dark eyes avid. "Secrets from me? Between my own dear father and my own dearer bride?"

"It's nothing, Jamie. Just that a few of the guests are people Mellie knows, and doesn't particularly like."

"Such as Alistair? He knows her. Surprised me until I remembered that he's a favorite at court, and travels with the *ton* of London. I'm not sure why Mellie wouldn't like Alistair. He's quite well set up—passingly handsome." Then he smiled slyly. "But I keep forgetting. Mellie's my own new bride. She wouldn't be interested in any other men, surely, not on her wedding day."

"Behave yourself, Jamie." Henning's voice was low, but it had the whiplash of command in it.

Mellie could see Jamie flush from anger to be thus humiliated in front of her.

"Father, I wish to have a long business talk with you."

Henning laughed. "Now? At your wedding feast?"

"Now." The mixture of fear, arrogance, and petulance made his voice rise unpleasantly.

In the background, Mellie could see Norwood hovering, his face black as a winter storm, his anger obvious to all.

"What business have we to discuss that is so urgent?" Henning asked his son.

"Money, Father. Now that I'm legally wed, as you required, I want my inheritance."

"When your charming wife presents you with a son, heir to all this after you, then you'll have control of your fortune. And not before!"

Jamie looked betrayed. "A son! But you promised . . ."

"Nothing, my dear son. You inferred too much. Merely standing before the bishop and putting a ring on Mellie's finger isn't enough. I will have a grandson.''

For one moment Mellie felt sorry for her new bridegroom, tricked into marrying her by thinking that he'd gain control of his fortune when the marriage lines were signed. Jamie would have to rise early in the morning to get ahead of his father.

It was distasteful to Mellie to stand there while the father she loved but couldn't have quarreled with the son she despised but was now legally tied to until death did them part. Her eyes strayed from the quarreling men and saw a very disquieting sight. Off to one side, almost hidden by a bower of roses, Lord Densbury was talking animatedly, with much graceful gesturing; and she could see that Norwood was near the boiling point. Then Densbury looked directly at her, gave a sketch of a bow, and turned back to Norwood, laughing.

Densbury was telling Jamie's lover that she had worked in a brothel—she knew that's what it was. Odious man! To think she'd admired him when she was younger. And if Norwood knew her secret, Jamie would learn it all too soon. What would the young viscount do when he learned that he'd been tricked in a second way by his father? That his new bride was a professional whore?

CHAPTER SIXTEEN

Mellie's wedding night was bitter and humiliating. Reluctantly Jamie ushered her to his own private suite which he'd been sharing with Norwood. The tutor was nowhere to be seen, thankfully. Mellie had gone to Jamie's suite with much trepidation, not knowing whether Jamie would have his lover with him to embarrass her. With Jamie, she couldn't ever be sure what to expect.

Jamie was seething with rage, his pretty face flushed and blotchy.

"A son! My miserable father demands that I father a son on you in order to get my own money. It is intolerable." He turned on Mellie, and for one dreadful moment she thought he was going to strike her. "He knows me! He knows that I have no interest in women. And yet he expects the impossible of me."

Trying to placate him, Mellie reminded her new husband, "Others like you have fathered large families, Jamie."

His lip curled with distaste. "I don't want you, Mellie. I can't say it any plainer than that."

"Well, whether you want me or not is scarcely the question, is it? You're stuck with me, and I with you, Jamie. Couldn't we have some sort of truce? If we must be bound as man and wife, we ought to make the best of a bad situation."

He turned on her, thrusting his face close to hers; but not in love, not to offer a conjugal kiss. His eyes were wild and bulging as he screamed, "I was tricked! Cheated! By my own father, and by you. He must be paying you handsomely, Mellie, to get you to agree to marry me. To have a son by me, by a man who loathes you."

"You don't loathe me anymore than I despise you," she snapped. "And if you want your inheritance, so that you can spend it on your fancy man, Norwood, you know the conditions."

"You're nothing but a whore!" he spat. "Selling yourself! But you call it a marriage of convenience—or whatever—to salve your conscience, make selling your body to me for my father's gold sound respectable.''

"How many marriages are for love?" she asked wearily. "It's only in novels, Jamie. You know that. How many love matches can you show me? Marriage is for other reasons, but seldom for romantic, passionate love.''

"But I was tricked," he stormed, pacing about his sitting room which was decorated in the latest rococo style. "I thought that all Father wanted was a marriage in name only. A proper ceremony, a license to show, a bishop to make it legal. Then I'd get my money which he has his grubby paws on. Now, after it is too late, I find that I'm expected to have an heir.''

"Jamie, it wasn't my idea. Don't shout at me.''

"I'll shout at you if I wish, and whenever I wish!" he screamed. "You're my wife. Didn't you pay attention in the chapel? Didn't you notice what you were promising? Or were you too busy counting your gold in your head to comprehend that we were being bound together for life?''

For a moment Mellie was tempted to tell Jamie the truth, that she, too, had been tricked into this marriage. That she'd had no choice—damned if she married him, damned if she didn't. But she was afraid that she might let slip the fact that she loved his father—even after this final betrayal, this marriage to his son, Mellie still loved Ritchie Jamison, Earl of Henning. Oh, how Jamie could take that fact and twist it, make it fodder for feeding his cruelties. No, she must never let him guess, or her life would be unbearable.

"Jamie, we're married. You know the terms of your father's agreement. When I produce your son, you get your money.''

But no sons were fathered that night. No matter that Mellie had known men at court who preferred men to women, but who fathered children. Jamie was incapable of consummating their marriage. Henning had given her too much credit.

Knowing that the night would be traumatic for both of them, Mellie tried to handle the situation as skillfully as she could. She decided that boldness, a show of wantonness, would be the wrong approach with Jamie. Instead, she was modesty personified, carefully disrobing behind the ornate screen which hid the washbowl and pitcher. When she came out, Jamie still stood there, his whole body set in rebellious lines. And he was still fully clothed.

"Do you wish to disrobe behind the screen, Jamie?"

"I don't wish to disrobe at all," he snapped.

"Jamie, we must make the most of a bad situation. Now, do behave. Your valet has laid out your nightshirt."

Jamie's bed was huge and high, so that she had to use a little walnut step stool to climb up onto it. Remembering the shy young man at Mrs. Mudridge's, her second contact, she decided that it might be best to gentle Jamie along, pray that they could have a semblance of normal relations, and hope against hope that she'd become pregnant.

Finally, Jamie muttered angrily, flung behind the screen, and came out in a few moments stark naked. "Why bother with the nightshirt. Remember, we're married," he said bitterly.

Mellie sighed, but held out her arms to him. Instead of heeding her invitation, he went to a chinoiserie cabinet, opened the door, took out a bottle of Madeira, and poured a brimming wineglass for himself. He sipped and paced, not looking at Mellie.

He looked male enough, she thought, his body no different from the scores she'd seen at Mrs. M's.

"Would you bring me a glass of wine, please, Jamie?"

Churlishly he said, "Pour your own. I'm not your servant."

Not really wanting the wine, only trying to ease the tension between them, she slipped down from the bed and got the wine. Then she went over to Jamie, hoping to lure him to their connubial bed.

"Come along, Jamie. It won't be so terrible," she said lightly.

The look he gave her was venomous. "I loathe you," he said, enunciating distinctly. "But I'm saddled with you. I want my money. So take off your gown. We're married, my disgusting wife."

She set down the wineglass and obediently removed the soft, silken gown with its yards of delicate lace, letting it fall in a pool of pale gold almost the color of the triangle now exposed to Jamie's eyes. Knowing he'd not take the initiative, she reached for the wineglass he was clutching like an amulet. Then she moved close, winding her arms about him, pulling him close, pressing her soft flesh against his. He stood like a stick, not even holding her in his arms.

Tilting back her head, she saw the distaste on his face, as if she were something unclean. Oh, God, how could Henning have done this to her?

"Come onto the bed, Jamie," she coaxed.

Reluctantly he followed her, and lay beside her, as impersonal as a stranger. She saw he had no intention of cooperating. It would all be up to her. With an inward sigh, she began caressing him, cradling his limpness in her skillful, experienced hands; but she got no reaction from him whatsoever. Nothing she did roused him.

"I wish you'd quit pawing me," he said savagely.

"Then you must cooperate," she said, just as angrily. "I can't produce babies all by myself."

"Gerald is heartbroken," Jamie said, almost sobbing. "To know I'm here with you, when I should be with him. To know that some stranger, a disgusting female chosen by my father, is here in bed with me, will kill him."

"I'm not interested in Gerald. But if thinking about him will rouse you, then think about him! Think all the lewd thoughts you can," she taunted, hoping that this might help.

For answer Jamie sat up and slapped her viciously across her bare buttocks. "Don't you talk about my Gerald, you rotten whore," he said. "That's all you are. You've sold yourself so that you can be the Viscountess Triller. Well, maybe dear father tricked you, too. Did he tell you we must produce a son and heir before you married me? Did he?"

Rubbing her smarting bottom, she said, "Yes, he did. And you won't get the money until we do. So you'd better try, anyway."

But nothing she did could rouse him even when, reluctantly, he did try to cooperate. The longer the night went, the angrier Jamie became at this ultimate humiliation.

"I hate him!" he muttered, as dawn finally lightened the windows of his frilly bedroom. "I should kill him. Then I'd inherit, whether I had an heir or not!"

Mellie gasped with horror. Was Jamie capable of this final evil? Or was it his anger talking, his humiliation? She must warn Henning to beware of his own son; for if Jamie killed his father, then she was lost.

Mellie was in a terrible quandary. Should she tell Henning that Jamie was incapable of consummating their union? If she admitted this immediately, Henning might well send her away. He might even arrange for an annulment, so that she would have no claim on Jamie. She'd be back where she was before she met Henning. How would she live? Or would it be better to wait a while? Was it possible that in time Jamie would be able to father a child?

She almost felt sorry for him. Why was Henning so anxious for the line to be continued through Jamie? Why hadn't he, himself, remarried? He might have another son, one who would inherit when Jamie died without issue. There was something hidden here

at Henning Hall, something about this entire ugly situation of
which she was unaware.

*Oh, Ritchie, why didn't you marry me? We could have had the
son you so desperately want, a real son, not such a popinjay as
Jamie. We could have been happy.*

Henning wasn't old. There was no reason why he couldn't produce a whole family of possible heirs to replace Jamie, to make
sure that the Henning line would continue, even though the
firstborn wasn't capable of continuing the line himself.

Jamie finally left her, going, perhaps, to the arms of his lover.
Mellie, alone at last, wept bitterly. A week ago she had been so
happy, thinking that she'd be lying in the strong arms of Lord
Henning, giving herself to him with joy. Instead, she had this effeminate, impotent son to husband. Even her time at the brothel in
Westminster had not prepared her for this fiasco of a wedding
night.

If Dora thought it strange that Jamie was not with his new wife
in their marriage bed, she gave no hint of it to Mellie.

"Milady, Lord Henning requests that you and the viscount join
him for breakfast in the upper dining room. I've already told the
viscount's man, Kenneth, that Lord Henning is expecting both of
you."

"Thank you, Dora. I'll wear the peach morning dress."

Mercifully, Henning asked Mellie nothing when she arrived at
the dining room before Jamie. Perhaps he realized that it might
take time for the marriage to be consummated. Or maybe he just
thought he'd wait until Mellie told him of a welcome pregnancy.
Well, poor Henning was going to have a long wait, she feared.
Perhaps he should have chosen one of the other, more experienced
girls at Mrs. M's to wed Jamie.

When Jamie arrived, surly and heavy-eyed, his father was
pleasant, with no coarse remarks about their wedding night. As
soon as the footmen had served them, Lord Henning dismissed the
servants.

"I have a surprise for you and Mellie, Jamie."

His son gave him a long, bitter look. "I don't much like your
surprises, Father dear."

"But this one I'm sure you'll enjoy. I've booked passage on the
packet to France for day after tomorrow. I thought a honeymoon in
Paris would be very romantic."

Paris! Mellie's eyes lit up. She'd always wanted to go to
Paris—but then her spirits fell. Not with Jamie!

"I shan't go without Gerald."

Henning's eyes narrowed, and Mellie thought there was going to be a row between father and son; but the earl kept his temper in check.

"I'd thought just the three of us—I have some business in Paris. We will stay with the Comte de Laq." He turned to Mellie. "You'll love Paris, my dear. And you can buy some of the latest fashions for your wardrobe."

"I said," and Jamie raised his voice, "I will not go without Gerald. It's bad enough to trick me into marrying Mellie; but now to spirit me away to France! Without Gerald! I will not go. You take Mellie on a honeymoon. I shan't!"

Unwittingly, Jamie had said the cruelest thing possible. Ah, how she wished she could be taking a trip with Henning.

"Don't be childish, Jamie," his father snapped.

"Childish? Dear Father, I'm a married man, remember? Here sits my beloved wife, with whom I exchanged wedding vows only yesterday. With whom I spent my wedding night." He was vicious now. "And I do not choose to spend time with her in Paris, unless Gerald goes, too."

The explosion Mellie expected did not happen. Instead, Henning said, "Very well, if you insist. Gerald goes, too. And your valet, and mine—and Dora, of course. So see to packing at once. We must leave early tomorrow, as I am not positive when the packet sails."

Mellie was stunned that Lord Henning had given in so easily to Jamie's demand. What a honeymoon it would be, with the man she loved and her husband and his lover! It sounded like a French farce, something to be booked into the Drury Lane, not something in real life.

But the flurry of packing did much to keep her mind off the possibilities of the nuptial chamber that night. In any case, although Jamie made a show of retiring with her, once the servants were dismissed, he curtly bade her goodnight and left, presumably to spend the night in Gerald's arms. If Lord Henning had hoped to get Jamie into a more romantic mood in Paris, then he'd ruined it by including Gerald.

Early next morning, Dora waked Mellie with the announcement that Lord Henning wished to visit her immediately. Just what was he going to say when he found that Jamie wasn't with her?

"I'll receive him in the sitting room, Dora. My robe. And brush my hair quickly."

When Dora showed in his lordship, Henning dismissed her curtly. "We'll ring when her ladyship is ready to dress for the journey," he told the abigail. When alone, he asked, "Is Jamie with Gerald?"

No point in dissembling. "I assume so. He left me as soon as Dora was gone last night."

There was a discreet knock, then a footman came in with a breakfast tray.

"Just leave it. We'll pour our own chocolate," Henning ordered. Then, as he and Mellie breakfasted, he said, "I guess you think me mad to include Norwood in our plans."

"Frankly, sir, I do. Maybe, away from the influence . . . ."

"You heard Jamie. He wouldn't go without his tutor." As Henning said the word, his mouth twisted as if he'd bitten into a bad piece of fruit. "I agree with you that having Norwood along will be disastrous. And he isn't going to Paris with us, I assure you. But I'll need cooperation from you in order to pull off my coup."

"But how—Jamie will balk, milord. He'll refuse to leave here. I know he will."

"Oh, Norwood will start with us, but he'll not get to the boat in time. First, I want you to feign a slight indisposition—not enough to postpone the trip, but you must feel ill enough so that you need Dora with you in the coach. Normally, she'd travel in the second coach with Kenneth and my valet—and the luggage. This time, my footmen have instructions to put my boxes, yours, Jamie's, and Dora's on our coach. There will be four of us, so there'll be no room for Norwood in the first coach. He'll have to ride with the valets."

"Jamie will probably ride back there with them."

"No. I'll lay down the law. If he wants any gold to spend in Paris, he'll leave here riding with his bride."

"And then, milord?"

"The second coach will fall behind, and will break down before it gets to Dover. Norwood will miss the packet."

"How clever of you." But would it work? Knowing Jamie, he'd probably stay at an inn in Dover rather than sail without Norwood.

As if seeing her doubts, Henning reached over and laid a hand on hers. "Trust me, Mellie. I assure you it will all go smoothly."

And with his hand touching her own, Mellie would have agreed with anything he said, even if he'd told her that black was white, so exciting was his touch.

CHAPTER SEVENTEEN

Jamie paced the deck of *The Black Hind*, peering through the gathering gloom to the dock below where the frantic activity of loading the ship for France made a kaleidoscopic scene.

"They should have been here hours ago, Father," he fretted.

Although still moored at the dock in Dover, the packet rocked in a manner which boded ill for the forthcoming crossing to Calais. "What can have happened to them? Maybe they were set on by highwaymen. We should have never gotten so far ahead of them." Then Jamie groaned and gulped.

"Are you feeling the swell?" Lord Henning asked, all solicitude. "Perhaps you should go below and lie in your bunk, Jamie. I fear it will be rough, if we're bouncing about this much in port."

"But Gerald . . ." he wailed, sounding more a callow youth than a married man.

"Jamie, the coachman is excellent, a guard was riding with him, armed with both pistol and blunderbuss. They may have had some minor delay; but there is plenty of time before the morning sailing. Stop fretting, or you'll be ill even before we leave Dover. Do go and lie down for a while."

By the light of the torches which blazed on deck, Mellie could see that Jamie was gray, with a touch of green.

"Dora will see to you if you feel ill," she assured him. "I'll stay here on deck and watch for the other coach."

Jamie turned reluctantly to go below, then made a mad dash for the railing, hanging over it and retching miserably. Dora, who was waiting near the companionway, hurried over to his side. "Come along, milord, I have some laudanum that will settle your stomach," she coaxed, leading Jamie below.

"That'll take care of him for the crossing," Henning murmured to Mellie. "I've told Dora to give him enough to make him sleep. He's a poor sailor, and it's going to be very rough, I fear. Do you feel all right?"

"Perfectly, milord. I never suffer from *mal de mer*."

"It may sound cruel to you, but I'm glad that Jamie is already queasy. I'd wondered just how I'd get the laudanum down him otherwise. When he wakes, we'll be either in France, or well out into the Channel, depending on how long it takes us."

"When I came from Hanover, the crossing was only about four hours, as I recall."

"I frequently make it in three. But as rough as it is, it may take eight or nine tonight. And we sail with the tide at midnight."

"Midnight! But I thought you said. . . ."

"Morning? So he wouldn't stew so much about Norwood. No, it's all part of the strategy. About now, Gerald Norwood is cooling his heels at the Ox and Cocks in Whitfield while my wily coachman sees to a loose spoke in the coach wheel."

"Milord, I'd hate to have you against me. I'll wager you are an astute businessman." She knew he was traveling to Paris on some kind of business. Jamie had mentioned that Lord Henning was a real wizard with investments, seeming to sense which endeavors to invest in, which to avoid, when to buy, when to sell. And he had interests on the Continent as well as in England.

"I can imagine no situation in which you and I would be on opposite sides, Mellie. You cooperated beautifully today, swooning about with your *sal volatile*—you even looked ill."

Mellie giggled. "I must confess, milord, that Dora and I accomplished that look with much diluted white lead. Poor Jamie. I hope he can enjoy Paris without Gerald. I for one intend to have a marvelous visit. I've never been to Paris."

"I'll show you the sights," Henning promised, making her pulse race. If only—oh, if only it was the two of them going there—no Jamie. What a glorious time they could have! Although Mellie thought she might see nothing of Paris under those circumstances, only the bedchamber she'd share with her love.

She wondered how soon Henning would realize that there would be no heir produced by this marriage? No, she shouldn't be so pessimistic. Maybe Paris would work a miracle on Jamie.

She was too optimistic. The crossing of the Channel in a storm took all of twelve hours. When Jamie's dose of laudanum wore off, he was sick again, suffering for the entire trip, so sick that he didn't seem to realize that Norwood wasn't on board. He asked for Gerald once, but Mellie lied and said that Norwood, too, suffered from seasickness. When they finally landed at noon the next day in Calais, Jamie was still so ill that they got him loaded into the hired coach and en route to Paris without having to explain why Norwood wasn't there.

The explosion took place in a private suite of rooms in the magnificent mansion of the Comte de Laq in the fashionable quarter of St. Germain. Jamie, fully recovered from his bout of *mal de mer*, fretted about Norwood's delay. "I can't understand it," he whined, pacing the polished parquet floor. "How does it happen that Gerald's coach is delayed again?"

Just then, Lord Henning entered their salon with an unobtrusive pair of servants behind him. "Jamie, Alphonse will valet for you while we're here." He indicated the younger of the men, decked out in the de Laq livery of maroon and gold.

"Thank you, but Kenneth will be sufficient, Father."

Then the truth hit Jamie. "They're not here? The other coach? If you're giving me a valet, that means . . . did they even sail with us?" His voice rose an octave, his face darkened.

"We had to sail with the tide, Jamie," Lord Henning said calmly. "Unfortunately, the second coach was delayed. I have no idea for what reason. If I'd not had this urgent business to attend here, we might have waited in Dover; but it was impossible to stay there past sailing time."

"You did it on purpose," Jamie said, his voice so low Mellie could scarcely hear it. "You arranged something—and my dear wife was a part of the scheme."

Quickly, Henning turned to dismiss the men servants before they heard the whole sordid squabble. Then he told his son, quite tartly, "Act like a man for once, Jamie. You're behaving like a spoiled brat. Now, your first visit to Paris can be enjoyable if you wish—or ruined. It is your own choice. We have been invited to a ball given by the Duc de Coaquin tomorrow night, and Madame de Bussy holds her salons every Friday. We may dine with her if we wish. All of the elite of Paris go there."

"Will we see Versailles?" Mellie asked eagerly.

"I'm sure it can be arranged; although, since Louis XIV died last year, there is not the brilliance attached to the court that there was. With young Louis still a child in dresses, it much detracts from court life. There is much activity in Paris now, though. The opera is well attended. And our host, the Comte de Laq, has told me that in two days there will be much street celebration because it is midsummer. The common folk dance in the streets, with special bands set up to entertain them in the food market, Les Halles."

"Who wants to watch commoners cavorting?" Jamie said,

pouting. "If I'd wanted that, I could have stayed in Kent to watch the Morris dancers. Or the maypoles."

"Don't sulk, Jamie. Enjoy Paris while you can."

The viscount's temper flared again. "I'd wanted a grand tour with Gerald, but you wouldn't hear of it!" he railed. "All of my friends have gone on tours, or are going. The Baron Alderbridge is right now in Rome. He told me they were taking the overland route through the Alps, carried in sedan chairs, because it is dangerous by sea, the pirates being numerous off the southern coast of France. And his cousin, Tom, is probably en route to Vienna. And I have to be saddled with a wife I don't want."

He stomped out of the suite, leaving Mellie with Lord Henning. "I'd hoped the romantic atmosphere of Paris would affect him," he said, his face drawn into tired lines.

Mellie longed to go to him, take him in her arms, and comfort him in the way Jamie refused to be comforted. How could she stand it, burning with desire for this man, yet married to his son. Ah, Paris was, indeed, full of romance. Unfortunately, it did her no good. Well, she'd make the best of it, enjoy the pleasures of the city by day, and try to make a man of Jamie by night, although she had little hope of success. Perhaps, by the end of their visit, without Norwood to distract Jamie, he'd manage what he'd so far been unable to accomplish. Once she became pregnant . . . .

"Are you too tired to see some of the sights?" Henning asked her. "We could hire a coach, or chairs. The Cathedral of Notre Dame is very beautiful, even though some who come to visit won't look at it because it is papist."

"I should love to see the sights," she said, eager to be with him, even as his daughter-in-law.

"Let me invite Jamie."

Her heart fell. She'd wanted the time alone with him. In a few minutes, Henning returned to say that Jamie was still sulking. "We'll go without him. He muttered something about seeing a Parisian tailor."

Paris! No matter that the king was a child and life at court was less brilliant than it had been a few years ago. Paris was still the home of the most fashionable people of Europe. Even London couldn't surpass it. Actually, George was rather a stodgy monarch, with his German ways and his ugly mistresses. Mellie soon realized that Paris was one vast salon of clever conversation, fashionable dress, and witty repartee. The balls were extravaganzas of invention, the homes of the nobility opulent and gracious.

As they returned from their drive that first day, they passed a truly lovely mansion in the same district where they were staying. There was such a crush of carriages and sedan chairs in the street, such hordes of elegantly dressed men going in the front door, that they came to a halt. Rapping on the roof of the coach, Henning called, "What is this, coachey? There must be some important event in progress."

The coachey leaned down from the box until he looked in at them, his head upside-down. "Ah, milord, that is the famous establishment of Madame Tilladet. She is having her girls model the latest fashions for her gentlemen clients. It is popular, no?" Then his head disappeared from sight.

Mellie's eyes widened with comprehension. "You mean—it is a brothel, milord?"

"Obviously. If he'd told me the name, I would have known. Madame Tilladet is famous in Paris. And much more elegant than Mrs. Mudridge, having been born into an old and honored Parisian family."

Mellie noted the address on the boulevard, a glimmer of an idea beginning to form in her mind. Madame Tilladet.

Back in the mansion of the comte, Henning inquired after his son, only to be told that the viscount had gone out for the evening. There was something about the way the footman said it that made Mellie wonder what was afoot. Once she and Henning were alone in their beautifully appointed salon, relaxing with glasses of wine, she asked Lord Henning if he had gotten the same impression.

For a few moments, she thought he was not going to answer. Henning sat there, turning his wineglass around and around in his fingers, his face no longer pleasant as it had been for their delightful outing. Mellie wished she'd not mentioned Jamie to him.

Then Henning looked directly at her, his face somber. It added years to his appearance, a preview of what he'd be like when he was an old man. "I should have remembered what a debauched city Paris is; but I'm selfish, Mellie."

"Oh, no, milord, not you!" She dared lay a hand on his arm, and he didn't pull away from her gesture.

"Many of the young nobles are like Jamie. I should have known that he'd find it out quickly. They seem to know just where to go—perhaps he bribed one of the servants. I'll wager he's with some pretty young man right now."

"Being untrue to Gerald?" she asked lightly.

Henning sighed, then put down his wineglass and laid his head back against the luxurious upholstery of his chair. He covered Mellie's hand with his own, sending such a surge of desire through her that she thought surely her hand must burn and alert him to her love. But he only clung to her for comfort, not love.

"I don't know if he finds other men or not, Mellie. It's such a distasteful thing for me to face—my own son—that I've not kept a proper surveillance over him, I fear. I don't know what he'll do. I'm beginning to think that this trip is a mistake. I had hoped . . . away from Norwood's evil influence . . . well, all I ask is a grandson. Then he can take a permanent grand tour with his precious tutor, for all I care." She could feel the muscles of his arm tighten with his anger. "It is very difficult for you, my dear," he went on. "But I shall make it up to you, once you bear his son."

"I have hopes, milord, that things will transpire as you wish, here in Paris." She didn't tell him of her idea, knowing he might not approve of what she planned to do.

Jamie did not come back until well after midnight, and when he did come into their bedchamber, he was almost too drunk to walk. Tight-lipped, Mellie rang for Alphonse, and ordered her husband put to bed. She thought the valet smirked as he turned away, and she wanted to throw something at him. Very well, if Jamie was going to make a spectacle of himself, she'd go tomorrow morning to see Madame Tilladet.

Not wanting anyone to know her destination, Mellie asked the comte's chair bearers to take her to a famous fashion house where she could shop, instructing the bearers to come for her in several hours. Once they were out of sight, she hired a public chair and gave the bearers the address of the famous brothel, not caring what they thought. These she instructed to wait for her outside Madame's mansion.

Presenting her card to the middle-aged maid clad in a gray Lyons silk dress with white embroidered apron and mobcap, Mellie said with authority, "Please tell Madame Tilladet that the Viscountess Triller urgently wishes to consult her."

The servant was well trained. Not by even the flicker of an eyelash did she show that few ladies presented themselves at the Maison Tilladet. She showed Mellie into a small but elegant salon furnished with delicate gilt chairs and tables.

Mellie had little time to wait. She'd scarcely settled herself when the maid returned and announced, "Madame Tilladet, the Viscountess Triller," and ushered in her mistress. Mellie had not known what to expect. Her experience with brothel keepers had been limited to Mrs. Mudridge. This elegant creature of perhaps forty was a far cry from that flamboyant, garrulous woman. Her dark brown hair, unpowdered, was dressed close to her head. She wore a sacque of a delicate taffeta, a deep peacock blue embroidered with large rosettes of deepest rose flowers, and a further overall design of small white leaves in clusters. The deep décolletage was framed with a narrow ruching of ecru lace, and the sleeve frills, fully six inches deep, fell in ecru gathers from the elbow-length cuffed sleeves. Her face was fashionably whitened, although she followed the Parisian style of heavy rouging not the vogue in London. Mellie was glad she'd worn her most elegant suit of lilac velvet with a cunning fitted basque jacket over a full skirt beautifully shaped by paniers.

"You wished to see me, your ladyship?" Before seating herself, Madame rang for the maid and asked that they be served coffee. As they sipped, she eyed Mellie curiously.

"I shall put my cards on the table, Madame. I need help and I am quite willing to pay you for assistance."

Madame's eyebrows rose slightly. "Indeed. I shall, of course, be happy to be of assistance, milady. But first, I must be sure of who you are. Am I right in thinking that you are the daughter-in-law of the Earl of Henning?"

Surprised, Mellie realized she was dealing with a very shrewd woman, one whose intelligence system was obviously far-reaching.

Nodding, she said, "The earl is my husband's father."

"And how may I help you?" Somehow, assurance that Mellie was connected with Henning seemed to please Madame.

"I shall tell you something which I trust you to keep in confidence. I am recently married to the viscount. Before that, when younger, I was at the Court of St. James where my mother was a lady-in-waiting to Melusina von Schulenberg."

"Recently granted the title Duchess of Kendal."

"You are superbly well informed, Madame. Between the time my mother was banished from court, and my marriage, my fortunes fell so low that I worked, briefly, for Mrs. Mudridge, in Westminster." Mellie paused, then asked, "Have you heard of Mrs. Mudridge, Madame?"

A wry smile flitted over the Parisian's face. "I have, indeed. You are being very frank with me, your ladyship."

"I am desperate," Mellie said. Quickly she told her of the strange marriage, and Henning's determination to have a grandson. "But my husband, the viscount, is—not interested in women," she finished delicately. "Our marriage has not been consummated."

"He will find many of his persuasion here in Paris."

"So I have learned. Madame, nothing I do rouses him. We can scarcely produce this heir to the Henning line unless we have sex together. I have heard that there are substances—powders—potions—which increase desire in men. If you can provide me with such, I shall pay you well."

"You think an aphrodisiac is the answer?"

"I hope so, Madame. But at home, I would not know how to obtain such a thing."

Madame Tilladet shrugged. "It is easy enough to provide. Whether it will help—I do not know. These creatures vary so in their sexual capabilities. He is completely impotent with you?"

"Completely."

"Has he a male lover? Or lovers?"

"His tutor, who," and Mellie grinned impudently, "missed the boat which brought us to Calais. Lord Henning hoped that the romantic atmosphere here might prove beneficial."

"Lord Henning—is he aware that you and the viscount have not yet had sex?"

"No." Mellie's reply was so short that Madame gave her a very shrewd look, but discreetly asked no questions.

"Then you can provide me with what I need?"

"I can provide you with an aphrodisiac, milady. Whether or not this is what you need—we shall have to wait and see, shall we not? Some of the men who come here use this powder regularly to enhance their pleasure. Your husband, does he have any liking for you at all? Does he make any sexual advances?"

"He loathes me. He feels he was tricked into the marriage, and consented only to receive his inheritance. After the ceremony, his father told him that the money would not be his until he had fathered a child on me—a male child."

"May I speak frankly, Lady Triller?" Mellie nodded consent. "Is it any wonder that your husband does not have success with you—sexually—after such treatment? I assume he was not interested in women even before the marriage."

"That is correct. But Lord Henning is determined that there shall be an heir to the title. Jamie's son."

"If you will excuse me briefly, I shall get the aphrodisiac."

Mellie, sure she'd be able to solve her problem, now began to have grave doubts. Madame Tilladet had given the impression that the aphrodisiac might not do what Mellie hoped it would. Well, it was worth a try.

When Madame returned, she carried a small alabaster jar. "This is quite potent, milady. Stir only the smallest bit, no more than the size of a pea, into his wine. Perhaps it would be wise to get him fairly drunk, first. Then give him the drugged wine. Then get him into bed and into you, as soon as possible. And good luck, my dear."

"The payment . . ." Mellie said, tentatively, reaching for her pocket.

"No gold, milady. But if you could ask your father-in-law something, and send the answer to me, I shall be amply repaid."

Puzzled, Mellie hesitated. "What question, Madame?" Then, in a burst of youthful frankness, she added, "He does not know that I have come here today. He might not . . . ."

"Approve?" Madame smiled in a very worldly way. "But he got you from a brothel, my dear. But, no matter. You can ask and not tell him who wishes to know. Your father-in-law, the earl, is renowned for his financial acumen. In Paris, they refer to him as a monetary wizard. His ability to know which ventures are good investments! Milady, he is incredible. Now, there is much talk, even from government sources, that France is going to invest heavily in the New World—in Louisiana, to be exact. Shares are selling briskly in the Paris Mississippi Company, to exploit the wealth of the colony. I have friends at court, and they advise me to buy now, for the shares are already rising. In fact, there is a curious phenomenon near the stock market now. I've seen it with my own eyes. There is a hunchback, a beggar, who plies his trade in that section of the city. He now charges stock traders to use his humpback as a desk when they write up stock orders. Speculators think it will bring them good luck. I think, frankly, the only fortune made may be by Bombario, the hunchback, for his rentals! I do not wish to risk my gold on some wild scheme which will fail. Ask the earl, milady. You can say you've heard of this new speculation in Paris, and wonder if he thinks it is sound. Then send me a message by hand, telling me what he advises. It will be ample payment for the little I have done for you."

Then, handing Mellie the jar, she added, "Unfortunately, this is also speculative. I can only hope you achieve your aims with it, milady."

Mellie took the sedan chair back to the fashion house, went in and ordered a gown made, and finally went back to the Comte de Laq's residence where she found her father-in-law but not her husband. Borrowing some of Madame Tilladet's story to use as her own, she asked about the hunchback, Bombario. "I heard this droll story when I went out today to shop," she said, not actually lying to Henning, but certainly stretching the truth. "Could it be true? They say that there is a stock—something to do with the New World—that is an excellent buy."

"Oh, the Mississippi Company?"

"I do believe that was the name, milord." Ingenuously she asked, "Is it a fortune maker? I might buy a share or two myself."

"Save your guineas for seductive gowns, Mellie. I know the man who is pushing that stock here in Paris. He's a Scot, John Law, and I've run afoul of him in England. I wouldn't invest in anything he has his fingers in unless I wanted to spend my final days either in the poorhouse or debtors' prison. Leave speculation to the men, Mellie."

But she had her answer, and was able to send off a note to Madame Tilladet before she had a chance to give Jamie the aphrodisiac. That night the comte had a dinner party for them, and then they attended the opera. Sometime during the evening, Jamie disappeared, and did not return to the performance. When they returned to the comte's mansion, he still was not home. Mellie, weary from the strenuous evening, got ready for bed, dismissed Dora, and then, herself, mixed the potion for Jamie to drink, leaving the glass of wine invitingly beside the bed. Then she lay down on the other side of the wide bed, wearing a very diaphanous night robe, to wait for her husband to return from whatever debauchery he had found to amuse himself. As tired as she was, Mellie dropped off to sleep, the candle still burning beside her.

She woke with a start, disoriented, strange noises frightening her. On the other side of the room, vague shadows writhed and gasps and moans filled the air. Terrified, Mellie opened her mouth to scream for help when she noticed that Jamie's scarlet brocade coat he'd worn to the opera was thrown on the bottom of the bed. Knowing, but not wanting to believe, she turned her head ever so slowly on the pillow until she could see the drugged wine she had left for him to drink. The glass stood there, empty. As her eyes grew accustomed to the dim light from the now guttering candle, Mellie was able to recognize Jamie and the new valet, Alphonse, enjoying each other, oblivious to her, oblivious to everything except their carnal urges which they were satisfying.

Sickened, she closed her eyes, pretending sleep. Later Jamie, nude and sweaty, crawled into their bed and began snoring almost before his head touched the fat, fluffy goose-down pillow, while his sex partner quietly dressed, picked up his master's discarded finery, and slipped out of the room like an evil wraith.

Mellie lay awake until dawn grayed the windows, sleeping only after she made the decision to tell Lord Henning that they should return to England at once. Instead of improving the situation, Paris had only exacerbated it.

CHAPTER EIGHTEEN

Unfortunately, Henning's business dealings were not yet complete, so Mellie couldn't persuade him to truncate their Paris idyll. Jamie was in a fit of blackest depression, with much talk to her of poor, dear Gerald, back home alone at Henning Hall. Mellie correctly interpreted this as an enormous burden of guilt because Jamie had been untrue to his lover with Alphonse—and perhaps with members of the Parisian aristocracy, for all she knew.

She did not try her experiment with the aphrodisiac again. The first time had been a fiasco. Even had she been awake when Jamie had drunk the drugged wine, she felt sure he would not have turned to her, but would have gone off looking for another man.

Lord Henning asked no details of her marriage, and she offered none. She was beginning to feel a desperation which no amount of gaiety in Parisian society could dispell. If she could not, somehow, help Jamie to consummate their farcical marriage, she would never become pregnant. How long Lord Henning would wait for that happy announcement, she dared not ask. It was a relief when they finally quit France and sailed for England. Even the weather helped them, for it was not stormy, the Channel was calm, and Jamie wasn't ill.

Life went on at Henning Hall, with Jamie putting on a good show, in public, of a happy marriage to deceive Henning. Never once did he mention their wedding night, nor the fact that she must produce his son in order for Jamie to control the considerable fortune that was his. Gerald Norwood remained there in the background, self-effacing; but Mellie knew that Jamie spent his nights with the tutor, not with her. And she knew that in a place like Henning Hall, it wouldn't be too long before some servant would catch on. Mellie thought that Dora, her personal abigail, was beginning to suspect that all was not bliss in the marriage bed.

Her father-in-law requested her company for a ride through the Kentish downs the next day, the first time they'd been alone since the wedding. Frightened at the prospect, she felt it necessary to tell Jamie. She found her husband in the music room, plucking in a desultory manner at the harp that stood there.

"I didn't realize you were a musician." She was surprised; for although he was giving only half-hearted attention to the instrument, Mellie could hear the excellent quality of tone. With work, Jamie could be an accomplished harpist.

"My dear father does not think harp playing is manly."

"But you are talented. Perhaps, if I spoke to him . . ."

With one of the lightning swift mood changes so typical of him, Jamie snarled, "Don't discuss me with my father! That's an order, Mellie. You promised to obey me. Remember?"

Annoyed, she snapped back, "I was only trying to . . ."

"To meddle. Once my money is my own, I'll do whatever I want. I'll hire the finest harpist in England—in Europe—to give me instruction. I'll play concerts in the Haymarket. But I want no favors from that unnatural beast who claims me as his son." Then he laughed, an ugly sound. "He sets great store in sons, as you well know. The great Henning line must be continued."

No longer able to control her curiosity, Mellie asked, "Why did he not have other children, then?"

"Because my mother refused to share his bed with him after she fulfilled her duty and produced the son he demanded of her. She found him so disgusting that she left. Surely you've been here long enough to hear the gossip."

"But now, with your poor mother dead, he might remarry "

"To his lordship, marriage means fathering sons."

"Come, now, Jamie, your father is a young man still."

The smile that crossed his face was utterly gleeful, and completely evil. "But he is sterile! The great Lord Henning, Sixth Earl of Henning, unable to produce a substitute for me. Oh, you don't know how delighted that makes me, Mellie. He drove my mother away with his beastliness. She used to hint of it to me—in a delicate, ladylike way, of course; but I learned what she meant. All she was to him was a brood mare. But then he was sick. Mother told me about it before she died. Someone passed the gossip on to her, knowing how she despised him. One of the tenants on the farm behind the Hall had a whole houseful of children, and they all came down with mumps, their jaws puffed out like squirrels loaded with acorns for the winter. And dear Father caught the fever from them."

"It's a common enough disease, Jamie." But Mellie remembered a discussion with Pamela and Tamsen, so she wasn't too surprised when Jamie went on with his story.

"It's common in children, true, Mellie. But if you escape it in childhood, and then your jaws swell when you're adult, more than that swells. I daresay his privates were as big as those round cheeses the farmers bring to market." He sniggered. "Father's manhood suffered more than his face, I can tell you. And now he can no longer father children—male or female. I'm the only product of his loins."

Poor Ritchie, Mellie thought. What a blow to his male pride. No wonder he was so anxious for Jamie to produce a son to carry on the Henning line.

"But I thought I heard you taunting him about having a long series of mistresses," Mellie said, confused.

"Oh, there's nothing wrong with his beastly urges, he still can romp with women all he wants to—and he wants to, believe me! That's why, when I saw you for the first time, I assumed that you were his latest doxy." Mellie winced at the vulgar term. "Well, I wish that's what he'd brought you here for, to warm his bed, not mine." He eyed her with distaste. "You're the type he likes, you know. Pale skin, cornflower blue eyes, lots of bosom for him to fondle, or whatever he does with his disgusting hands. Poor Mama, to have been subjected to such beastliness from a man little better than an animal, always after her, wanting her in his bed morning, noon, and night, pawing her, doing all those nasty things to her that she so hated."

"It must have been a blow to him when his wife left him, took away his only son, and then he found he could have no more."

"That's why he came running to fetch me when Mama died. I was his son—the only one he'll ever have—his heir."

"If you hate him so, why did you come here to live?"

With utter arrogance, he said, "It's my right, Mellie. All this is mine—or will be someday. And it can't happen too soon for me. If poor dear Father catches a chill and dies of lung fever, I shan't wear a crepe weeper on my hat!"

"Jamie, that's wicked."

"Wicked." He caught her arm in a bruising grip. Harpists have strong fingers. "Do you call what he's doing to me nice? That's wicked, Mellie. Forcing me to marry you—or any woman—can you imagine what it has done to poor Gerald? He's all to pieces."

"He needn't be," she said drily. "He still has your favors. I certainly don't." Then she remembered why she'd come to find her husband. "Your father wants me to go riding with him tomorrow. What shall I say if he quizzes me closely about our relationship?"

Jamie's eyes narrowed. "No need to tell him anything. It's none of his business, Mellie."

"But . . ."

"But he's paying you to have my child. Right?"

She couldn't bring herself to answer him.

"Don't stand there tongue-tied," he yelled at her. "He's bought you as a brood mare to give him a grandson. You thought I didn't know about you, sweet Mellie?" He smiled, and her blood ran cold. "A member of the demimonde, that's who he chooses for a wife for his only son. A whore! A professional! Not just a silly girl who bestowed her favors on her friends, but a woman from one of the most notorious brothels of London."

"Who told you?" she whispered, sick at heart.

"Gerald did. Oh, how he hates you, Mellie. Hates you and hates my father for doing this to me."

She remembered seeing Lord Densbury and Gerald Norwood with their heads together at the wedding banquet. Her worst fears were realized.

"Do you deny this, Mellie?"

"No, I don't. Jamie, you don't know the circumstances . . ."

"And I don't want to know them. Spare me the sordid details." Then his eyes narrowed, and reached out and caught her delicate wrist with those surprisingly strong harpist's fingers. "Have you had a child?"

"A child? Good heavens, no!"

He flung her hand from him so hard that it banged against the back of one of the elegant chairs grouped around the harp. Sullenly, she rubbed the bruise.

"Too bad. I'd thought perhaps, since he's so anxious for a grandson that he paid a whore to marry his son, he made sure that you aren't barren." Then a horrified look crossed his face. "My God! What will I do if you *are* barren?"

"Since there's little likelihood of my conceiving with you, why worry?" she spat at him. But it was something that had never crossed her mind. Now it was an added worry. Presuming Jamie eventually was able to consummate their marriage, what if she were barren, could not bear a child? Then what would Lord Henning do?

She was surprised that Jamie smiled. "No need to worry about me, dear wife. I find you most unattractive in an intimate way. Decorative enough for public display; but you could never woo me away from my darling Gerald. But my father is not the only one who can practice trickery." His laugh was gay enough, but it sent shudders through Mellie. Now what was he planning? Nothing that she'd like.

"Gerald has had the most delicious idea. I'm delighted with him. I should have thought of it myself; but I've been in such a deplorable state of mind, with this ghastly wedding, with a wife foisted on me, and demands for a son, that I've not been thinking straight."

He paused, waiting for her to ask what Gerald had suggested; but Mellie, tired of Jamie's posturing, disgusted with his blatant sexual abnormality, wouldn't give him the satisfaction of asking.

"Not curious, dear little harlot wife? Ah, but since it affects you so vitally, I'm sure you want to know all about my dear Gerald's brilliant idea."

Tired of this shabby charade, Mellie turned to leave, stating coldly, "I am not interested in anything Mr. Norwood has to say. I'd thank you to keep his nasty ideas to himself. I'm sure that nothing he thinks up will be agreeable to me."

Jamie moved, though, to block her exit from the music room. "Not so fast, dear wife. I wish to talk to you. And it is your duty to listen to your lawful husband."

"Oh, Jamie, stop your nonsensical posturing." She was so annoyed with him that she didn't make any attempt to soften her tone.

"Nonsensical posturing! Look who's talking: the darling young woman from the Court of St. James. Ha! Does my father know that you and your sluttish mother were banished from court because she spent her time trying to lure decent men away from their wives?"

Wearily, she said, "Your father knows all about me. Now, if you'll please let me by, Jamie. This conversation is too distasteful for me to endure another moment."

"Oh, poor, dear, delicate little whore who is my wife. But you must listen, whether you like it or not. Because it will free you, too—free you from me, as I'm sure you pray to be freed. My father will have no further demands on you once you've produced this male child he has determined you shall have. You'll be free of me, free to spend your payment—and I know he's promised to pay you—anyway you desire, far, far away from Henning Hall. So Gerald, with my best interests at heart, as always, has come up with this fabulous plan. We'll get some healthy, lusty, earthy young man to act as my proxy. As you've worked in a brothel, surely one man is as good as another to produce the desired result—a son. My stupid father won't know the difference. If you produce a son, he'll assume it is mine. So—have you any preferences? Any special man who has caught your fancy? If so, we can arrange it all very discreetly."

She stood there, appalled. Each time Mellie was convinced that nothing worse could happen to her, she learned all too devastatingly that she'd been wrong. There was always one more indignity to which she could be submitted.

"If you haven't any special choice, I'm sure that my friend Alistair—Lord Densbury—could be persuaded to spend as many nights as necessary in your bed, to make sure that you become pregnant with *my* son!"

CHAPTER NINETEEN

Mellie was a flash of scarlet as, mounted on a lively little bay mare, she galloped through the extensive park that stretched down the hillside behind Henning Hall. Behind her, thudding along on a big chestnut hunter, was Lord Henning. It was exhilarating to race along the wooded path. Mellie heard Henning shout something, but the wind rushing past her ears swept away the words. She lifted a gloved hand to let him know she'd heard his call, assuming he wanted her to wait so that they could ride together. Normally she'd have reined in immediately, anxious to spend as much time with Ritchie as possible; but there was something about the early late-summer morning, the crisp feel of the air, the motion of vibrant horseflesh under her, that made Mellie more reckless than she would ordinarily be. Instead of trying to check the mare, she tapped her flanks with the riding crop, so that the animal surged ahead, sweeping around a bend in a mossy trail.

Disaster lay in their path. There was an unexpected fence, and although the mare gallantly picked up her feet and sailed over it, Mellie, not ready for the jump, went flying over the horse's withers when the mare landed after clearing the barrier cleanly. Mellie managed to tuck in her head and pull up her knees so that she made a ball of herself; but even so, and even landing on a mossy bank beside the bridle path, she had the wind knocked out of her lungs. Moments later, the chestnut soared over the fence as if it weren't there, and Henning reined in roughly, tossing the lines over the horse's head as he leaped from the saddle before the beast had come to a complete standstill.

"Mellie, Mellie, are you all right?" He fell to his knees beside her, catching her in his arms. When he realized that the breath had been knocked from her, he turned her so that his knee was in the small of her back and pulled her shoulders back sharply, forcing her to suck air back into her lungs.

Then he cradled her in his strong arms. Mellie could feel his

150

muscles like iron, and she reveled in his strength, and in her closeness to him.

"Are you all right?" he begged. "Are you hurt, Mellie?"

Much as she hated to admit that she was only shaken by the fall,
for she wanted nothing more than to lie there in his arms, his face
close to hers, so that the blood raced through her veins from his
nearness. Mellie knew she had to say something to relieve his
anxiety.

Shakily she said, "I'm quite all right, milord. A bit shaken up is
all. It was a stupid thing for me to do, racing along an unknown
trail that way."

"I shouted to you, trying to warn you, but . . ."

"I heard you call, but didn't understand the words. And the ride
was so exciting, that I—I—" She couldn't go on. His nearness,
the look on his face, his sudden awareness of her which she
sensed, took her speech away. Then, with a sound almost like a
groan, he crushed her to him, and his mouth sought hers, hot and
hungry, in a kiss which she passionately returned. Time stood still
for Mellie. All she knew was that the man she loved was raining
kisses on her mouth, her eyelids, burying his face in the soft curve
of her throat above the neck cloth of her riding habit.

It was wildly exciting, and she abandoned all sense of shame,
yielding to his eager caresses. But abruptly he pulled away from
her, almost tearing her clinging arms from about his neck.

"No! My God, what am I thinking of?" His voice was thick
with emotion, his face flushed, his eyes wild. "I—how can you
ever forgive me? It is unthinkable . . ." He sprang to his feet,
walked away from her, while she lay back on the mossy bed, her
emotions seething. Never had a man aroused her as he had; and although she had endured many intimate embraces for pay in the
brothel, she had never realized the tremendous power of such passion. It caught her up, sweeping her along as if she were a leaf
floating, spinning, whirling, on the crest of a raging mountain
stream in spring flood.

Her breast heaving, her breath coming in gasps, she longed to
cry out to him, "I love you! Don't leave me now!"

But remembering the look of horror on his face as he'd thrust
her away from him just now, Mellie remained silent.

It seemed forever that he stood apart from her, not looking at her
as she lay on the soft green moss she'd hoped would be her bed of
fulfillment but which now symbolized only her couch of bitter
frustration. Then Henning turned, remote and unfriendly, his

strong, muscular figure silhouetted against the sky which showed through the branches of the beech trees lining the path.

"I forgot myself," he said, his voice now tight and cool. "You must forgive me. You are young and attractive—and I, God help me, am a normal man. It could have happened with anyone. My fear for your safety—the proximity . . ."

Mellie wanted to scream, "Stop! Don't say such cruel words to me, my beloved." But she remained mute, her heart finally quieting, chilled by the abrupt change in Henning.

Then he approached her, almost reluctantly, Mellie thought. Reaching down, he helped her to her feet, careful to keep his distance. "Are you all right? Can you ride?"

She longed to lie, to say she'd hurt her ankle so that the earl would be forced to carry her cradled in those strong arms. She wanted nothing more than to lean against him, feel the hard strength of his body, the thudding of his heart as he responded to her closeness; but Mellie took her cue from him.

"I'm sure I can sit my horse, milord." And she pulled her gloved hand away from his, preferring to leave him before he could reject her again.

"Wait here until I bring your mare." Then he swung up onto the chestnut and cantered on down the path.

It gave Mellie a few minutes to compose herself. She wished the passionate episode had never happened. Now, for the rest of her life, she'd know that his lordship was attracted to her, while she was legally tied to his miserable son. How could a man and his son be so different? They were exact opposites, two sides of a coin.

Then Henning was back, leading her skittish little mare. He made a step with his hands and tossed her up into the saddle, as impersonal as if he were a hired groom. Was it possible that this was the man who, only short minutes ago, was holding her and kissing her so passionately?

Without even asking if she wanted to ride further, he headed back for the Hall. Well, the morning ride had been ruined for Mellie, so they might as well return to the house. No doubt he realized this as well as she did.

When they were within sight of the stable wing, Mellie remembered what she'd wanted to tell Henning. She slapped the reins on the neck of her mare so that she caught up with her companion before they reached the house.

"Milord, I must talk privately with you, before we go inside," she said.

He gave her a cold stare. "There's really nothing to discuss, Mellie. I should have remembered that I brought you from Mrs. Mudridge's brothel. I'm not blaming you. I have only myself to blame."

It was as if he'd poured a pitcher of cold water on her. Mellie gasped at the hurt his words caused; but she remembered that she loved him, and must accept whatever he said to her, no matter how cruel.

Trying to match him in coolness, she said haughtily, "I was not referring to our ride, milord. I must talk to you about Jamie."

A look of shock went over his face. "I never thought—are you with child, Mellie? That fall from the horse—we must get you to bed at once. I can call the doctor from Canterbury . . . ."

"No, no, not that." His face fell, but she forged ahead. "Do you have any idea how much Jamie hates you, milord?"

His dark eyebrows raised like a blackbird's wings. "Hates me? Hate is a strong word, Mellie. Oh, I know he resents the strictures I've put on his inheritance; but it is for his own good. He will live to thank me."

"He may live to thank you, but you, milord, may not live to receive those thanks." Her voice was bleak.

"What are you trying to say, Mellie?" He looked at her sharply.

"He—told me he could get his inheritance if you died. Then he'd not have to endure this odious marriage with me. Receiving his inheritance would not hinge on his fathering a child."

Henning frowned, then laughed out loud, to her consternation.

"But I'm quite hale and hearty, Mellie. Just turned forty, with many more healthy years ahead of me, I trust. It's just wishful thinking, a childish way of getting out of his responsibilities, that puts such words in Jamie's mouth. No, I don't intend to drop dead to satisfy my son's pique."

"Milord, aren't you afraid you might go to an early grave?"

With one of his lightning changes of mood, anger flared in Henning's face, and his voice was harsh. "Are you hinting that my own son would kill me for his money?"

"It has been known to happen, milord." She sat there on the little mare, controlling her with firm hands on the reins, staring him down.

"I don't want to hear you mention such an abomination, ever again. Just do what you've been brought here to do—give Jamie a son. Then he'll understand my feelings about keeping the Henning line viable."

"Of course, milord."

She could have wept with frustration; but Mellie wasn't going to give the earl that satisfaction, not now, not after what had happened, not after all the harsh words he'd thrown at her. Perhaps, though, when he was alone, with a chance to think about what she'd said in a calmer atmosphere, rather than one charged with the emotion that had embroiled them, he might decide that Mellie's warning was a valid one, worth heeding. She hoped he'd take care that no fatal accident gave Jamie what he so desperately wanted. Silently, Mellie begged, *Guard yourself, my darling. Always be on guard!*

"I hope I do not have to wait overlong for news that my grandson is on the way." He said it as a warning.

"These things sometimes don't happen instantaneously." She let her temper show a bit. No need to take all of his insults without fighting back. "Do not expect miracles, milord. They've gone right out of style."

"Well, I'm naturally impatient. I don't expect to wait forever, Mellie."

What would his lordship say if she told him of Jamie's latest scheme, thought up by his lover, Norwood? How would Henning feel if she had the male child he kept demanding, only to learn that it had been fathered by someone other than his precious son? Mellie was suddenly so angry with Henning that she was tempted to go to her husband and agree to his repugnant suggestion, that she get pregnant by someone else and palm the bastard child off on Henning as theirs. It would certainly serve Lord Henning right to be so deceived.

Without another word, she gave the mare a sharp cut with the riding crop, so that she almost bolted to the stables where the groom helped Mellie dismount. Catching up her scarlet riding skirt with one gloved hand, she swept across the cobbled courtyard and into the house.

She'd warned Henning about Jamie. Now it was up to him to take precautions to stay alive. Yet, once in her room, with Dora helping her to disrobe, Mellie suddenly burst into tears, sobbing bitterly at the fate that was hers. Why was Henning so determined to have this grandson? She'd have been willing to live with him, childless, happily.

"Milady, what is wrong?" Dora asked, sympathetic; but underlying her sympathy was avid curiosity. "You aren't expecting, are you?"

It served to turn Mellie's tears off abruptly. "No, I'm not," she snapped. It wasn't a subject she chose to discuss with her abigail, certainly not now, after what had just happened.

Then Dora discovered a huge bruise on Mellie's hip.

"Milady! Whatever have you done? . . ." She stopped abruptly, as if afraid she'd already pried too much into Mellie's private affairs.

"The mare threw me." Better to tell her the truth quickly, or Dora might have all kinds of tales to tell below stairs that Jamie was beating his new bride. "It was my own carelessness and stupidity. I raced on a new path, and came to a fence quite unexpectedly."

"Are you all right, milady? I can bathe the bruise for you."

"I'm perfectly all right, Dora. I didn't realize I'd bruised myself until you called my attention to it. Actually, I landed on a bank of moss."

"It's good you aren't expecting, milady. Riding can be dangerous, you know. A miscarriage. . . ."

"Dora, I'm all right," Mellie snapped, her temper frayed. "Stop worrying about me. I'm healthy. I just took a fall when I didn't anticipate the jump. That's all. I'll live."

"Yes, milady." Properly squelched, Dora scurried about, murmuring, "I'll take the riding habit and brush it, milady." She was halfway out the door when she stopped short, one hand over her mouth. "Oh, milady, I forgot. His lordship the viscount, wants to see you when you are available. He's in the music room."

"Thank you, Dora."

Her abigail had dressed her in a charming morning gown in the popular sacque shape, the soft printed silk flowing full from the shoulders in back. It was of a delicate peach color, with flowers of blue and a deeper peach embroidered all over it. The frills were of a lace almost the same color as the flowers.

When Mellie began the long walk to the music room, she discovered sore muscles that she'd not noticed at the time of her fall. Well, she'd feel all right in a few days. Physically. Emotionally, Mellie wasn't sure she'd ever feel right again. Was Henning truly attracted to her, or was it only an animal passion roused by her closeness when he knelt beside her on the mossy bank? Until that moment, Mellie had despaired of arousing any emotion in Henning—love, lust, anything. He'd been so circumspect when he was with her. The perfect gentleman. But now that she knew what depths of passion could sweep through him, she longed for such an episode to happen again. Next time, she'd make sure that he fulfilled his passionate desires. If it was only lust he felt for her, she'd accept that rather than nothing; but Mellie longed for the earl to love her as much as she loved him.

It was with such thoughts in her mind that she approached the music room where Jamie was once again playing the harp.

Without missing a note, Jamie looked up at her and pursed his lips appreciatively. "You are looking well today, dear wife. Glowing. Positively glowing. Could this possibly mean that you've found a lover so soon? I do hope so. It could be the solution to our problem, a lover."

Dashed down from her pinnacle of rapture, Mellie said rather shortly, "No, I haven't taken a lover. I think one lover in this household is quite sufficient at present."

He strummed loudly and discordantly for one moment, then set the harp aside. "My, my, in a real pet, aren't we? Well, it has naught to do with me if you choose to be in bad temper on such a lovely day."

"Dora said you wanted to see me," she reminded him, annoyed by his words.

"Is that so strange? Remember, we're newlyweds."

"How could I ever forget?"

"Tut, tut, dear Mellie. I think you find life dull here in Kent after your exciting existence in London. Work at Mrs. Mudridge's must have kept you much busier than you are here in the country."

She stared balefully at him, longing to push his pretty face so hard that it would be imprinted on the back of his silly skull.

"So I thought we'd have an entertainment here at Henning Hall. A masked ball. I do so love dressing up. It will be the grand occasion to introduce my charming bride to all of the young bloods in the county. I hope you'll form some liaison with one of them, and manage this odious pregnancy without further bother to me."

"And what if your father learns of this deceit?"

"What can he do about it?" Jamie asked arrogantly. He reached into one of the deep pockets of his emerald green coat and brought out a chased silver snuffbox. Delicately putting pinches of snuff in each nostril, he sneezed into a lacy handkerchief. "My father will close his eyes to anything, if you produce a child. Unless you mate with someone's blackamoor page, and produce a child so dark as to be obviously not mine, he'll accept it as his legal grandchild. Mellie, he is completely warped on this idea of the succession. If he'd not had me, I'm sure he'd by now be in Bedlam from worrying that he had no one to inherit his precious earldom.''

What could Mellie say to this?

''But let's talk of the ball. I do adore masquerades, don't you? So much can happen when your face is hidden by a mask.'' He smiled suggestively. ''You can allow the young men all sorts of liberties—and perhaps one will wind up in our bed.''

''With you?''

His nostrils flared and his face darkened. ''Don't be too smart with me, dear wife, or I'll invite all of the stable boys to share your marriage couch.''

CHAPTER TWENTY

The masked ball was at its height, the great Hall ablaze with hundreds of white wax tapers. Behind the mahogany screen of the minstrel gallery, the musicians kept up a lively succession of gavottes, minuets, and mazurkas. The dancers whirled through the figures, bright costumes in myriad designs concealing identities.

Mellie was dressed as a Cathay princess, her entire face covered by a gauzy veil. Jamie had chosen to dress as an Indian from the colonies of America, his costume devised, as was Mellie's, by Gerald Norwood, who had quite a flair for designing clothing. Norwood, by contrast, was garbed in the austere gray of a Puritan, which amused Mellie; for it was so inappropriate to Norwood's personality. She had little contact with her husband's lover, which suited her admirably. She'd seen a bit more of him in planning her costume for the ball; but the two of them, at best, maintained a state of armed neutrality toward each other.

Henning was dressed as a young, not yet corpulent, Henry VIII. When Mellie learned this, she wished she'd chosen to come as Anne Boleyn, but it was too late then to change her plans. And perhaps too obvious. The one thing she must conceal from Jamie was her love for his father. Life would become unbearable if Jamie should learn of her secret desire for Henning.

While they were receiving the guests, Mellie whispered to Jamie, "Who are all these people? I didn't realize that you had invited so many."

He shrugged. "It was an open invitation. More always come than actually receive cards. Friends have friends down from London, and of course they bring their guests. Others have sojourners from the Continent. I won't know the names of more than half the guests, and my father may not know the other half."

"Heavens, anyone could come. A highwayman could walk in and we'd assume he was a genuine guest disguised as a knight of the road."

Jamie giggled. "It happened in Sussex, believe it or not. At Aldingham Manor, I think. The thief whipped out a jolly huge pistol and relieved all the guests of their jewels and gold. And then he escaped scot-free into the night."

Jamie was in good humor tonight, even dancing with Mellie for the first gavotte. He was a marvelous dancer, light on his feet and graceful as a woman; but she much preferred it when Henry VIII claimed her for a fast mazurka. It was the first time since the fateful ride that he'd even touched Mellie's hand, and her heart thudded so loudly that she was sure Henning could hear it over the sound of flute and cello.

"It's good to see such a lively rout," he acknowledged. "I'd almost forgotten how enjoyable such an evening can be."

Was his arm about her waist tighter than absolutely necessary? Did he clasp her hand with more warmth than he did his other partners? Mellie longed to respond, to cling to Henning so that she would arouse his passion; but she remembered how he had rebuffed her the day that she'd been thrown from her horse, so she was reluctant to show her feelings again. He must know how attractive he was to her. She was sure now that he found her equally alluring. If only there were no Jamie, no false marriage, no demand for a child from the loveless union. If only—but Mellie was all too aware that life was not made up of "if onlys." It was harsh and cruel, even when that harshness was covered by a veil of seeming happiness and good fortune.

Still, she could dream of Ritchie Jamison, Lord Henning. Perhaps such dreams would sustain her through the bad times.

The high point of the evening was to be the awarding of prizes for best costumes for man and woman. Jamie had given Gerald Norwood the task of choosing the winners.

"Why should Gerald decide?" Mellie complained.

"He's more clever at costumes than either of us." This was one time when Jamie asserted himself quietly and with authority, so Mellie was forced to give in to his decision. Although she didn't like Norwood and his place in her life, she did have to admit that her husband's lover was the most skilled in costuming of anyone at the ball.

"And no one will know it is Gerald who has chosen. I wanted to give him public credit," Jamie added, "but he thinks it not wise. It might cause complications which we don't want nor need now. Once I'm Earl of Henning. . . ."

A chill came over Mellie, as if a cold vapor had escaped an open tomb. There it was again, the subtle threat to his lordship's life. And warning him had gotten her nothing but abuse from Henning. She must be ever vigilant, to prevent Jamie from harming his father, causing his death. Did Jamie hate Henning that much, did he want the title for himself so desperately, that he'd consider patricide to become earl?

Suddenly Mellie felt very alone, even though surrounded by the swirling masses of guests. There was no one in the whole world to whom she could turn for help. Henning would not listen to her allegations against his son; and except for Henning, she hadn't another friend in the world.

The prizes were to be awarded on the stroke of midnight. About a quarter before the hour, Norwood beckoned to Jamie, and Mellie followed him so that the three of them were isolated in a hall corner behind a screen set up to mask the door through which the servants came bringing wine to the guests.

"Well, dear Gerald, who shall win the prizes?"

"If she weren't the hostess, I should award first prize to your wife."

"Thank you, Gerald." She was quite surprised; but then it was Gerald, himself, who had drawn the design that her dressmaker had used to sew the Cathay princess costume. He was actually giving the prize to himself!

"So who is the lucky lady?"

"I think the one dressed as Good Queen Bess," he said. "She actually looks like portraits of the queen."

"I'd hate to have to choose, there are so many lovely costumes," Mellie admitted, glad now that Norwood was the one to make the choice. "And for the men?" She knew that Henning wouldn't be chosen, nor Jamie—although both looked quite handsome—because they were the hosts.

"Lucifer, after his fall," Norwood said without hesitation.

It was a clever choice. Mellie had noticed the man with the shining robes and the huge, artificial wings—as well as the tiny attached horns on his forehead, and the pitchfork and tail he sported.

"Tell the musicians I want a fanfare exactly as the clock strikes the hour of twelve," Jamie instructed his lover.

The prizes were a charming enameled patchbox for the woman, and a chased silver snuffbox for the man. Neither Mellie nor Jamie had any idea who the winners were behind their masks, although Henning had told Mellie that he thought that Good Queen Bess was the Baroness of Chester.

There was a raised dais at the end of the great Hall under the minstrel gallery, and Mellie and Jamie went there to be ready for the midnight unmasking and the awarding of prizes. Footmen had been told which two guests to bring forward, and the atmosphere was charged with anticipation as all of the guests awaited the stroke of twelve, the traditional hour for unmasking.

Mellie was to give the award for best woman's costume, which she did very prettily to Good Queen Bess, curtsying as if to genuine royalty. The winner was the Countess Alicia Edwards, not the Baroness of Chester, and she was gracious in her acceptance of the pretty patchbox.

Then Jamie beckoned to Lucifer. "Behold the fallen angel!" he cried, with a flamboyant gesture. He stepped forward and drew the winner up onto the dais where Lucifer, facing Jamie, removed his mask.

Mellie, standing a bit behind them, gasped. The two men's profiles were identical. And more than that—they had the same coloring, the same facial shape, the same hair and eyes, every feature identical.

Jamie, apparently not seeing the resemblance to himself, murmured, "Forgive me, milord, but I do not recall having met you. I do not know your name."

Mellie was sure that the man dressed as Lucifer was well aware of the resemblance between himself and the young Viscount Triller.

"Lord Carstairs, milord," he said softly.

Jamie turned and announced, "I present Lord Carstairs, best-dressed man at this masked ball."

In the blaze of candles, there could be no mistaking the twin-like looks of the young man and the older one. Mellie heard a buzz, and saw many sly smiles and faces hidden by hastily snatched kerchiefs; while gossips whispered behind fans.

Her eyes sought one face in that crowd. Quickly spotting the flat velvet cap worn by Henning, she saw that he, too, had recognized the implications of this similarity between Jamie and the man, Lord Carstairs. Henning's face was contorted with rage. For one moment he stood there as if rooted to the black and white checkered marble floor. Then he turned and pushed his way rudely through the crowd, making quite a commotion as the guests closed in behind him. A few titters were heard, then muffled.

And another face showed itself with appalling fury. Gerald Norwood, Jamie's lover, half-hidden behind an artfully contrived floral bower, glared at the tableau on the dais.

Lord Carstairs accepted his prize, bowed briefly to Jamie, more deeply to Mellie, and then moved into the crowd of guests, a knowing smile on his face.

By now Jamie realized that something was wrong; but he still didn't see his own resemblance to Carstairs.

"Seems I've seen that fellow before," he said to Mellie, "although I can't for the life of me remember where."

"In your own mirror," she said before she had thought out the implications of her answer.

The sudden comprehension in her husband's eyes was devastating. She thought Jamie might strike her; then she thought he might have some sort of seizure. Fortunately, Norwood appeared at his side and muttered something which Mellie couldn't hear. In the next moment, he spirited Jamie out of the hall, much to Mellie's relief. She'd been afraid that Jamie might cause a scene in front of all the assembly.

It left her alone, though. Henning was gone, so was Jamie. A harlequin, still masked, approached and held out his hand for the next dance as the musicians struck up a minuet. She had already taken his hand when Mellie realized that this was Alistair Lord Densbury.

She tried to withdraw without attracting attention; but Densbury held tightly to her hand.

"You might as well unmask. I know you," she said coldly.

With his free hand, Densbury took off his domino. Softly, so that no one else could hear, he told her, "Smile, Mellie. Smile if it kills you. Don't let your guests have the satisfaction of knowing how upset you are to find that your husband is not only fonder of men than of women, but that he also is not Henning's son at all."

"You lie," she spat at him, realizing that he was enjoying her discomfort.

"Come, now, Mellie, dear, I've heard the rumors before. Now that I've seen the two of them together, I know that the gossips, for once, are right. Jamie is no more Henning's son than I am. He is the natural child of Lord Carstairs. But I can also understand why he'd prefer to think that Henning is his father. Carstairs is a most unlucky gambler. His estate has been sold to pay his gambling debts, and he exists only by his wits."

"Did Lord Carstairs realize when he came tonight? . . . ."

"I'll wager my last guinea that he did. No doubt he has some scheme in hand to get money from Henning. To guarantee that Carstairs will keep quiet.''

They moved through the figures of the dance automatically, continuing the distressing chat as they moved back together each time.

"Every tongue in the county will be wagging," Mellie said, aghast.

Densbury shrugged. "No more than they'd wag if they knew your history, dear Mellie.''

"Sir, you are no gentleman," she said coldly, wishing for the dance to end so that she could get away from her odious partner without causing any further sensation.

"And you, my dear, are scarcely a lady. How are you enjoying your marriage to Jamie, by the way? Knowing you, it seems, shall we say, incongruous? Do you share quarters with what's-his-name—the tutor?''

Mellie wanted nothing more than to slap his arrogant face; but she pasted on a smile and chose not to answer his despicable questions.

"Come, Mellie dear, you should be kinder to me. If you shared your favors, I might be better able to keep gossip about you to myself.''

It was blatant blackmail, and Mellie knew it. Thankfully the set ended just then, and she curtsied to Densbury, murmuring, "I must see to my other guests, milord.''

She circulated through the great Hall, noting that all too many conversations died as she approached. Carstairs's arrival would be the talk of Kent for weeks. She wondered where the impecunious but bold Lord Carstairs was now. Looking for those enormous gilt wings, she saw Lucifer disappearing through a door that led to another wing of the house. Moving as quickly as she could, Mellie got a glimpse of him as he went into the library. A footman came from the room, and she stopped him.

"Is Lord Carstairs seeing someone in the library?''

Did the footman give her a knowing look? Mellie felt her flesh crawl, as if ants tracked over her. Was it going to be like this for long, this suspicion that everyone knew about Jamie and Carstairs?

"He asked to see his lordship, the Earl of Henning, milady. His lordship told me he'd interview Lord Carstairs in the library.''

"Perhaps you'd best take them some wine," she suggested. "Claret, I think.''

"Of course, milady."

Mellie went back to her guests, but her mind was awhirl. Densbury had said that Carstairs lived by his wits, and hinted that he'd try to get money from Henning. Mellie hoped that Henning refused the despicable fellow; but the alternative, to have Carstairs publicly acknowledge Jamie as his son, was unthinkable.

She kept a surreptitious watch to see when Lucifer returned to the festivities, but he did not reappear. Jamie and Norwood both were absent, as well as Lord Henning. There was an air of gleeful anticipation, almost a lip-licking, as the gaily clad guests waited to see the next act of the drama unfold. But after about an hour, it became apparent to even the least perceptive that there'd be no public denouement tonight. With both hosts, as well as the chief villain, out of sight, the ball wound down rather quickly. Mellie was a gracious lady of the manor to the departing nobles, murmuring little lies about Jamie's having felt ill—"A fever, I fear, hopefully short-lived"—and finally the guests were all gone, except Alistair Densbury, her nemesis.

"You must excuse me, milord," she said as prettily as she could, fearful lest she antagonize him, recognizing that he was malicious and spiteful, and that he could do her great harm if he chose to gossip. "I am excessively weary." She laid one hand gracefully to her forehead. "I'm sure that Parkins will see you out."

Densbury grinned evilly. "But didn't you know? How remiss of Jamie. He's invited me to stay for a few days. To enjoy the pleasures of Henning Hall," and he made a leg as he smiled that sly, knowing smile at Mellie.

Aghast, she could think of nothing to say. Had that devil of a husband already enlisted Densbury to try to get her with child?

No! She would not submit to such a gross scheme. If she never had this child Lord Henning was so anxious to see, if her remaining childless meant that she'd be sent away, penniless, no matter what her fate, she'd not be a party to this deception.

Yet, even as she thought this, even as she tried to keep her expression calm and polite, instead of allowing Densbury to see that she was horrified, deep down Mellie acknowledged that it was one way out of her own predicament. She didn't want to return to London to Mrs. Mudridge or some other procuress. She didn't want to live in a poky little garret room over a grubby shop in London's slums. Would it be any worse to share her bed with Densbury than it had been with a succession of men at Mrs. Mudridge's? And if she proved quickly fertile, then it could all be put behind her. Once she produced the desired male child, she was assured of a life of ease. She'd not even have to stay with Jamie. She'd have fulfilled her function—as a brood mare—and with the income Henning promised, she could live comfortably in fashionable London—or in Bath—or even on the Continent.

Without Ritchie Jamison, Lord Henning. That thought tore at her heart. She couldn't leave here, she couldn't!

Her immediate need, though, was to get away from Densbury before she said something irreparable. Fortunately, the butler hovered nearby.

"Parkins."

He approached, bowing. "Yes, milady. Is it all right if I have the maids begin to clear?"

"Of course. And Lord Densbury will be staying the night. Put him in. . . ."

"The Rose Room, milady. His lordship, the viscount, has already given instructions."

"Of course." How like Jamie not to tell her. It sounded more and more as if he actually intended to go ahead with his plan. Well, he'd find that two could play at such games.

"Goodnight, milord," she said, curtsying to Densbury. "Have a footman show his lordship to his bedchamber, Parkins."

Parkins motioned up one of the footmen and the liveried fellow led Densbury away. She hoped for good.

"Is his lordship, Lord Henning, still up?"

Parkins was the perfect butler. His face was blank of any expression. "I think he has retired to his private suite, milady. You would not wish to disturb him so late?"

"No, of course not." Odious butler. She'd been sorely tempted to go to Henning, see what he told her of his interview with Carstairs. See what Carstairs had threatened, if he'd had the temerity to threaten her Lord Henning!

"I'll have Willem light you to your bedchamber, milady."

"Thank you, Parkins, and goodnight."

On the way, they passed another of the footmen coming along carrying a tray with a cut-glass decanter of brandy and one glass.

Mellie noticed that the footman went on toward Henning's private suite. It looked as if his lordship intended to drown his problems in brandy. Would that she could, too!

CHAPTER TWENTY-ONE

She was back in the poky garret room overlooking Chancery Lane in the house near Lincoln's Inn Fields. The master had slipped into bed with her, and his fumbling hands . . . Mellie woke with a start to find that someone was in her bed, someone who reeked of wine and whose hands were pawing, just as that oafish man's hands had pawed at her innocence. Surely it wasn't Jamie.

"Who . . . what? . . ."

"Oh, hush, Mellie. You'll wake the whole house and make us the laughingstock of. . . ."

"Alistair Densbury! Get out of my bed!"

For answer he grabbed at her, although he was fumbling in the dark; so Mellie managed to wriggle away from him. This was like one of the sillier of the farces imported from France to the Drury Lane Theatre. Throwing back the bed covers, she slid out on the far side of the high bed, eluding Densbury momentarily. Quickly she felt for the candlestick on the marble-topped bed stand and lighted the taper, to show Densbury, his face flushed from alcohol and lust, struggling to free himself from the bedding so that he could pursue her.

"I warn you, Alistair, get out of here this instant!"

Her cold tone seemed to cut through his alcoholic haze; but instead of intimidating young Lord Densbury, it only inflamed his desire. She saw anger on his handsome but dissipated young face.

"Don't play the shy miss with me, Mellie. Remember, I'm doing you and Jamie a favor."

So Jamie had told Densbury. She might have guessed.

"A favor! You are utterly despicable, Alistair. And so is that miserable husband of mine. Now get out of here before I ring for my abigail and ask her to have two of the sturdiest footmen throw you out bodily."

"That's right, selfish to the last. Can't let your poor maid sleep, have to wake her. And the footmen, too."

Mellie raised cynical eyebrows. It was not in character for Lord Densbury to be worrying about the welfare of mere servants.

But he wasn't finished yet. Wheedling, he said, "It's not as if you were the sweet, innocent young virgin, Mellie." He scowled blackly. "You played this stupid game with me at Mrs. M's." A nasty smile twisted his face so that it was no longer good-looking. "Demanded my money back from her, I did." He sneered. "You certainly were no prize in bed, dear Mellie."

"Then why do you bother with me, now?" she demanded.

He grinned, shrugged. "Habit, I guess. You've been throwing yourself at me from the time your bosom budded, while you still were at court."

"Oh!" Outrage and anger shook her so that she couldn't speak. The fact that there was truth in what he accused her of only made her more furious. That handsome, lusty face leering suggestively at her, undressing her with his eyes as she stood, lightly clad in a flowing, rather sheer night robe of pale yellow China silk, was maddening.

"Imbecile!" she cried when she could talk. Reaching out almost blindly, her fingers closed around the neck of a carafe of white wine which Dora always left at her bedside. Without even thinking, she flung the wine into Densbury's face, causing him to gasp as the liquid stung his eyes and filled his nose.

It would have cooled a less ardent bed partner; but not Densbury. The wine only served to fuel his rage. With a lightning quick movement, he flung himself to the edge of the bed and snaked out a long, muscular arm to catch Mellie's other wrist in a grip of iron. Inexorably, he dragged her to the bed, and Mellie knew he intended to force himself on her, whether she acquiesced or not.

For one moment she quailed. Why fight him? He was stronger than she, obviously able to overpower her as he'd done that horrid night in her bedchamber in Westminster. Jamie had put him up to this odious assault. Well, Jamie would never father a child on her. Perhaps she should submit to Densbury. Maybe, if she didn't fight him so, he would be more gentle and loving than he'd been that first time. If he gave her a child, it would come from good stock. Could this be any worse than having to submit to the stable hands, as her dear husband threatened?

Then Densbury took his free hand and, catching at the low-cut neckline of her night robe, gave it a tremendous yank, ripping the delicate fabric to the waist, exposing her proud young breasts to his greedy eyes and hands.

It was too much. If he had approached her in a more gentlemanly fashion, if he'd courted her, at least pretended some interest in her other than bedding her to oblige Jamie, she might have decided that Densbury was as good as any of the young noblemen she knew to achieve the objective—get her with child to ensure that Jamie received his inheritance and she was paid the pension Henning had promised. But this—it was too crude, it brought back painful memories of her other intimacy with Densbury.

"Miserable clod! Let go of me," she muttered through clenched teeth. When Densbury only laughed and tugged her closer, she lost her balance and felt herself sprawling onto the bed. As the young lord tried to mount her, she lashed out at him with the empty wine carafe which she still had in her hand, hitting him a glancing blow on the temple which stunned him momentarily.

He loosed his grip on her. Mellie pushed him away and fled from her room while Densbury struggled to a sitting position on the bed, his eyes unfocused, shaking his head to try to clear it after the blow she'd dealt him.

She scarcely noticed where she ran. Any moment Mellie expected to hear Densbury thundering after her. She fled through the long gallery with the family portraits now hidden in shadow. Her torn gown was slipping from her shoulders, so that she had to clutch the ragged edges together over her bosom to keep from exposing herself. An occasional tall night taper set on a candle stand cast faint pools of flickering light on the floor. She didn't know where she was going; but unconsciously Mellie was fleeing toward the wing where Henning had his own private suite.

Gasping with fright and other unnameable emotions, she raced, her feet bare and cold, down the final passageway. A faint line of light shone under the door to Lord Henning's suite. Without thinking of the possible consequences, only knowing that she had to escape Densbury's unwelcome advances, Mellie pounded urgently on the door, praying that Henning wasn't too far gone in his brandy to hear her importunate knocking.

At first she thought that Lord Henning was not going to let her in. From inside the suite, she heard an angry voice call out something, although she couldn't understand the words. Again she knocked. There was a stumbling noise and a crash, as if something had been knocked over. Then, nearer, Henning's voice called out, "Who's zer?"

"It's Mellie, milord," she gasped, trying not to wake the rest of the house, suddenly conscious of how she must look in her ripped night robe and bare feet.

"Mellie? What? . . ." But he now sounded closer to the door.

Mellie looked back over her bare shoulder fearfully, not sure that Densbury wouldn't come racing around the corner at any moment to claim her.

"Hurry, milord," she begged. "Hurry!"

She tried the doorknob, but the door was locked. She pounded frantically on the door panel, no longer caring if anyone heard her or not, so afraid was she that Densbury would appear before she reached the safety of Henning's suite. Then there was the rattle of a key in the lock and the door was flung open wide to show her a Henning she'd never seen before. He was ready for bed, clad in a silken robe of wine brocade. His hair was brushed free of powder, showing its own deep brown color, with traces of silvery gray at the temples. It was pulled back into a short queue tied behind his neck with a wine ribbon. His face was flushed and he reeked of brandy. Clutching the door, he swayed drunkenly.

Without waiting for an invitation or his permission, Mellie darted into his sitting room, quickly closing the door behind her and leaning against it. She still clutched the torn nightdress to cover her heaving bosom.

Henning leaned forward and peered at her through half-closed eyes. "It's Mellie," he muttered. "Lil' Mellie. Should be in bed with Jamie, lil' Mellie. Can't give me a grandson unless you're in bed with my son. . . ." Then to her utter dismay, Henning turned from her and a terrible sob was wrenched from him. "My son . . . thought he was my son . . . must have a s——" He staggered into the room and his broad shoulders shook with racking sobs.

Mellie followed him timidly, scarcely knowing what to do. The room was handsome, but completely masculine, with hunting prints on the walls, as well as a fine collection of pistols. The furniture was massive Tudor oak, the carpet a fine Turkey red. Heavy red velvet drapes covered the long windows. Although there was no fire in the fireplace on this summer night, Henning sprawled in a great armchair in front of the massive brown marble chimneypiece. The brandy decanter stood on an oak stand at his elbow, and he sloshed more of the deep amber liquid into a goblet and drank it down as if it were spring water.

Then he looked up and his eyes widened as if he thought Mellie might be an apparition.

"Mellie. Come here," he ordered, words slurred by the brandy he had consumed.

Mellie moved slowly, drawn by the animal magnetism of the man, even while she was faintly repelled by his drunkenness.

"Must talk to you," he muttered. "Talk to my daughter-in-law." Then he groaned and covered his bloodshot eyes with one shaking hand. Again he sobbed, one terrible, gulping sound that tore at Mellie's heart.

It was more than she could bear to see him so distressed. With a rush, she flung herself to her knees beside him and cradled his head against her bosom, forgetting that she was nearly nude. All she could think of was her overwhelming love for him, her desire to comfort her beloved Henning in his hour of terrible distress.

"Oh, Ritchie, my darling, my love, my heart," she crooned, "don't cry. I can't bear it when you cry. Whatever is wrong, it can't be that terrible, it can't." She rocked gently to and fro, a mother comforting a weeping child.

Her words penetrated his drunken fog, and he pulled away from her angrily, rejecting her solace.

"Can't be terrible? What d'you think . . . laughingstock of all Kent." He groaned, closed his bleary eyes as if to hide from some unpleasant truth too horrible to envision. "Not my son . . . everyone saw . . . not my son . . . Jamie . . . that rotten blackguard Carstairs. . . ."

His face, already flushed wine-red with drink, turned so dark a red that Mellie feared he might have an attack of apoplexy.

Catching at his shoulders, she pleaded urgently, "Don't pay attention to a lying, scheming opportunist like Lord Carstairs."

"Don't you see?" he shouted at her, the cords in his neck standing out, his voice hoarse with emotion. He, in turn, caught Mellie's shoulders in a vise-like grip, making her wince with pain. "Everyone saw. Jamie is the spit and image of that no-good . . . he used to be here when we were first married. . . ." His voice dropped to a whisper, infinitely sad. "I thought he was my son. Jamie. I thought. . . ."

He loosed her so abruptly that she almost fell against his knees. Then he caught up the empty goblet. Discovering that he had drunk up the brandy, Henning flung the crystal goblet into the fireplace, smashing the delicate glass into tiny, sparkling shards. "Not my son," he muttered, "not my son." Then, shouting so loudly that Mellie clapped her hands over her ears to keep from being deafened, he yelled, "Jamie belongs to that rotten Carstairs!

My wife . . . she betrayed me with him . . . cuckolded by a no-good rogue.'' Henning shook his head, a look of utter bewilderment on his face. "I don't understand. She— I can tell you this, Mellie—she hated sex. Hated it. Submitted to me because it was her duty, but it was like making love to a doll. A lifeless mannikin. So why would she take Carstairs into her bed? Why? Why?'' He slumped back in the chair, his head lolling against the high carved back. Eyes closed, face relaxing into gentler lines, Mellie was sure he'd fallen asleep.

Heartsick at his discovery of Carstairs's perfidy, desperate to know how this twist of fate would affect her relationship with Jamie and with his father, this tormented man now sunk in drunken slumber, Mellie reached out a trembling hand to touch Henning's cheek. He moved his head at her touch, and Mellie froze, fearful that he would wake and once again reject her love.

Henning settled back into sleep.

"Oh, my dearest, my dearest, if only I could do something to help you,'' she murmured, caressing his face, her touch as gentle as a mother's hand with a babe.

His eyes opened, and he stared at her for one long moment. Then his face twisted in anguish, and he caught her to him, crushing her against his chest, burying his face in her golden hair. "Oh, Mellie, Mellie, what have I done?'' he cried in agony. "I married you to my son—the man I thought was my son—pretending that I had chosen you for special reasons, to help with Jamie's sexual problems. But in truth I chose you because you are so lovely, so utterly, devastatingly desirable.''

Her flesh and bones seemed to melt, her blood was a torrent of liquid fire rushing through her veins, as his lips found hers. Her own lips parted, and their tongues were darting flames, lighting the fire of passion, igniting all the nerve ends of her body, making her supremely aware of her physical self.

With complete abandon, she shed the torn nightdress as if she were shedding her skin, baring her lush, eager flesh to Henning's skillful hands. His hot, urgent lips kissed her breasts, and her nipples hardened under his inflaming touch. Mellie let her own hands embrace him, sliding in under his robe, to find that he was nude, his body hard and ready.

"Oh, Ritchie, now,'' she moaned, as she drew him down with her onto the Turkey rug.

Impatiently, he flung his robe aside as her soft white thighs opened to welcome him. It had never been like this before for Mellie. She had had many men use her luscious young body to satisfy their lust; but it had been all one-sided. She had closed her mind to them, pretended an ecstasy she did not feel. Now her whole body was quivering with desire, and as Henning entered her, she cried out at the intensity of the sensation. Their bodies moved in the ever-quickening rhythms of love, and she wrapped her legs about him and held him close as her need mounted and she arched her body to melt with his. When her climax came, she convulsed beneath him, her wild movements bringing him to orgasm, also.

Nothing that had been done to her at Mrs. Mudridge's had prepared Mellie for this supreme moment of love. No man had roused her; and although she had cleverly simulated fruition, coached by the other whores who worked there, Mellie had never before known any of the joys of love.

"Oh, my darling, that was heaven," she murmured, holding him in her arms, still embracing him with her legs, willing him to stay in her as receding waves of sensation swept through her loins.

"I've wanted to do that from the first time I saw you," he gasped, as they lay, still joined, and his hands caressed her breasts, traced the hollow in the small of her back, slid over the silky skin of her softly rounded buttocks.

Her hands in turn explored him, felt the crisp curl of hair on his chest, the strong lines of his body. Their lips met in a deep, long, passionate kiss, and Mellie felt her passion begin to rise again, even as she felt Henning, still within her, stir and swell.

This time they loved slowly, prolonging the exquisite sensation until Mellie was almost in a frenzy of desire. She moaned as Ritchie quickened his rhythm, and she gave herself utterly to him, eagerly, matching his need with her own. And again there was the wild, overwhelming climax that made her realize that this was all that mattered in life.

Sometime later Henning gathered Mellie into his arms and carried her to his bed where they made love yet again.

Their passion was a surging tide much too strong and elemental to resist, even if they had tried to deny themselves this ultimate ecstasy. It was a night of fulfillment, of raging emotions, of tender love, so exquisitely sensuous that Mellie thought she might die of such consuming fire. She knew she would never be so happy again in her life. It would be impossible to reach such heights of rapture ever again. Nothing in her experience had readied her for the tremendous power of such a love as this. It was a night of giving and receiving, of loving sharing, of ultimate delight.

She woke at first dawn to find Henning's head cradled on her breast, his arms still embracing her. He slept peacefully, his face unlined by care or despair. The overwhelming passion of Mellie's love had washed away the bitter realization of Jamie's lineage, leaving him completely relaxed and happy.

Mellie wanted nothing more than to lie there, entwined in her lover's arms, to await his awakening to more sweet love; but she knew that it would not be wise to be found in his bed by the gossiping servants. There was much to be decided, now that Henning knew his so-called heir was not his son at all. She had no idea what legalities would be required to declare Jamie illegitimate; but her heart sang, for no longer would Henning expect her to consummate her marriage with his homosexual son—no, not his son! Jamie was the son of Lord Carstairs. And somehow, sometime, when she'd been freed from this travesty of a marriage, she and Henning could be man and wife.

Now, though, she must slip quietly from her dear love's arms and from his bed, and hurry back to her own bedchamber before Dora came with the jug of hot water for her morning ablutions. Easing herself out of Henning's sleeping embrace, Mellie crept from the bedchamber into the sitting room, making sure that Henning's manservant was not yet about. With the greatest caution she opened the door onto the passageway, peering down its length to make sure it was empty. Then she fled on bare feet to her own room, not meeting any of the servants along the way. Once inside her own suite, she leaned against the door, panting from exertion.

A horrid thought came to her. Would Densbury still be in her bedchamber? She tiptoed through her own sitting room and peeked into the adjoining chamber. No, there was no sign of him. Apparently, she'd only stunned him; and when he had found her gone, he'd taken himself off to the Rose Room.

She intended to make something very plain to Jamie today. She would not be a party to this deceitful scheme of his, to have her gotten pregnant by any likely young blood, just to fulfill the requirements of his marriage.

After the rapture of a night of ecstasy with her darling Ritchie, she had no intention of allowing any other man to be intimate with her. Until she could be Henning's true wife, she would deny herself to any other man, no matter if she was legally married to Jamie.

With this resolve, she crawled into her own bed and fell fast asleep.

CHAPTER TWENTY-TWO

Mellie woke when the sun was high and Dora had brought in a cup of steaming chocolate to rouse her with the aroma.

"Oh, Dora, it's a beautiful day!" she cried.

"Yes, milady. You must have had a marvelous time at the ball."

"The ball?" For one moment Mellie didn't know what her abigail was talking about, her mind was so full of her lover. Then, seeing the startled look on Dora's round face, Mellie quickly said, "Oh, yes, the ball was magnificent. The costumes were very imaginative."

"I heard. . . ." Then Dora quickly turned away to pour hot water from the porcelain pitcher into the washbasin.

"Heard what, Dora?" Mellie could hear the sharp note in her own voice, saw Dora wince as if she'd struck her.

"N-nothing, milady."

So the story about Carstairs was already being chattered about among the servants. Well, the talk would go on for a while, until Henning made some proper settlement of the matter. Mellie couldn't wait, although she realized that her own position was now precarious. If Jamie wasn't Henning's legitimate son, was her marriage to Jamie legal or not?

While she puzzled over this and sipped the chocolate, lounging back luxuriously on the down pillows Dora had plumped up behind her, Mellie heard a tap on the door, a servant's discreet knock. "See who it is, Dora."

There was the murmur of voices, then Dora approached her bed. "His lordship, the viscount, wishes to breakfast with you, milady."

The last person Mellie had any desire to see now was Jamie; but she knew that there was much they should discuss, albeit it unpleasant.

"At his convenience," she told her abigail.

Shortly thereafter, Jamie arrived accompanied by his lover, Gerald Norwood, who looked as if he'd spent a sleepless and troubled night. Jamie greeted Mellie with a cold, distant bow, with Norwood echoing him. So it was to be that way. Very well, Mellie could be just as cool. She nodded to both men, waved them to seats at a small table.

"I'll breakfast in bed," she said firmly.

Jamie gave a little shrug as if to say he didn't care what she did. He carefully waited until the footman had served them all with buttered toast and chocolate, then dismissed both the footman and Dora, without even asking Mellie's permission. It must be a serious discussion, if he bothered to get the servants out of hearing. Usually he talked away as if they were statues.

"Well, wife," he started abruptly, "we're in a pretty fix," was his petulant opening. "Would you were with child."

Mellie, assuming he was going to berate her for refusing Densbury last night, decided to take the offensive. She didn't mind Norwood's hearing her, as it was his idea that Jamie find her a substitute for himself.

"Jamie, if ever you send another of your drunken, boorish friends into my bed again, I'll. . . ."

She saw the look of surprise on her husband's pretty face, and even Norwood looked blank instead of knowing.

"Whatever do you mean, Mellie?"

"I mean last night, when. . . ."

"Someone was in bed with you last night?"

"I had to hit him over the head to get rid of him," she said, her voice dangerously low. "And if ever you try that nasty trick again. . . ."

Jamie held up an admonitory hand. "I don't know what you're talking about, Mellie." He turned to Norwood. "Do you Gerald?" At Norwood's negative, he turned back to face his wife. "If someone tried to climb into that bed with you, then it was no doing of mine; although he'd have been rendering me a great favor." He gave that sly smile she hated so. "Who was it? I should give him a little token. . . ."

"I tokened him!" she snapped. "I hope with a lump as big as a goose egg on his hateful head."

"Perhaps you gave him reason to believe you'd welcome his advances," Norwood murmured maliciously.

"Get out!"

"I invited Gerald to breakfast with us," Jamie said.

"Then uninvite him," she ordered. "I will not put up with your fancy man. The sight of his face makes me ill."

Norwood turned pale with rage, his green eyes glittering, while Jamie flushed dark at her audacity.

"Gerald stays."

"Gerald goes—or I invite Lord Henning here and tell him in front of you both that you are trying to cheat him by sending your horrid friends to sleep with me."

"You wouldn't dare."

Mellie felt a great swell of power, and she smiled a little, superior smile. "I most certainly would dare. I have nothing to lose, Jamie. You're the one who would suffer if your father learned of the scheme you two have thought up." She turned and stared at Norwood, letting her lip curl with scorn. "Get out of my bedchamber, and stay out of it, Gerald." She'd not do him the honor of calling him Mr. Norwood. "Mister" was for equals. She'd use his given name as if he were a servant.

Then she leaned back and smiled, watching the gamut of emotions on both their faces. Jamie was furious; but he knew he was beaten. To prod him, Mellie reached a hand for the bellpull which hung at the head of the bed.

Defeated, Jamie said, "Run along, Gerald dear. I'll come to you as soon as I can."

If looks could kill, Mellie would have dropped dead; but Norwood's animosity didn't bother her now. She'd finally gotten the whip hand with Jamie, and she intended to keep it.

"I can't understand why his lordship allows Norwood to stay on here."

"I told him that if Gerald left, so would I."

She gave him a look of loathing. "Well, what do you want? I assume you didn't invite yourself to breakfast just to admire my beauty."

"We must do something about Carstairs," Jamie said.

"*We* must? What has it to do with us? He has approached your father—or, I should say more correctly, Lord Henning." She smiled, a cold, terrible smile, now that she had Jamie at her mercy. "You are nobody, Jamie. Lord Carstairs' son. No fortune. A title—but nothing to go with it. I wonder if our travesty of a marriage is even legal? You aren't Jamie Jamison at all." She laughed, almost hysterically.

In a flash he was up and standing over her, one hand raised to slap her face. "Don't say that!" he warned. "Don't ever say that,

Mellie. I'm Henning's legal son. And I intend to stay just that. I'm entered on the records as his son. I'm heir to Henning Hall, and the estate, and I will be the Earl of Henning someday—soon, I pray!"

"But, after last night, everyone knows. . . ."

"Gossip! Not legal facts, Mellie. Gossip!"

Before she thought, Mellie said, "But Carstairs intends to make trouble. He has approached Lord Henning. . . ."

"I'll fix him," Jamie said darkly. "I'll fix both of them. I won't be cheated out of my inheritance now!"

Mellie felt a cold hand clutch at her heart. When Jamie said such wild things, it frightened her terribly. Her love for Henning was so consuming that she dreaded any threat to his safety; and Jamie, with his veiled menaces, chilled her blood. Was he actually capable of physical violence? She thought so. There was a berserker quality in him which terrified her. With Henning's refusing to believe that Jamie posed a real threat to his life, the burden of protecting her lover must fall on Mellie.

Steadying her voice, to keep Jamie from knowing just how much his ravings frightened her, Mellie said, "Jamie, stop posturing. If you so much as make a threatening move toward Lord Henning, you'll be thrown into prison."

He gave her a pitying look which was worse than his anger. "Really, Mellie, I wish Father had chosen a more intelligent wife for me. Surely you don't think that I'll make the earldom mine, only to spend my time as Seventh Earl of Henning in prison? Or gain my title, only to lose it as I hang from the gallows on Tyburn? No, my dear wife, subtlety is the order of the day."

"I don't even want to hear you utter such nonsense," she cried, wishing immediately that she'd had sense enough to keep her mouth closed. If Jamie weren't encouraged to boast about his plans to remove her darling Ritchie from this life, she'd not know how to counteract his nastiness. She must be wise as a serpent in order to save Henning's life. "If you keep on saying such wicked things, someone will hear you," she warned. "And you know gossip. It will fly to his lordship's ears; and then where will you be? He may well decide to let Lord Carstairs claim you as his own issue."

She watched Jamie's face carefully, for he was poor at concealing his feelings. If she needled him sufficiently, he might let slip whatever plans he had for killing his father. Across the pretty face swept storm clouds of emotion.

"He'd never believe such gossip," Jamie said sullenly.

This was all too true, for Mellie had already tried to warn Henning against Jamie; but she had no intention of telling her husband this.

"Come, now, Jamie, Lord Henning isn't stupid. He knows how disgruntled you are over the way he's treated you. He's quite aware that you think he cheated you and tricked you when he married you off to me. He knows how filled you are with overweening ambition, how much you want to get your hands on your fortune. Do not sell him short. Don't be misled by the fact that he so desperately wants a son to carry on the Henning name. He won't stand still for the threat of patricide."

"Who'll tell him what I'm saying?" Jamie stormed. "I don't go spouting such talk to the servants."

Now it was her chance to give him a pitying look.

"You say all kinds of indiscreet things in front of the servants, Jamie, because to you they are part of the furniture. You surprised me this morning when you dismissed them. One day you'll slip and say something truly incriminating before a footman who has ambitions to become butler—or one who needs enough gold to emigrate to the American colonies. And that is the day you'll topple, Jamie; for the man will run to his lordship and tell him what you've been saying, to curry favor for himself."

She could see that she'd shaken Jamie's composure. If she frightened him sufficiently, he'd not dare try anything against the earl.

"I can keep my mouth shut as tightly as the prison gates at Newgate," Jamie told her. "And I don't intend to catch up a carving knife and do in my father at dinner in front of a table full of guests. Please give me credit for more ingenuity than that, Mellie. No, I want him dead, but not at my own expense." Then he gave her a terrible smile, one that made her breath catch in her throat so that she felt faint but dared not reach for her vinaigrette lest Jamie guess how frightened she was. "I shall practice all subtlety, dear wife. And, if you are clever, you'll cast your lot with me instead of with my father. I might be willing to allow you to stay on in your nominal role as wife. There are times it might be advantageous for me to have a hostess, if you make no demands on me physically. Behave yourself, do as I say, and you'll be Countess of Henning some day soon. What do you say, dear wife?"

Every fiber of her being screamed out to curse him, to strike him, to flee from his invidious suggestion; but Mellie held her emotions in check. Right now, the most important thing in her life was Ritchie Jamison, Lord Henning, her only love. If she allowed herself to show Jamie her true feelings, she would alienate him completely. Only by keeping some semblance of friendship with her husband could she hope to gain his confidence. Only if he trusted her was Jamie likely to tell her his plans to do away with his father.

It took all of her willpower, all of her skill as an actress, to smile at Jamie. She'd learned her lessons well at Mother Mudridge's brothel. She'd had to smile at the men she despised, laugh at their humorous sallies, pretend to be moved by their lust, even while she detested them. Very well, if she could do that for the casual buyers of her flesh, surely she could do it now, when there was so much at stake.

Oh, Ritchie, forgive me, she begged silently. *I am not betraying you. I only pledge allegiance to Jamie and his evil plans in order to save you. I love you so desperately. If anything should happen to you, life would no longer be worth living. If you die, then I want to die, too.*

If Jamie planned to use a serpent's guile, then she must match him in duplicity, must surpass him in deceit.

Putting an unbelieving face on, she said, "I don't think you have any clever plans at all, Jamie. You are just bragging to boost your ego. Remember, if a word of your intentions reaches his lordship's ears, he may well cut you off, disinherit you, tell the whole world that you are Carstairs's bastard. Then you'll be nothing."

"I'll think of something," Jamie muttered, glowering at her. "And Gerald will help me."

Gerald. For a moment she'd forgotten the older man. Norwood was clever. In one way, he was the enemy, much more so than Jamie. It was Norwood's enormous influence over his lover that made Jamie what he was. She must be careful how she handled Jamie; for he'd certainly tell Norwood everything she said. He might see what she was doing and persuade Jamie not to trust her, nor take her into his confidence.

"Gerald is clever; but you are the one who will suffer if anything goes wrong with your plan, Jamie, and murder is suspected. You are the one with the most to gain from the death of the Sixth Earl. You are the logical suspect. The constables aren't all dolts. The magistrates are not universally corrupt. You may learn this to your sorrow when you are up before a hanging judge!"

"Let's have less talk of hanging," he said, shuddering delicately. Then, as if frightened by vistas that she had unveiled,

Jamie flung out of the bedchamber, leaving her alone with her terrors and her thoughts.

If she could convince Jamie that she, too, wanted Henning's death, she might be in a better position to protect him from his own son's hand; but to do this, Mellie would have to be a better actress than anyone appearing in the Haymarket!

CHAPTER TWENTY-THREE

Mellie was plunged from the heights of elation and exhilaration to the depths of despair. All day she'd hoped to see her beloved Ritchie; but he kept to his room. She heard one of the footmen and Henning's valet joking about a "big head" after last night's brandy. She knew that Lord Henning had been very drunk when she went to him. No doubt he was suffering today for his excesses last night—his excesses of drink, not his excesses of love!

With her whole being she longed to be with him, to feel the comfort of his strong arms around her, holding her close, to know the heat of his kisses, the depth of his passion, the ecstasy of their coupling. She mooned about like a lovesick maid, hoping for a glimpse of him; but to no avail. Finally she called Dora to dress her for dinner. Surely his lordship would put in an appearance then.

"What will you wear, milady?" Then, with an odd mixture of boldness and shyness, Dora said, "You seem very happy, milady, after last night."

"Oh, yes, I am!" Then, realizing that she must be more discreet than that with her abigail, or the whole house would buzz with gossip, Mellie added, "It was a magnificent ball."

With a sly little glance out of the corner of her eyes, Dora said, "And I'll mend this nightdress for you, milady," holding the silken gown which Densbury had ripped from neck to waist.

Mellie felt her face grow hot; but she said with all the dignity she could muster, "If it can't be mended, throw it away, Dora," knowing very well that Dora would keep it for herself, reveling in a real silk nightdress. Then, to get Dora's mind off the gown, she said, "I think I'll wear the new yellow taffeta over the emerald green petticoat for dinner. And the new green leather slippers."

"I'll dress your hair high, and pin on a pompon of yellow roses from the garden, if you like."

"That would be lovely, Dora." Lord Henning would look at her with love, she knew.

181

But Lord Henning looked at her the way he'd looked at her every evening for dinner since she'd come to Henning Hall. He was polite and distant, with absolutely no indication of their night of love together. At first dismayed, Mellie only picked at her meal, taking a few bites of the peeper pie made from newly hatched turkey chicks, and passing up completely the sirloin of beef garnished with veal burrs, the sweetbreads stuffed with the livers, hearts, and gizzards of woodcocks. She tasted the candied carrots, but did not eat the turnips and cabbage boiled together. Lord Henning, Jamie, and Norwood ate prodigiously, although Jamie complained that he preferred asparagus to the turnip mixture, even though it was considered a cheap food fit only for the laboring class.

In place of eating, Mellie drank much more wine than usual, so that by the time the pudding was brought in, she was feeling quite tipsy, and the cook's fancy molded creation shaped like a hedgehog stuck all over with slivered almond quills and sporting currant eyes almost turned her stomach.

Was his lordship only being ultradiscreet, treating her as usual? Or had last night been—what? A drunken encounter, fueled only by the brandy he'd drunk in such quantities before she'd gone to his room? A lapse that he would pretend had never happened?

Mellie was in a frenzy of anxiety to be alone with him, to hear him say once again, "I love you."

They all drank their coffee in silence, but the atmosphere of the formal dining room was crackling with tension. She felt that Jamie, perhaps egged on by his lover, Norwood, had some plan; but he didn't mention anything other than casual gossip about people who'd been at the ball. There was no mention at all of Lord Carstairs, or the horrible dilemma into which that rogue had plunged all of them. Were they just going to ignore the situation, hoping it would go away if they didn't talk about it? Or had Lord Henning already paid off Carstairs so that he was sure that the man would disappear from sight, and, hopefully, from the memory of the nobility of Kent?

When Parkins brought the port, Mellie made as if to rise from the table and retire to the drawing room; but Lord Henning said, "Stay, Mellie. We must have a discussion, all of us; and since it affects you, also, I wish you to attend."

"Yes, milord."

Her heart leaped with hope. Although Henning had been quite matter-of-fact, perhaps he intended to tell Jamie of his great love for her. No doubt he was about to inform his so-called son that since Mellie married him thinking he was truly the Viscount Triller, heir to the earldom of Henning, the church would annul their marriage. If she further explained that her marriage to Jamie had never been consummated, it would surely be grounds for annulment or legal divorce through the courts.

"Do you wish me to stay, milord?" Norwood asked.

Mellie thought the tutor seemed wary as a doe drinking her fill at a pool in the woods. She'd never talked to Henning about Norwood. His lordship wasn't stupid. He knew the role the tutor played in his son's life. Some men might not have allowed him to stay on at Henning Hall, especially after Jamie's marriage to her; but Henning apparently knew his son—or the one purported to be his son—well enough to know that, without Norwood, Jamie would refuse to stay. It actually was clever to allow Jamie's lover to live here. No doubt the earl hoped that once Jamie was married, he'd lose interest in Norwood. Mellie was sure this would never happen; or if Jamie fell out of love with Norwood, he'd only take up with some other man. Paris proved that.

"We are in a quandary," Lord Henning said. Then he sipped deliberately at his port.

"How so, Father?"

Henning scowled at Jamie. "Come now, Jamie, don't play the fool with me. You're no dullard. The whole country will be buzzing after last night. What a rotten piece of luck that Carstairs was chosen as best-dressed. Why did you pick him out, Jamie?"

Jamie looked as if he could die. Either he must take the blame for the fiasco, or place it squarely on his lover. Mellie, although she had little love for Jamie, had none at all for Norwood. Spitefully, she spoke up.

"It was Gerald who made the choice."

She got a venomous look from Jamie for her trouble. Norwood, however, seemed unconcerned.

"I chose the best costume, milord—barring yourself and Jamie. I had no idea who hid behind Lucifer's mask; and had I known the name, it would have meant nothing to me. I'd never seen Lord Carstairs before."

Impatiently, Henning waved a hand at the tutor. "I know it is foolish to try to place blame in this situation, Mr. Norwood. And I honestly think that Carstairs would have arranged to be seen with Jamie before the evening was over, even had he not been given the prize. It was all part of his plan. He approached me, you know—out-and-out blackmail. He wants money to emigrate to the American colonies."

Mellie was watching Jamie's face. He said nothing, but she felt that this wasn't to his liking for some reason. She, herself, thought paying off Carstairs a good solution. Therefore she said, "Milord, would it not be best, perhaps, to pay off the scoundrel, get him far, far away?"

Henning twisted his mouth as if he'd bitten into a spoiled game pie. "Probably, although it does go against my grain to give good money to a bad fellow."

Again Jamie had that look. Mellie thought of it as his coiled-spring look, as if he could scarcely contain himself from speaking out.

"Well, Jamie," Lord Henning said, "what do you think?"

The young man said nothing at first. Then he smiled. "I think I don't want to belong to Carstairs. If you pay him, it shows you think he is my father, so why pay? Let him talk all he wants to. We will just ignore him. The gossip will settle down, Father dear, when a new scandal raises its head—and scandals happen every day."

Henning's face was a turmoil of emotions. He was annoyed at Jamie's flip reply; yet Mellie knew there was relief, too. Henning wanted to believe Jamie was his, even now. And Jamie wanted it, too. She distrusted the young viscount. Somehow Henning was playing into Jamie's hands. She recalled the times Jamie had wished his father—or the man supposed to be his father—dead. She wanted to cry out, "Don't listen to Jamie, my dearest. He means you ill." But she'd already tried to warn Henning that Jamie wanted to kill him, and had only angered the earl with her words.

And quiet in the background, Norwood sat, a spider in a sticky web. Whatever was good for Jamie was good for him, and Mellie knew that he exercised a lot of influence over the younger man. They both had their hands turned against Henning; but he thought only of the continuation of the line. He'd better think about himself, soon, or he might not live to see this grandchild he was obsessed with having.

"And when do I receive happy news that you are expecting?" Henning asked Mellie, almost as if he'd picked the thought from her mind.

Drily, she said, "Milord, you shall be the first to know."

How could he? After last night, did he still expect her to continue with this travesty of a marriage? Perhaps she should tell him in no uncertain terms that Jamie would never father a child, tell him of the fiasco with the aphrodisiac; yet she held her tongue. She could feel Jamie's eyes on her, almost daring her to say something; but again she didn't trust her husband. He might well counter with an accusation that she had taken a lover, even though it was a blatant lie.

Last night Henning had said over and over again that he loved her. Tonight, here, Mellie feared that if Henning had to choose between her and Jamie, he'd choose Jamie. She wasn't going to risk forcing him to make that choice.

"Very well, then, I refuse to pay Carstairs and let him talk?" Lord Henning asked.

"I think that is wisest, father. What can he prove? You and mother were legally married. It is merely a quirk of nature that I seem to resemble him more than you. Perhaps you could find a portrait of one of mother's ancestors—or your own—who looks like me."

"Be serious, Jamie," Henning snapped. "There is no such picture, and you know it."

"But I know an artist in London who can paint lovely pictures, and make them look very old. He's quite clever at it, father."

"That's dishonest," Henning thundered.

"And it puts your father in line for more blackmailing," Mellie hastened to point out, wondering if this was part of Jamie's plan to force money from his father.

Jamie shrugged. "I was only trying to help."

"You can help me most by giving me a grandson. The Henning line must continue no matter what the circumstances are. Ours is an old and honored name—regardless of who bears it." He gave Jamie a pointed look and then rose from the table. "Very well, when Carstairs comes around again, as he said he'd do, I'll send him packing."

Mellie thought it would be better to pay off the man and let him go to the colonies; but she held her tongue. She was now so heartsick from Henning's treatment of her that she wanted only to get away so she could weep in solitude.

Jamie had further ideas about Carstairs, though. "I think it unwise to allow Lord Carstairs to return to Henning Hall, Father. Just send him a note saying you have no intention of paying. Call his bluff. It is the best way to handle him."

Mellie thought Jamie too insistent; but Lord Henning seemed pleased that Jamie was taking such an interest in the matter, and even more pleased that the viscount wished to be his son. *Ritchie, Ritchie,* she wanted to cry, *he wants only to be Earl of Henning. He wants you out of the way; for currently you and you alone stand in the path of his inheritance. Oh, beware, Jamie will play you false!*

Jamie went on, "I'll be glad to draft the letter for you, if you wish. You needn't bother with it."

"Very well, Jamie, and I thank you. Then, if everything is settled, we can adjourn this little family session." He smiled at Mellie; but there was no passion in the smile. It was only the indulgent expression of a man for his young, beautiful daughter-in-law.

What had happened? Had his lordship been so far gone in drink that he did not remember anything that happened last night? Could it be possible that he was completely unaware of the passion between them? Mellie wished she could die. If he were not truly in love with her, then her life was going to be increasingly dreadful here at Henning Hall.

Or had she dreamed it all? There'd been no sign of Alistair Lord Densbury today. Perhaps she was losing her mind. Mellie remembered her mother in Bedlam. Pray God she wasn't going to wind up there, too. In a sudden panic, she hurried after Jamie and Norwood, determined to find out if she had imagined Densbury last night. If she had, then she might have imagined her love with Henning, too. The torn nightdress! That had been real, hadn't it? Now her head was pounding from tension.

"Jamie," she called, pursuing the two men down a long passageway. "Jamie, wait. I must speak with you."

He stopped, looked back, then said something to the tutor who hurried on alone. Mellie was glad that Norwood wouldn't overhear what she had to ask her husband.

"Well, what is it, Mellie?" He was impatient with her, his manner abrupt, his face forbidding.

"After the ball, last night—Densbury stayed." At the last moment she chose not to phrase it as a question.

"That's right, and I thought he was going to spend several days here with us; but he left very early, even before I was. . . ." A comical expression crossed his petulant face. "Good God, it wasn't Alistair, was it? The man in your bed? The one you tried to brain?"

"Yes, it was," she said, cross with herself for mentioning it, for now it gave Jamie another bad mark against her.

"What did you hit him with?" Jamie asked, his voice silky and dangerously low.

"A wine carafe, if you must know. Jamie, I won't put up with such nonsense. I swear, if you send one more of your rakehell friends to my bed, I shall tell Lord Henning exactly what is going on."

He smiled, a very superior smile, which chilled her. "And I shall tell my father that you lie, that you entice these strange men to your bed while you deny me my conjugal rights. He'll believe me, not you. He found you in a brothel, and he'll think you've reverted to your professional ways."

"Oh, you are despicable."

"And you are an interfering busybody, dear wife. I planned a dramatic entertainment, with Densbury to help with it. He is quite good at theatricals, is Alistair. And all because you suddenly choose to be virtuous, I've lost his talents. It's not as if you hadn't already shared your bed with him."

"Yes, I'm sure he couldn't wait to tell you," she said, bitterness like gall in her mouth. "He's a good friend for you, Jamie, cut from the same flawed bolt."

He turned on his heel and left her, then. Her only consolation was that she had not imagined Densbury's attempted seduction last night. So, if that had truly happened, then surely she had not dreamed the later part of the night, with Lord Henning. She could still feel his hands on her breasts, could still remember the well of sensation which he had plumbed to the depths. Yet he acted as if it had never happened.

Perhaps it was Henning who was mad, not she. It seemed impossible for him to have been so passionate and loving last night, so cold today—unless he suffered some mental disorder which made him two separate and distinct personalities, with one of them in the ascendancy sometimes, at other times, the second.

And what was Jamie planning? There was some skullduggery afoot concerning Lord Carstairs, she was sure of it. There were vibrations emanating from her husband that warned her that he and Norwood were up to something which boded no good for Lord Henning. It wasn't natural for Jamie to say he'd take care of Carstairs himself. Surely Henning, with his greater experience, should know that the suggestion rang false.

She considered going back, broaching the subject with the earl. She thought it wisest to pay off Carstairs, help him to emigrate to the colonies. There'd be gossip; but with Carstairs out of sight, the tittle-tattle would soon die down.

She remembered, though, trying to warn Henning about Jamie's bad intentions once before. It had earned her nothing but reproach from her beloved Ritchie. No, better to keep her own counsel. But Mellie was determined to spy on Jamie, if necessary, to find out what evil plans he had for his father. Forewarned, she might be able to prevent disaster.

CHAPTER TWENTY-FOUR

"Let us go up to London, dear wife," Jamie suggested.

Mellie, who had been haunting Jamie's footsteps, hoping to overhear him discussing his plans with Norwood, had scarcely spoken to her husband since the morning after the ball, now a week past. She'd had no luck whatsoever in divining what plan Jamie was plotting with his tutor; Jamie had ignored her, even as she had ignored him. The only thing she'd heard in her discreet spying on her husband was talk of the dramatic entertainment he and Gerald Norwood hoped to have in late autumn.

"London? You wish me to accompany you to London?"

Jamie scowled at her. "Is it so strange that a man and his bride should travel together? Remember, Mellie, we still must put up a front for the world; and that world includes my loving father." The scowl darkened, giving his long, pointed face a satanic cast. "I think it would be wise if we pretended, at least, to share our bed at times. Father will hear the gossip from the servants. He's no fool, Mellie. He knows that if we don't share a conjugal bed, there's no chance of our producing this brat he insists on seeing before I have my inheritance."

She was stunned. Since the humiliating wedding night, Jamie had made no further pretense of sleeping with her, except when they were put together by their host in Paris. Now what did he have in mind? Was he planning again to have sex with her—or to try? Remembering how abysmally he had failed on their wedding night, and the results of her too clever ploy in Paris, Mellie shuddered inwardly. How could she bare her body to him, how could she tolerate his touch, his fumbling efforts at consummation, after her experience with Henning? Well, it would be the brothel all over again, turning off her mind, ignoring what he did with her body. Mellie was sure there was more to this proposed trip to London than Jamie was telling her.

She considered refusing to accompany him. If she went to London with Jamie, she would not see her dearly beloved Ritchie. Even though he treated her as he would a daughter, Mellie remembered their night of blazing passion. If she were here at Henning Hall, there might be more opportunities for her to lie in his arms, have him make love to her.

On the other hand, the way he now ignored her, perhaps absence would indeed make his heart grow fonder. Mellie could scarcely ply her father-in-law with brandy in order to fire his passion! Ah, bitter thought. Was it only the strong spirits that had inflamed him? Would any woman have served Henning as well as she in his drunken lust? It was too terrible to think about. No, she remembered his protestations of love, his tenderness despite the drink which coursed through his veins. Ritchie loved her. She knew it. It was the only thing which made living here bearable, with her effeminate husband and his male lover.

Very well, she'd go to London with Jamie. If he were planning some disaster for his father, she might be able to prevent it if she were with him, possibly privy to his secrets. And it would be exciting to be in London with money to spend, with a titled husband, once again with a place in society. How she'd love to go to court, flaunt her good fortune in the faces of those who had enjoyed her downfall. Yes, a trip to London might be exceedingly gratifying.

"Very well, Jamie, I should enjoy a trip to London. When will we go?"

"Tomorrow. We shall make an easy journey of it. I have no wish to tire myself unduly by arriving the same day."

"That is fine with me." She remembered the long, wearying trip she had made here with Henning. It seemed years ago, not just weeks. And perhaps the trip with Jamie would not be too deadly. He could be good company if he chose to put his mind to it.

Then Jamie ruined everything by saying, "Gerald is so looking forward to London. He gets quite bored here. And he missed the trip to Paris, poor dear. The plans for the ball kept him busy and happy; but now he longs for the pleasures of the city."

"Gerald's going along?" What a dismaying development.

"You didn't think I'd go to London without him, did you? Honestly, Mellie, sometimes I wonder at you. One would think you had lead a sheltered life, convent-raised, instead of having been a brothel whore. I know I said we must pretend to share a bed occasionally—but I can't abide you, and you know it. I must have dear Gerald with me for love."

How she longed to slap his smug face; but Mellie controlled herself. This was one time when she must keep track of what Jamie was doing. There was something in the wind. She could feel it, a tension that had begun building at the masquerade. Once Jamie learned that he was not Henning's son, that his natural father was Lord Carstairs, the air at Henning Hall had been charged, as if a summer thunderstorm were brewing. Mellie had to know what kind of lightning strike Jamie had in mind for her dearest Lord Henning. Although he had no desire to be acknowledged as the son of Lord Carstairs, Mellie knew all too well that Jamie had no love for the man who was supposed to be his father. All Jamie wanted was to become Earl of Henning and to inherit Henning Hall. If he could manage to remove his father, then he would be Earl of Henning. Would Jamie stoop to murder? Mellie wasn't sure. Maybe it was all bombast. Given an opportunity to kill his father, perhaps Jamie would not be able to go through with it. She had no way of knowing; and Mellie wanted no opportunity to find out first hand. Jamie was wicked enough, spiteful enough, desperate enough to do his father grievous harm, if he thought that was the only way he could get what he wanted. His ambition was frightening. There were so many ways in which a man could be killed without its seeming to be murder. Poison in a game pie, and everyone would think the game had been hung too long. Accidents of all kinds could take place in a large house or on a large estate. If Henning's horse threw him, as Mellie's had thrown her, he could break his neck—or have his neck broken by someone hidden in a convenient copse. Or the earl's coach could be waylaid by a knight of the road, and Henning shot in the flurry that always surrounded a highway robbery.

Better to stay close to Jamie, even if it meant being in Norwood's company, also. There was one pleasant thought. Norwood hated her as much as she despised him. No doubt he was as unhappy to learn she'd be going to London as she was when she found out he'd be there.

"Ask Father for some money," Jamie ordered. "Tell him you want to buy some new gowns. Women always want new gowns. He's much more likely to give it to you than to me."

"I have so many gowns now, I haven't even worn them all," she protested, determined that she wouldn't ask Henning for anything, most particularly not for money.

Jamie scowled at her. "You can be incredibly provoking, Mellie. He has plenty of money. Didn't you know that he is reputed to be a real financial wizard? According to London gossip, everything he lays his hand to makes money."

Of course this had to be true. Mellie remembered how Madame Tilladet wanted no money from her for the aphrodisiac, only Henning's feelings about the Mississippi venture.

Jamie grinned at her in a companionable way. "In fact, I hope to pick up a bit of extra spending money for myself by asking Father for stock tips before we go. Which companies to buy into. He'll be impressed that I am taking an interest in the business end of Henning Hall. He chided me once that I had no concern for such mundane things as the making of money. Well, he was right, much as I hate to admit his lordship is ever right about anything. I haven't the faintest interest in buying and selling, in shares or merchant banks, in interest rates. I can't get excited about cargo ships with hogsheads of brandy or barrels of whale oil. All I want to know about is the end result—money. Money in my purse for me to spend."

Mellie, not very conversant with such matters herself, said, "But what do you intend to do? Invest your allowance in—in something?"

"Good God, no! No, I sell information."

"What do you mean, you sell information?"

"To investors. They all know how astute Father is in such matters. So, for a price, I tell favored friends which enterprises Father thinks are money makers."

"Jamie! That's. . . ."

"Dishonest? Not really. If Father lets slip certain inside information, and I, in turn, let it slip further, and my friends make money on these slips, I think it only fair that I receive something for my wagging tongue."

"You are despicable."

"True," he said quite cheerfully. It seemed to please him when he shocked her. "And it works the other way, too. If I know someone I wish to harm, then I let him overhear false information, so that he'll invest his guineas in what he thinks is something Father endorses, and then he loses a packet." He shrugged, smiled. "It's quite a good way to get back at one's enemies, Mellie."

Although it shocked Mellie to hear him be so brutal about it, she couldn't help thinking what pleasure it would give her to be able to furnish one of these snippets of false information to the hated Duke and Duchess of Seybrook. It might be nice to see their money disappear in a bubble of unwise speculation. Knowing how impressed they were with themselves, and realizing how expensive it must be to maintain their position in the *ton* they'd be finished socially if they were poor.

And Densbury! How she'd like to see bad things happen to him. Mellie wasn't sure, though, that having him fall on lean times financially would satisfy her need for revenge against the handsome young lord. He had betrayed her too thoroughly to be satisfied with less than some sort of actual, physical downfall for him. Wickedly, she hoped that he caught the French pox from one of the prostitutes whose favors he bought with his ready gold. That would be a just sentence for such a sinner as Alistair.

Meanwhile, Jamie kept pestering her to ask Lord Henning for money to spend in London, and Mellie kept refusing, to Jamie's increasing fury. As it turned out, she got the money without even asking for it.

At dinner that day, over the roast goose, before the butler had even sliced the baked ham, Jamie mentioned that he thought his bride needed a change of scenery. "I thought we'd go up to London tomorrow for several weeks."

"I'll send a rider today to alert the servants, so they'll have the house ready for you," Henning agreed quite readily.

"House?" Mellie asked, confused. When Henning had bought her from Mrs. Mudridge, he'd lodged her at the Oxford Arms while they remained in London. Had he acquired a house in the city since then?

"Oh, didn't I mention it?" Jamie asked, quite casual about the whole thing. "Father has quite a nice mansion on Little Queen Street, off Great Queen, near Lincoln's Inn Fields."

"I'm sure you'll be very comfortable there," Lord Henning interposed. "We travel up to London frequently, so the house is ready on short notice. I just like to alert the butler so he can lay in fresh supplies for the cook. It's not like living here, with our own fresh meats and produce from the estate. Living in London requires more shopping—more planning."

"Very well, then, Father, we'll leave tomorrow; but not those early dawn departures of which you are so fond. I think we'll break the trip in Rochester."

"Yes, it will be much less tiring for Mellie," her father-in-law said.

Did he remember their long, arduous journey here in June? Ah,

Mellie remembered it. She'd thought she was coming to Kent to be the Countess of Henning. The lovely bridal gown was to be for her marriage to her beloved Ritchie. How little she'd known then. How naive she'd been. Now she was to travel back to London a married lady, but married, alas, to the wrong Jamison.

"Mellie, I'll give you some pin money," Henning was saying, his tone indulgent as if he were a loving uncle and she an adored niece.

Before she had a chance to answer, Jamie cut in, "That's very good of you, Father. I'm sure Mellie will want to have some gowns made for the autumn season." He turned to her, his smile all that a new bride could wish. "We must do more entertaining here in Kent. Life must be dull for you, my dear wife, after the excitements and entertainments of London."

"Oh, I'm quite contented here," she protested, earning a scowl from Jamie which he skillfully kept from his father's eyes by turning his head so he faced her.

"And we'll spend more time at the town house in London, too," he promised. "The high season is much more interesting in the city than stuck out here in the middle of nowhere."

When Mellie saw the amount of money that Henning had allowed her for a new wardrobe "and ribbons" she wanted to return part of it; but Jamie was adamant. "We can use every cent. I can lose that much at White's in a single whist game, if the stakes are high."

Having played whist there evenings with Jamie, Norwood, and Henning, Mellie said, "You'd lose at whist any place, with stakes high or low. You really are a poor player, Jamie. Whoever plays with you for a partner loses. And as for this money, your father gave it to me." She felt quite high-handed. "If you don't behave yourself, I shan't give you as much as a ha'penny."

"Miserable little vixen," he spat, no show of love now that his father was no longer with them. "Fortunately Father was more generous with me than usual. And if I'm lucky at the tables, I may come back to Kent a rich man. Or if I'm luckier than that, I may just stay on in London. Gerald likes it better there. And perhaps in London we'll find you a lover who'll produce the desired results." He looked at her tiny waist with loathing. "Once you are with child, you can retire here and vegetate, if you like. Just don't expect me to stay here with you."

"Dear Jamie," she said sweetly, her voice dripping sarcasm, "I can think of nothing lovelier than to have you removed forever from my presence.''

There was much packing to do. Dora was excited over being able to go up to London with her mistress, for she explained that she had an ''understanding'' with one of the underfootmen at the house on Little Queen Street. ''We walk out in Lincoln's Inn Fields,'' she confided, ''when the weather is pleasant.'' Then she added hastily, ''With your permission, of course, milady.''

Mellie, madly in love with Lord Henning, certainly had no desire to stand in the way of Dora's happiness. ''If you love him, and he loves you, Dora, you have my blessing.''

''Ah, milady, I hope you'll be happy, too, someday,'' Dora said in a rush of goodwill. Then, aghast at what she'd blurted out, Dora blushed crimson and muttered, ''Of course you're sure to be happy now, just married to the viscount,'' but sounding as if she didn't mean it for a minute.

And Mellie, who wished to shout to all the world that she loved Lord Henning, had to keep silent. She compared Jamie's feeble, unsuccessful attempts at sex on their wedding night to his father's virility, and wanted to sit down and sob in bitter frustration. Once initiated into the raptures of sex with a man she loved, Mellie burned to make love with him again. Chastity was not for her. With her passionate nature, Mellie thought at times that she could not bear it if she could not soon again share Henning's bed with him, know the bliss as their bodies joined in that greatest expression of love between man and woman; yet she was tied to an impotent husband, and Henning made no effort to satisfy her passion.

CHAPTER TWENTY-FIVE

"You aren't taking two carriages?" Lord Henning asked. "Jamie, you can't possibly travel clear to London with Mellie, her abigail, you, Norwood, and your man in one carriage. Not even the berlin will hold all of you and your boxes."

"Father, stop worrying." Mellie could see how annoyed Jamie was to be criticized. "Gerald and I are planning to ride horseback."

"You'll wish you hadn't if it rains," his father said drily. "And since when did you choose the saddle to the comfort of a coach?"

Jamie just raised his eyebrows at that, and Mellie had a hard time to keep from giggling. Coaching was the most uncomfortable abomination ever invented. She wished she'd thought of riding! But no doubt everyone would think it unseemly for a young matron to ride all the way from Canterbury to London when she could ride in a jouncing, swaying, poorly ventilated box which is what carriages were.

"Stay with the coach," Henning ordered his son. "There are highwaymen everywhere."

Jamie looked bored and sounded it as he answered. "The coachey and the footman both will be armed, Father. Don't worry so."

"I wish you'd told me sooner that you weren't taking two coaches. There's safety in numbers."

"We'll be all right!" Jamie flounced out of the house, boot heels clicking on the marble floor.

"Well, Mellie, enjoy your stay in London," his lordship said, bending over to kiss her cheek, a very fatherly salute. But even this casual farewell made her breath come faster, and she longed to throw her arms about his neck, to cling to him, press her eager body against his until she felt his own respond, and to kiss him passionately. *What would he do?* she wondered, *if I did embrace him that way, did allow my true feelings to show?* Would he re-

196

spond as he had that day when her horse threw her—as he had the night of the ball when they writhed and gasped in the clutch of passion? Or would he repulse her? She dared not test him.

"Milord, I shall miss Henning Hall," was all she allowed herself to say.

He laughed indulgently. "It's a pretty dull place here, Mellie. Brighter now that you are here, of course. I shall find it most boring while you and Jamie are in London."

It was little enough; but Mellie clung to those few hints that Henning would miss her.

"Why don't you join us?" she asked impulsively. "Surely your bailiff can look after Henning Hall for a while, manage the estate for you while you take a short vacation."

He smiled but shook his head. "Not this time, Mellie. Perhaps, in a few weeks, if Jamie doesn't decide to come riding back, I might drive up to London."

It was not much of a promise; but she knew every moment of her stay she'd be watching, hoping, for Lord Henning to arrive.

Then Dora was at the door to tell her the coach was ready, and Mellie had to leave Henning, much as it grieved her to do so. Weeks without seeing him! How could she bear it? And now she had another hateful worry. How many eager young women from the village would he have in his bed while she was gone? As virile as he was, Mellie knew he'd not remain celibate, it wasn't his nature to be without a woman. She raged with jealousy, her hands shook slightly, she surprised herself at the corrosive nature of this new emotion. If she ever found one of those young sluts with him, she'd scratch out her eyes, pull out her hair, take a riding crop to her luscious plump young buttocks.

She was so swept with jealousy that she scarcely noticed what Dora chattered about as they drove toward Canterbury through the soft air of late summer. "Oh, milady, I never dreamed I'd get to ride in the good, sprung coach with you." Then she lowered her voice, laughing. "Kenneth is annoyed that he must ride outside while I get to sit inside. If we'd taken two coaches as usual, Kenneth and I would have both ridden inside in the second one." Kenneth was Jamie's valet. "I told him to be glad he didn't have to ride a horse all the way to London, as his lordship is doing."

Although her heart was aching at leaving Henning behind, Mellie couldn't help but enjoy the lovely morning, with the sun slanting down through the tall trees lining the road. Jamie and Norwood cantered along beside them, seeming to enjoy the morning ride.

Mellie was wearing the same brown traveling costume she'd worn when she came to Henning Hall those two months ago; but this trip was not the same. Dora was pleasant enough, but she was a poor substitute for Lord Henning. Mellie let the abigail chatter on while her mind wandered.

She dreamed of a time when she and Henning could be together. Jamie wasn't there. Mellie didn't dwell on that part of the vision. She just imagined life with Lord Henning as his wife; or as his mistress, if marriage was not possible. All she wanted was happiness, and that meant a chance to love her darling Ritchie whenever she wished, as often as he wanted her. Was that too much to ask for when you were sixteen and beautiful? Her marriage was a farce. Her past was so bad she wanted to forget every sordid minute of it. She longed for love. One blazing night of passion was not enough to last her all the rest of her life. All it had done was to awake her emotions, to show her that physical love with a man could be the most beautiful, all-consuming thing in life; that the men who had bought her body were nothing, they didn't matter, only Henning was real.

As mile after weary mile jolted by, she was lost in a dream of life as it would be for her someday, somehow.

They broke the trip at Faversham, stopping at a cozy inn with a thatched roof and roses climbing over the trellised entrance. A sign swinging in the breeze proclaimed it to be The Brown Bull. A stagecoach had pulled in just ahead of them; but Jamie engaged a private parlor for Mellie and Norwood, leaving the servants to dine in the main taproom.

After a good meal of a joint of mutton and roasted capon, with potatoes and cabbage, and a rich fruitcake, all washed down with a passable claret, Jamie said, "I think that Gerald and I shall ride on ahead, Mellie. It is boring to have to stay back with the berlin. We'll see you at The George in Rochester. We'll have better chance to get some private accommodations if Gerald and I get there early."

"But your father said. . . ."

"Bother what Father said," Jamie snapped. "There's absolutely no danger to you. The coachey has a blunderbuss in the box. Father is just being an old granny woman, eh, Gerald?"

"It's much more dangerous at night," Norwood said. "It would take a bold highwayman to venture out by the light of day. You'll be quite safe, milady." His tone made it obvious that he didn't care in the least if Mellie were accosted, raped, and carried off bodily by an entire band of villains.

Since there was nothing she could do to stop him, Mellie shrugged, poured another glass of claret, and said, "Suit yourself. If your horse goes lame, we may not bother to stop for you as we pass you on the road."

"Dear wife." Jamie reached out as if to give her face a loving caress; but instead he tweaked her ear painfully.

Miserable man. If he spent all of his time with Gerald, they could plot all sorts of wicked things against Henning, and she'd never know it. She'd expected them to ride in the coach with her, and all those hours would have given her a chance to pick up some bit of information from their chatter. Now, tucked away in the berlin with Dora, she had no chance whatsoever to learn anything.

When they went outside The Brown Bull, Mellie was surprised to find that it was quite overcast.

"Oh, drat, it looks like it will rain," Jamie chafed.

"You'd better give up riding and come in the carriage with us," Mellie suggested sensibly. "There's plenty of room for both of you," she added ungraciously, not really wanting to ride with Norwood. Just being around him raised her hackles.

"But our horses. . . ."

"Can be tethered behind the coach." Sometimes he was such a child.

There was one of those nonverbal exchanges between the viscount and his lover, a look which they seemed to understand.

"No, we'll ride on. Hopefully we can reach Rochester ahead of the rain."

Mellie shrugged. If they wanted to be soaked, it was their business. And it would be nice to get to The George and find a private bedchamber which she and Dora could share. Mellie didn't for one minute expect Jamie to share it with her. Probably the main reason he and Gerald were going on ahead was so that they'd have more time for their beastly sex together. Her lips thinned and her nostrils pinched as she remembered that grotesque scene in the dimly lighted bedroom in Paris when Jamie, inflamed from the drug she'd so naively provided, satisfied his lust with Alphonse. If Dora thought it strange that Mellie and Jamie didn't share a bed, well, there was little Mellie could do about that. Jamie might have said they should put up a pretense of sleeping together at times; but she noticed that he was in no hurry to implement his own suggestion.

Would he ever try again to have sex with her? Or was he still depending on her to take a lover to produce the desired child?

The party set off for Rochester, still many miles to the west. Depending on the weather, they might even have to break at Sittingbourne, take tea while the horses were changed. The fresh team moved along smartly, but they had gone no more than three or four miles when the sky grew as dark as night, and thunder rumbled in the distance. By now, Jamie and Norwood were long out of sight, having ridden off from The Brown Bull at speed on their rested mounts.

As the thunder came nearer, Dora cried, trembling, "Oh, milady, should we stop? What if lightning strikes a tree and it falls on the coach?"

"Have you ever known this to happen, Dora?" Mellie asked, laughing. Storms never frightened her. On the contrary, there was something exhilarating about the slashes of lightning that cut across the black, boiling clouds, and the sharp rattle of thunder made her feel alive. Even the rain from a summer thunderstorm couldn't depress her, it was too violent, too alive, to dampen her spirits. Besides, she was gleeful that Jamie and Norwood were riding somewhere ahead in this torrential downpour.

Dora covered her face with her gloved hands and shrieked at every rumble. Mellie could feel the poor girl tremble. She could have rapped on the roof of the carriage to attract the coachman's attention and asked him to stop at the first cottage where they might shelter; but Mellie felt at one with the storm and reveled in the elemental nature which was venting itself outside the carriage.

"Let me pull the curtains, milady," Dora begged; but Mellie selfishly forbade it, wanting to be able to watch the storm in all its awesome power.

She was much annoyed, then, to feel the coach slow down and come to a stop.

"Why is he not going forward?" she fretted.

"Oh, milady, maybe the road is washed away," Dora moaned. "At least if we are stopped, nothing can happen to us."

As if to make a liar of the poor, terrified abigail, there was the sound of a shot so close that both of the young women jumped.

"Milady—milady—was that? . . ."

"A shot? It certainly sounded like it," Mellie said grimly, "although it might have been a bolt of lightning striking a tree, or a branch snapping off in the storm." She was more annoyed than frightened, not knowing what was going on; but she intended to find out. Pressing her face to the glass window set into the coach door, she tried to peer out; but the wind had come up, now, swaying the standing coach with hard gusts which spattered rain so heavily on the dusty glass that it became almost opaque. She thought she could see horses moving about, but she wasn't sure.

"I think that his lordship, Viscount Triller, and his friend, Mr. Norwood, have ridden back to join us," she told Dora. "I guess the storm got to be too much for them."

"But the shot?"

"It probably was a branch cracking off, Dora," Mellie decided, which did little to reassure the maid. Just then the handle of the coach door rattled, and she added, "Ah, here they are, eager to get out of the rain. Pull your skirts close, Dora. They'll drip water all over us, and they may be muddy to boot."

Mellie leaned forward to greet her bedraggled husband. The door was pulled open, letting in a gust of rain which caught her full in the face, blinding her for just a second. "Really, Jamie," she sputtered, angry that he'd let the rain beat in on her.

Beside her, Dora let out a scream that startled Mellie so that she almost fell out of the open door. Whirling around, she discovered that someone was climbing into the coach from the opposite side, a large, burly man with dripping tricorne pulled down over squinting eyes, and a black kerchief tied over the bottom part of his face, hiding nose, mouth and chin. He clutched a long, wicked-looking pistol, and Dora cringed back against Mellie, whimpering now that she'd stopped her shrill screaming.

Snapping her head around again to her own door, Mellie found that a second highwayman, as muffled as the first, was pushing into her side of the coach. Lord Henning had been right. And that imbecile, Jamie—then she laughed. It was Jamie and Norwood, trying to play a trick on them.

"Ah, ye like us, do ye, milady," growled the one on her side. "Good, then after we takes your gold and baubles, we'll have some good romps, eh, Ned?"

The other guffawed. "Told you that empty cottage'd be a bonny place to bounce a woman. And if she screams, no one'll hear—nor find the body until we're long gone."

Dora suddenly went limp, slumping over Mellie's lap.

"Silly girl, to faint when it's only. . . ." But then Mellie saw the hot amber eyes that glittered at her above the soiled kerchief tied over his face, she really looked at the rough brown coat, the torn black trousers, the scuffed boots with rusty spurs on them.

This wasn't her husband—nor his lover! They were actually being attacked by highwaymen.

Mellie's head swam and she thought that she was going to join Dora in a state of unconsciousness. Then the villain reached out and fumbled under the flared peplum of her fitted basque traveling jacket.

"Where's yer pockets, me pretty birdie? Give me your golden guineas. . . ."

"And then he'll give yer somethin'," Ned guffawed. "Oh, ye'll remember him. Big's a stallion they claim he is. A caution with the ladies—they can't get enough of him."

Dora moaned and stirred. Mellie suddenly saw red. She wasn't going to hand over her gold to these ruffians, and she'd had her fill of "romping" with men not of her choice. She wasn't going to allow these bandits to rape her, nor Dora. Pretending to swoon, she shrieked loudly and fell toward the man who was just inside the door on her side. Her dead weight knocked him from the coach where he fell to the muddy road, striking his head on the step as he fell with the sound of a splitting ripe gourd.

"Here, now, none of that!" cried Ned, grabbing Mellie and hauling her toward him. She let her body go limp instead of resisting him, until she was practically sitting on his lap. Then, quick as a striking adder, her hand flashed out and seized his pistol. Pointing it directly at him, the round, cold end of the muzzle against his temple, she grated, "One move and I'll blow out your brains."

But the man wasn't frightened. As carelessly as if he were brushing away a horsefly, he pushed the barrel of the pistol away.

"Now, now, none of yer tricks. I likes me women full of fire, I does. It's more fun to tame 'em, hurt 'em a bit, make 'em beg fer mercy," and he pulled her close, planting a wet, sour kiss on her lips, holding her there until Mellie thought she'd surely suffocate while he used one hand to pinch and maul her breasts, forcing his hand down the front of her dress to get at her tender flesh.

In a panic, realizing how strong the highwayman was, knowing how little she could actually do if he chose to rape her, which was obviously his intent, she aimed the pistol once again, even as he kissed and pawed her, and pulled the trigger. The blast nearly shattered her eardrums. The highwayman called Ned slumped down, and Mellie saw to her horror that she'd blown a hole through his skull with bits of shattered bone and pinkish gray matter all over the wall of the coach. The robber was quite dead.

Sudden revulsion seized her and she moaned, pushing frantically at the dead body. Slowly, slowly, it slipped away from her, sliding out of the coach door. The last thing she saw were Ned's blank eyes, wide with shock, as the dead body toppled into the muddy road.

Her stomach revolted, and Mellie clung to the frame of the coach door, vomiting into the road, onto the dead body. Finally, when the spasms ceased, she fell back onto the seat, fumbling for the pocket that he'd not found, to get her sal volatile. A few whiffs restored her, and then she held the vinaigrette under Dora's nose until the abigail, roused by the pungent odor, opened her eyes.

She looked blank for a moment, then her eyes widened with horror at the huge pistol on the seat, the bits of bone and brains, the gouts of blood, on the carriage wall and seat. Dora began to moan, and her eyes rolled up in her head.

"Stop it, Dora," Mellie said sharply, thrusting the smelling salts under her nose, "stop it or I'll slap your face. We have to do something to help ourselves. There may be others in this gang of brigands." Reaching up, she rapped sharply on the roof of the coach with the butt of the highwayman's pistol. "Coachman. Where are you?" There was no answer.

"Milady," Dora said, voice quivering from shock, "there was a shot . . . the one we thought might be lightning striking a tree. . . ."

It conjured up the mental image of Ned, dead eyes staring as he'd slid out of the carriage, and Mellie quickly sniffed at the smelling salts. It wouldn't do to faint in front of Dora. She laid the pistol on the seat beside her, handy.

"I shot the one man—the other I pushed out of the coach and he hit his head."

"You shot. . . ." Dora's face went chalky, and Mellie held the vinaigrette under her nose again until the poor little abigail's eyes watered; but it kept her from fainting.

"Oh, drat," said Mellie. "Now I'll have to get out and see what has happened to our guards." She should have realized that the coachey and the footman, both armed, would have done something to protect them if possible. Unwilling to get out on the side where the man she'd shot lay dead, Mellie cautiously exited through the other door, glancing down at the other knight of the road, still crumpled where he'd fallen when she pushed him out. There was a lump as big as a goose egg on his temple, and his greasy tricorne had fallen from his equally greasy brown hair; but the kerchief still masked the bottom of his face. Mellie could see that he was breathing. She must hurry. If he regained consciousness, she and Dora could still be in serious trouble. Two horses stood on either side of their own team which were restless in the harness.

"Coachey?" There was a quaver in her voice which Mellie tried to suppress. "Guard?"

There was no answer. The rain had slacked off now, but it was exceedingly muddy in the road. Without the footman to place the stepping stool for her, Mellie knew she'd probably sink in over her slippers in the muck underfoot; but she had to find out what was wrong. Her face squeamish with distaste, she stepped gingerly down from the high coach, clinging to the door for support. As she feared, the mud oozed over her slippers, sucking at them as she stepped forward so that she could see the high coachman's box. A figure slumped forward, half off the seat. Unable to see him well, Mellie pulled up her skirts, got a precarious footing on a spoke of the front wheel, and pulled herself up so that she could see into the box. The coachman was sprawled back, a bullet hole through his head right between the eyes. The footman, beside her, had apparently been reaching for the blunderbuss when the highwayman had loomed out of the stormy gloom. He'd been hit on the back of the head. She could see blood and matted hair; but he was breathing, for the stentorian sounds rattled in his throat, a frightening sound. Mellie realized that he needed medical attention immediately.

Then Dora's timid voice called, "What has happened, milady?"

There was no point in trying to spare the girl. "The coachman is shot to death, the guard badly wounded."

"And what of Kenneth, milady?"

"Kenneth?" Good heavens, she'd forgotten all about Jamie's valet.

"He's not up here."

"I think he was to ride in the basket with the boxes."

Wearily, Mellie climbed back down to the muddy road and crept along, clinging to the side of the berlin, until she could peer into the luggage basket on the back. There, laid out like a corpse on a bier, face white, but obviously alive and breathing, was Jamie's valet. At first thinking the man had been wounded, Mellie tried to see if there was blood on his clothing, or signs of bullet holes. Then she remembered that she and Dora had heard only one shot earlier, the one that had killed the coachey. As Kenneth didn't seem to have been bashed over the head, Mellie came to the conclusion that he had fainted. In annoyance she called to Dora, "Hand me my vinaigrette, please. This silly creature has fainted dead away like a woman."

A few whiffs of the smelling salts, and Kenneth came around, white-faced and glassy-eyed.

"A lot of protection you gave us!" Mellie slashed at him, not waiting for him to fully regain his senses. "The coachman shot dead, the guard clubbed—and you faint!"

"Coachman . . . shot . . ." His eyes rolled up and he slumped back in another swoon.

Oh, let him lie there in the rain, Mellie thought, furious. She crawled back into the coach momentarily to get out of the wet. "Kenneth has fainted," she said. "It's up to us to help ourselves. Do you know where we are, Dora?"

The abigail, taking courage from her mistress, peered out into the now lightening gloom. "I think there's a village not far ahead, milady. And if there isn't, we might as well make for Sittingbourne, rather than go back to Faversham. His lordship is ahead of us, not behind. Surely, when we are late, he'll ride back to see why we're delayed."

Mellie wasn't at all sure that Jamie would come looking for them, but she didn't suggest this to Dora who was already upset enough.

"Very well, I shall drive on to the village."

Dora's eyes opened saucer wide. "Y-you, milady? Drive? The berlin?"

"Yes, the berlin. How else shall we get help, Dora?"

"Someone will come along. . . ."

"That's what gave us all this terrible trouble in the first place— someone came along. I don't choose to sit here and wait for more highwaymen to accost us. I shall drive, and you shall hold the blunderbuss."

Dora shrieked, and crawled back in the corner of the carriage as far away from her mistress as she could get. "M-me? The blunder—oh, no, milady. I'm scared to touch it."

"Touch it you shall. I can't take you up on the box with me, because there's already the dead coachman and the guard there, and we're not strong enough to move them. I'll just have to find room. If that ninny, Kenneth, were worthy of the name *man*, he'd be up in that box holding the reins. But if a hare hopped across the road, he'd probably have apoplexy. No, I'll drive. You'll sit here with that gun. If I shout, you point it out of the window. Understand?''

''Yes, milady,'' Dora said faintly, not sure whether she was more afraid of the blunderbuss or her mistress.

Mellie got out into the rain which was pouring hard once again and slogged to the highwaymen's horses. Catching the reins, she made them fast to the basket where Kenneth lay moaning as the rain beat down on his face. Looking at him in disgust, Mellie struggled back up into the box of the berlin. The guard was still unconscious. If she could dislodge the coachey's body, she'd have more room; but although she hadn't minded pushing the dead highwayman from the coach, she couldn't bring herself to do the same to a Henning Hall coachman. She scooped up the blunderbuss and leaning far over to the side, called, ''Dora! Take this musket. Instantly!''

Two reluctant hands came out of the coach door, the gun was pulled inside, and then Dora closed the door, shutting herself in.

From where she sat, perched on a few inches of seat between the dead coachman and the wounded footman, Mellie was appalled at how far down the road looked. Well, she'd just look ahead, not down. She had to do something. If they sat there, the coach might mire down in the mud, they might be accosted by more robbers, they might even, God forbid, be struck by lightning or a falling tree. She picked up the reins. Mellie had occasionally driven a pony cart when she was still at court and she and her mother wanted a little drive through St. James's Park. And she rode, of course. But she'd never driven a team of four hitched to such a heavy carriage as the berlin. Very well, today was the first time! She picked up the reins and shook them. Nothing happened. ''Giddap!'' she called. The horses might have been dead, for all they responded. The coachey's long whip was in the stand beside him. Taking it out, Mellie found that she could scarcely hold it, it was so long; but she wound the reins about her neck, then caught up the heavy whip with both hands and, after a false try or two, managed to crack it over the flanks of the near right-wheel horse. Improving with practice, she next flicked the lead horse, and finally managed to get the team to lean into the harness and start the heavy coach to rolling along the rain-slicked, muddy, bumpy road.

If the village Dora remembered had been any distance ahead, Mellie might never have made it; but fortunately the first thatched stone cottage loomed out of the rain in less than a mile.

Hoping to attract attention, Mellie kept shouting, ''Help! Someone help us! Help!'' but the noise of the rain and the wind carried her voice away. Soon the cottages were closer together, although no one was outside in the rain. Any other time she would have met several other coaches, or passed riders, on this busy Dover Road; but everyone seemed to have chosen to sit out the storm in a cozy tavern. As she thought this, Mellie saw ahead, arching across the road, an inn sign, swinging and creaking in the summer storm. She'd be able to get help here.

Pulling on the reins with all her strength, she managed to get the team headed toward the inn courtyard from the rutted road. As if they were eager, too, to interrupt this rainy journey, the horses turned willingly into the cobbled yard and stopped of their own accord even before the ostlers came running out.

"Help, we've been attacked by highwaymen," she shrilled to the first of the boys.

Then, as if the knowledge that help was now at hand released her, Mellie slumped back onto the coachman's seat in a swoon.

CHAPTER TWENTY-SIX

Mellie opened her eyes to a familiar face. She thought that it was the night of the masquerade ball, that she had dreamed everything she'd experienced since then; for looking down at her was her nemesis, Lord Alistair Densbury.

She was just ready to make some cutting remark, to let him know that she had no intention of allowing him in her bed, when he said, "Ah, she's reviving. Are you feeling a bit better, Mellie? After such a ghastly encounter. . . ."

Then it had happened?

Feeling like the heroine of a French novel, Mellie said, "Where am I? What are you doing here, Alistair?"

"You're in a private parlor of The Hobbled Donkey in the village of Hunter's Green. I am here because I just happened to be having a pot of ale in their taproom when one of the ostlers rushed in to say that highwaymen had attacked a coach. I rushed out with the other drunks, and there you were, draped gracefully over a dead coachey and a footman with a terrible headache—and your abigail was screeching something and waving a blunderbuss at everyone in sight. Then, as a final bit of trim on the pudding, there was Jamie's man, Kenneth, asleep in the basket." He shook his head, and his hazel eyes gleamed wickedly. "Upon my word, Mellie, you do get yourself into the most unusual predicaments."

"It's no joking matter," she said crossly, and tried to sit up. Densbury slipped an arm around her for support, which she found she needed, as her head was spinning.

"Where's Dora? I want my vinaigrette," she said petulantly.

Densbury made a beckoning gesture and a buxom barmaid in a low-cut gown of maroon came forward with smelling salts.

"Your abigail's with cook, milady," she murmured. "She's havin' the vapors, she is."

"Well, so am I," Mellie snapped. "Abigails aren't supposed to have vapors."

"Yes, milady. I'll get her, milady."

"Bring some wine first," Densbury ordered.

He waited until Mellie was sipping a glass of claret before he asked, "Why in God's name were you traveling without suitable escort, Mellie? The roads aren't safe these days. I know Jamie's witless about such things; but I do think Lord Henning would have had more sense."

"Don't blame Lord Henning," she said, flying to his defense. Then, afraid that Densbury would suspect something, she hastened to add, "He wanted us to travel in two coaches, for safety. But Jamie and that miserable Norwood insisted on riding."

There was frank alarm on the young lord's face. "Were they killed by the highwaymen, too?"

"No such good luck!" she said, and Densbury burst out laughing. She could have smacked his foolish face. "It's not funny, Alistair," she snapped. "If they'd been riding with us, those two villains wouldn't have dared stop us."

"And where is Jamie by now?"

"God knows. He meant to stop at The George in Rochester. Claimed he'd get better accommodations for our party if he rode ahead." Then, noticing for the first time the state of her clothing, Mellie cried, "My suit! It's ruined. And my slippers. Where are they?" She peered down at her silk-shod toes in dismay.

"I sent the maid off with them to dry them by the fire and try to brush them clean. What did you do, walk all the way from Faversham?"

Reaction set in. "Oh, Alistair, I killed a man! I shot him dead!" She shuddered, blanching at the ugly memory.

Densbury took one look at her, snatched up the wine bottle, and poured her another glass. "Here, drink this."

She drank the claret obediently, then sighed. "Now what? Will they string me up in Tyburn for murder?"

"Don't be ridiculous, Mellie. You were defending yourself. But give me the details, so we can send the constables off as soon as possible."

Quickly she told him of the dreadful affair.

"And one man was still alive? One of the thieves?"

"He was breathing. Frankly, milord, I didn't bother to render assistance. By now he may be dead. If so it will save the hangman the bother of putting a noose about his wicked neck."

"Always charitable, eh, Mellie?"

Her eyes narrowed with anger. "I'll reserve my charity for those who deserve it, not those who come to rob me and rape me." She looked him right in the eye as she said this.

He had the good grace to look chagrined. As if wanting to change the subject in a hurry, Densbury said, "Let me go talk to the constable. I'll tell him what you've told me. He and some men can ride back and pick up the one robber's body, and see if the other one will live to hang."

"His name was Ned," she said, half to herself. "The one I shot. That's what his companion called him. I've never killed anyone before, Alistair."

Suddenly the tears streamed down her face, and she let them flow unchecked. She was not sorrowing for the dead thief. He deserved his fate. Rather she was crying for herself. Her life was to have been so good once she met Lord Henning; but what had happened? Married to a member of the third sex, afraid that Jamie would kill her lover, and now she'd been driven to murder a man. Very well, she was defending herself. No one would place any blame on her. But Mellie knew that for many a long year, there would be times she'd not be able to sleep at night, with the ghost of Ned, dead eyes staring at her, to trouble her rest. She had done what she had to do in killing him; but it was not a pleasant thing, nor one of which she would ever boast.

While Densbury was gone, Mellie tried to brush some of the mud from her bedraggled traveling suit. She discovered that the top button was missing from the jacket, no doubt having been ripped off when Ned pawed her bosom. The suit was ruined; but until she could change clothes, it would have to do. She hoped Dora got over her vapors soon. She could use some help.

Soon Densbury was back. "I've sent off messengers to The George at Rochester, and also to Henning Hall."

"Henning Hall! Why did you do that?" Henning would be livid when he heard what had happened.

"Because the coachman is dead, and the footman has a cracked skull. They're Henning's men, Mellie. He'll have to see to them."

"Of course. I wasn't thinking. . . ." What would Henning do when he learned that Jamie had deserted her to ride on ahead with his lover? Then she had a sudden, very bad idea. Could it have been planned? Had Jamie arranged for the carriage to be stopped by those villains? But why? Surely not for a small share in the money she carried. No, it was absurd to think of such a thing. If it had been Lord Henning, himself, who'd been attacked . . . the thought frightened her. She hoped this wouldn't put ideas into Jamie's head. He'd even mentioned the fact that his father might be killed by a knight of the road one of those times when he was bemoaning the fact that Henning wouldn't turn over his inheritance to him at once. Now Mellie could see how easy it could be.

"I told the messengers to say you'd be at Falconhurst," Densbury added. "You can scarcely continue your journey until you are calmer."

"Falconhurst? I thought you said we were in Hunter's Green."

"No, no, my home, Falconhurst. It's not far from here. You'll be more comfortable than you'd be here at The Donkey."

"No, I think I'd better. . . ."

"I swear I shall not annoy you, Mellie." He laughed, rubbing his head. "What did you hit me with, anyway?" He reached over, took one of her slender, white hands in his. "You must have an iron hand hidden under that soft flesh, my dear Mellie. And all I wanted was a romp in bed."

She snatched her hand away from him. "I hit you with a wine carafe, if you must know. And I prefer inviting men to share my bed, not having them creep in like bedbugs."

"Then I'm lucky you didn't shoot me as you did the highwayman," he joked. Seeing how distressed she was, he added, "Sorry, Mellie, it isn't a joking matter, the highwayman."

"Very well, I accept both your apology and your invitation, as long as it doesn't involve sharing my bed with you." She added with malice, "I hope Jamie does come back looking for us and can't find us. It would serve him right to worry."

"Don't count on it," was Densbury's dry reply. "Oh, begging your pardon, milady. I shouldn't speak ill of your beloved husband."

The look she gave him spoke volumes.

"Let me make all necessary arrangements. Meanwhile, I'll have the innkeeper send you in some food. I think it would help to steady your nerves."

"And send that silly Dora to me, too, please. If I can shoot a man and be recovered by now, she has no right to prolong her vapors!" Mellie said with considerable asperity.

Densbury amazed her. After what had happened the night of the masked ball, she'd think he wouldn't have the gall ever to speak to her again. Yet he was here, taking charge, actually helping her, and he even managed to joke about that fiasco in her bedchamber.

She really should be grateful to him. If he hadn't tried to force her, she'd not have fled to Henning's arms.

Her thoughts quickly changed to happy memories of what had happened with Henning, the searing, soaring, all-consuming passionate love. Would Ritchie come flying to her aid when he heard from Densbury's messenger? Or would he delegate the responsibility for the dead and wounded servants to his bailiff, while he stayed at Henning Hall? *If he comes here,* Mellie thought, *I'll know that his cool, impersonal manner with me is all a pose to hide from the world the fact that he loves his son's wife.*

Wife! She was more truly Ritchie's wife than Jamie's. If only she dared tell Lord Henning the truth, that her marriage with Jamie had never been consummated, nor was it likely to be. What would he do then? Would he arrange an annulment and take her for his own bride? Oh, how she longed for such a happy ending to her story. Surely she deserved some happiness.

By the time Densbury had made all suitable arrangements, it was late in the day. There was no sign of Jamie. Was he so engrossed with Gerald Norwood that he was oblivious to the fact that Mellie should have arrived at The George in Rochester long since?

And when would Lord Henning get the word of the attempted robbery and the dire consequences of that affair? It would take a rider on horseback several hours to get back to Henning Hall. Then more long hours for Henning to come to Falconhurst, if he chose to do that. Falconhurst, which was situated several miles east of Sittingbourne, was just about equidistant from Rochester and Henning Hall beyond Canterbury. Presuming that Alistair had sent messengers in both directions at about the same time, and further postulating that Henning and Jamie would set out at once for Falconhurst, father and son could arrive simultaneously.

Mellie grinned hugely. It would be interesting to be there when the two Jamison men met. Even if Henning weren't concerned solely for her safety, there was the poor dead coachman, and the wounded footman who might never recover properly, according to the doctor Densbury had called in. Lord Henning could scarcely be pleased to lose one or two of his servants because Jamie disobeyed orders.

He'll come here, Mellie thought. *He'll have to come.* But then what? Would he take her back to Henning Hall, or allow her to continue to London? If she didn't manage to keep close to Jamie, she'd have no way of finding out his plans to dispose of his father. Thinking about it, Mellie had to admit that it sounded terribly melodramatic. If she told anyone that Jamie was planning his father's death, they'd have her committed to Bedlam. Henning himself hadn't listened to her warnings.

As a last resort, could she kill Jamie to protect her lover? It was a dreadful thought, one she wished immediately to erase from her mind; but it persisted, a little coiled viper, ready to strike. Kill Jamie. She'd already killed one man today. Just thinking about that ghastly experience made Mellie's gorge rise. Apparently she became pale, also, for Dora, who was stewing about, in and out, fretting until they got underway for Falconhurst, came into the private parlor just then, gave Mellie one look, and whipped out the sal volatile.

"Pale as a ghost, that's what you are, milady," Dora said. "Shouldn't you lie back with your feet up on this ottoman?" She pushed a clumsy, overstuffed stool of red plush in front of the settee where Mellie sat. Dora had unpacked one of Mellie's boxes and had gotten out a fresh suit for her to wear. It was of deep purple wool which clashed horribly with the furnishings of the parlor at The Hobbled Donkey; but Mellie was glad to be out of the muddy, bloodstained outfit. She hoped that Dora would burn it once they got to the house in London. She certainly never wanted to wear it again. And her ruined shoes were drying, but even Dora said they'd never be wearable again.

"I don't want to be fussed over, Dora." Poor girl, if she knew what murderous thoughts were going through her mistress's mind, she'd need the smelling salts for herself.

"Do you think we'll be leaving for Falconhurst soon, milady? If we wait many more hours, it will be pitch-dark and I'll see a highwayman behind every bush and tree."

"I'm sure that Lord Densbury will provide us with a suitably armed escort, Dora. Quit dithering. Be glad we have somewhere to go for tonight instead of having to take on an unknown coachey and drive to Rochester."

"Kenneth says he's going to leave his lordship, the Viscount Triller, milady. Claims he didn't take the position to fight off highwaymen." Dora snickered. "He fought hard, didn't he, milady?"

"Well, at least we have one little joke about an otherwise horrifying, tragic experience, Dora."

"And now we're going to Falconhurst. I've been talking with cook. She says it is a magnificent house. Will we be there long, milady?"

"I don't know. It depends on the viscount, and Lord Henning. Lord Densbury has sent riders to alert both of them."

"Oh, milady, his lordship, the earl, he'll be in a rage, I daresay."

Mellie thought it very possible.

CHAPTER TWENTY-SEVEN

Mellie first saw Falconhurst by the light of a gibbous moon. She and Dora were in the coach from Henning Hall, but Densbury had provided a new coachman and another footman. Poor Kenneth still rode in the basket, complaining bitterly the entire way from The Hobbled Donkey to Densbury's ancestral estate.

Densbury himself chose to ride inside with Mellie and Dora, keeping up light conversation in an attempt to take Mellie's mind off the appalling adventures of the day.

"Mother will be delighted to greet you, Mellie," he assured her. "She's not been too well, and doesn't get out much; so she enjoys visitors."

Mellie wondered if Alistair had dared tell his mother, the Duchess of Amberton, her history. Hopefully not. She knew he'd gossiped to Jamie and Norwood about her, an unforgivable offense; yet here she was, accepting his hospitality, and thankful for it.

The carriage turned off the Dover Road and traveled along a tree-lined approach to the estate of the Duke of Amberton and his son, Alistair, Marquis of Densbury. Under the spreading elms, most of the moonlight was screened out, making an eerie, faintly lit tunnel of the ancient trees. Then, almost without warning, the road led through a high stone arch and Falconhurst lay before them, the moonlight casting a sheen of silver over the ancient stone walls. The main block of the house bulked dark against the sky, three stories topped by a battlement and many chimneys. The graceful proportions were augmented by bays on either side, and curved colonnades led the eye to the lower wings. It was larger than Henning Hall, from what Mellie could see by moonlight.

The entrance was lighted by flaming torches, and the windows of the ground floor blazed with lights from hundreds of wax tapers.

"I see we are expected," Densbury said.

"It seems most discourteous to disturb the Duke and Duchess at this late hour. It must be well past midnight, Alistair.'' Mellie longed for a comfortable bed, so that sleep could wipe away the terrors of the day. Would she ever again enter a copse along the road without expecting a highwayman to block the way, pistol in hand? Thinking of the episode, she shuddered.

''Is the air too chill, milady?'' Dora asked, noticing her mistress shiver.

''Here, let me lay this shawl over your lap,'' Densbury suggested, taking up a soft woolen blanket from the seat beside him. He leaned over to wrap Mellie in the warm shawl, sliding a hand along one thigh as if by accident. Then he touched her hand, whether by accident or design, she could not tell.

''Good God, your hands are like ice! Well, we'll soon have you indoors, my dear. And I'll make sure that a footman lays a fire in your bedchamber. Nights are cool, now.''

''That will be comforting, Alistair.'' It wasn't a cold night, but she felt chilled to the very bone.

''I'll leave word with the butler that you aren't to be disturbed, even if both Jamie and Lord Henning arrive before morning,'' he promised. ''After today, you need sleep.''

Mellie couldn't understand the change in Densbury. Previously he'd been an outright cad. Now he was solicitous as a lover. Her mouth twisted cynically. No doubt this was a new approach to her bed. He'd had no luck the other way. Well, Alistair, Marquis of Densbury, was going to be in for a big disappointment if he thought she'd yield to him now. Not after Henning.

Would he come here? She hoped and prayed that he would; yet Mellie was all too aware that a confrontation between Jamie and his father now, over the trouble with the highwaymen, could turn ugly.

''Jamie may not come back here,'' she said bluntly. ''He and Norwood may be too busy to bother with me.''

Densbury gave her a startled look, then glanced out of the corner of his eye at Dora, who sat quiet as a mouse, taking it all in. Mellie had quite forgotten that the abigail rode with them. Oh, well, if Dora hadn't caught on by now that something was amiss with the newlyweds, she was stupider than Mellie thought.

Then, gallantly, Densbury said, ''Ah, he'll leave you to me, then.'' A mischievous grin made him appear very young. ''I'll make sure that there's no wine carafe in your bedchamber.''

Drily she told him, ''I can always use a silver candlestick—or a shoe heel—or a china chamber pot, if necessary.''

"Upon my word, Mellie, you should be in the army. You'd have routed the French in short order."

"Just don't forget that," she cautioned.

It was as she'd thought. Densbury hadn't abandoned his campaign to get into her bed, he'd only changed tactics. *I'll pay you back for what you've done to me,* she promised herself. But she didn't let any of her feelings show in the smile she gave him. Let him think he was winning her, if he wanted to. The disappointment would only be that much greater when he found she had no intention of taking him as a lover.

Perhaps, when Jamie got the message that she was being taken to Falconhurst, he wouldn't come for her at all. He'd be only too happy to have her exposed to Densbury's blandishments, hoping that Densbury would win her, and do Jamie's duty for him. *While Jamie takes his pleasure with Norwood,* she thought bitterly. *Oh, Ritchie, your plan is doomed, and was from the start. Why didn't I refuse to marry Jamie when you told me that was why you'd rescued me from Mrs. Mudridge? I could have told you that I wouldn't go through with such a travesty of a marriage. I could have left Henning Hall; but I hated poverty, I was sick of grubby living, and so I truly sold myself, more so than when I was in the brothel.*

Her pensive thoughts were interrupted by their arrival at the massive entrance porch with marble columns supporting the flat roof.

Bowing servants ushered them into the beautiful entrance hall. At the farther end, Ionic columns supported a small balcony with a beautiful metal railing, and niches held vases of the finest porcelain, their designs in muted colors on a white background. It was a gracious room, even more elegant than Lord Henning's lovely home.

The butler murmured something to Lord Densbury, who said, "My mother would be pleased to greet you briefly in her boudoir, Mellie. Then I'll have you and your abigail shown to your room. I know you long for rest."

Mellie was suddenly conscious of the fact that she was not impeccably groomed. "I look terrible," she murmured.

"Mother understands what has happened. And you look stunning, Mellie. You would even if you were wearing the drab homespun of a milkmaid."

"Thank you, milord." There was a mocking note she was unable to keep out of her voice, and Densbury heard it. The smile that lit his face was just as mocking as her voice. *At least we understand each other*, Mellie thought.

Then Densbury escorted her up an exquisite spiral staircase off the entrance hall to the first floor, leading her along a wide corridor well-lit with candles.

"It still seems late to call on your lady mother."

"She doesn't sleep well. Don't worry. If she hadn't wanted to see you tonight, she'd have said so. Mother can be quite plain-spoken."

Then he tapped on a white lacquered double door. A pretty young maid opened it, dropping a curtsy to them. "Her Grace is expecting you, milord." She dimpled prettily. Her hair was as blonde as Mellie's but her eyes were brown, not blue. She had a full-blown figure, much of which was showing in her low-cut, green-striped gown. Mellie noticed that Densbury was eyeing the maid almost greedily, and she was sure the maid knew it and invited those hot eyes to assess her charms.

"You are looking well, Ettie," he said, bringing a blush to the peaches and cream complexion. "Now, if you'll tell Her Grace that we are here. . . ."

They went through a beautiful sitting room directly into the Duchess of Amberton's boudoir. It was a striking room with Gothic windows set deep in thick walls. Densbury's mother was sitting up in her bed which was tucked into one corner of the room. The canopy of blue and white brocade was draped from a small half-round cornice of dark blue, and the lining of the same midnight shade made a fitting backdrop for the duchess. She sat propped up by a mountain of swansdown pillows as if she were royalty granting an audience. Mellie swept her lowest curtsy as Densbury said, "Mother, may I present Melusina, the Viscountess Triller."

The duchess wore an exquisite robe of the same warm apricot color as the walls. Her head was completely covered by a round cap of the finest lace, with lappets over her ears, and a bow under her chin. Densbury said she was not well; but she was painted as if for a ball, and her eyes, the same hot, hazel eyes her son used to such advantage with the ladies, burned into Mellie's brain.

"Sit down, milady." Mellie sat on a small chair of polished mahogany and tried to put on a social smile. "I understand you killed a man today."

It was so abrupt that Mellie thought she'd fall off the chair from shock. The duchess was leaning forward, eyes glittering, lips moist as if she'd been licking them in anticipation.

"I get out so seldom," Densbury's mother went on, her words rushing as if they couldn't wait to be said. "So I look forward to hearing of other people's excitements."

Mellie had heard of evil creatures called vampires who sucked their victims' blood. She was sure that the Duchess of Amberton had hidden fangs. How ghoulish she was!

"I would prefer a quieter life, myself, madam," Mellie said rather coldly.

"No, no, you must live life to the fullest, experience everything possible!" cried the duchess. "And I must live vicariously from your adventures. So, tell me exactly how you felt after you'd killed this highwayman. Exactly!"

Mellie was very tired, emotionally drained from the horrors of the day, so she said the exact truth, as asked. "I felt ill, Your Grace. I leaned out of the carriage and vomited until I was bringing up nothing but bile."

"Oh, really? I should have thought it might be quite exhilarating to kill a man."

"I assure you, it is not." Mellie remembered the spattered blood, bits of bone and hair, and brains. "It is an experience I could have done without."

But it was as if the duchess wasn't hearing her. "Murder. To commit murder. The ultimate sensation, even greater than having a man in you—to kill a man. Marvelous."

Mellie's lips tightened and she had difficulty in keeping her temper with this older woman. *She's as mad as my mother, but she's rich enough to stay out of Bedlam.*

"This man you killed—you shot him?" She turned to her son who was leaning indolently against the chimneypiece. "You did say she shot him? That was the message I received."

"Yes, Mama, she shot him. With his own pistol, I gather. Our little Mellie is quite adept at defending herself."

"Not always," she said with considerable bitterness. Who knew that better than Alistair?

"Did the man bleed much?" the duchess persisted, her face avid. "Where did the bullet strike him? Did he die instantly? Cry out? Imagine, knowing a lady who has shot a man. I shall be the envy of all my friends."

"Your Grace, I only wish it could have been you who killed the highwayman, and not I,'' Mellie said quietly but with considerable dignity.

"Oh, yes, that would be splendid! But I fear I shall never be so fortunate as to be able to kill a man."

Had she known what her hostess was like, Mellie would gladly have stayed at The Hobbled Donkey rather than come to Falconhurst with Densbury. The experience with the bandit had been shattering enough without having to describe it in all its gory detail to this hideous woman.

The duchess seemed to sense that Mellie was not going to supply her with any of the sordid facts of the killing. She leaned back on the pillows, murmured faintly, "I am very tired, now," and closed her eyes, an obvious dismissal.

"Goodnight, Your Grace," Mellie said, rising and looking around as if she wanted to make sure she could escape from the cloying imprisonment of the room.

Densbury walked across to the bed, leaned down and kissed his mother on the forehead, murmured, "Goodnight, Mama, sleep well, now," and led Mellie from the suite.

Once outside the door, Mellie said with considerable asperity, "I should like to retire now, if you would be good enough to call my abigail."

"You wouldn't care to share my bed?" He didn't touch her, but the look he gave her was almost tangible. All too easily she imagined his demanding hands on her body.

"Alistair, if that is why you brought me here, if that is your idea of hospitality, then have my coach prepared at once and I shall go, with Dora, driving myself if necessary, back to that little inn where you found me."

It didn't seem to bother Densbury in the least that she was so annoyed with him. He only smiled, shrugged expressively, and murmured, "Well, it was worth a try. You might have said yes. I'll just have to make do tonight with Ettie."

He extended a hand to escort her back through the maze of opulent corridors filled with choice pieces of furniture, the walls hung with paintings and tapestries, until he came to her own guest chamber.

"I think they've put your abigail in the dressing room on a pallet for the night, as she doesn't know the house and might have difficulty in finding her way about."

"That is quite satisfactory. Thank you, milord."

"And you don't wish to be disturbed if Jamie arrives?"

"He'll keep until morning."

"I daresay." Densbury made a leg, then said, as Mellie was opening the door to her chamber, "You really should take a lover, Mellie. Everyone knows about Jamie. No one would think a thing about it. You are a normal young woman, and I'm sure you need a man. I'm just as sure that Jamie isn't giving you what you need. I understand that your father-in-law is expecting you to produce an heir—is he that blind, Mellie?"

"I don't care to discuss my father-in-law with you."

"As you like. But remember, if you do take a lover—which is the only way out of your dilemma—do drop me a line. I might well be available."

It infuriated Mellie. "You surprise me, milord. I thought I was not a satisfactory bed partner. As I recall, the only time you shared my bed, you demanded your money back from your dear friend, Mrs. Mudridge, may God rot her wicked soul."

Any other gentleman would have been demolished by her words; but nothing seemed to repress Lord Densbury. With that smile on his face, that wicked gleam in his eyes, he countered, "But apparently you became quite adept at your profession, from what various of my friends told me. Just my bad luck not to go back to Mother M's before you left."

"Oh, you are impossible."

She went inside, closed the door harder than was necessary, and when she found a great brass key in the lock, she turned it, making sure that it rattled against the metal so that Densbury would know she'd locked the door in his face.

No matter whether Jamie came to Falconhurst or not, Mellie was determined to leave tomorrow even if, as she had threatened, she had to drive the coach herself.

CHAPTER TWENTY-EIGHT

Breakfast with the Duchess of Amberton was a command performance, one that Mellie would gladly have ignored if she hadn't felt obligated to show courtesy to her hostess. It was nearly eleven when a footman came with the invitation to have chocolate with Her Grace. Densbury was nowhere in sight when she was escorted into her ladyship's boudoir once again. This morning the duchess was sitting at a dressing table while her abigail dressed her hair. Mellie was given a chair nearby, with a small tray of breakfast set on a drum table beside her.

"Ah, good morning, my dear. You seem quite well this morning, as if the terrors of yesterday had flown." Then she picked up an ivory comb and rapped her dresser's knuckles. "Imbecile. You are pulling."

"Sorry, milady," mumbled the poor woman.

"Your husband, the viscount, has not arrived?"

"If he has, I have not been notified." Mellie didn't tell the duchess that she'd given express orders not to be disturbed even if Jamie did get there before she woke.

"Such a strange marriage. You don't mind my saying that, do you, my dear?" Again that avid light was in the hazel eyes which were the only feature she shared with her son. "Jamie has been the talk of London. His mother hated men, you know." She cackled in glee. "I would have liked Ritchie Jamison for myself, but he chose Isabella instead because her father was Duke of Rothfield. She and I had gone to Miss Zinn's Select School for Young Ladies in Canterbury. I knew she wasn't for a lusty young man like Ritchie Jamison—you should have heard her tales of woe to me. I'd not let any grass grow under my feet once Henning was out of my grasp, but married Amberton, which made me a duchess rather than a mere countess! Oh, you wouldn't believe how she complained about what she delicately called his 'animal nature.' All his talk was about having a son—and he was determined not to waste any

222

time. She moaned about his beastly behavior every night—and often in the morning when she woke up, there he was, ready and waiting. She prayed for pregnancy, so that she could escape such an ardent husband. To hasten it, she took up with Carstairs."

"But if she didn't like men. . . ."

The duchess winked, an altogether obscene expression. "She hated Henning so by then that she gloated over cuckolding him. The moment she conceived, she broke off with Carstairs—and ordered Henning from her bed! Cleverly, of course. Told him that any further coupling might make her miscarry. And Ritchie was such a fool about having an heir that he allowed her to get away with such nonsense. I told her that Amberton expected me to satisfy him, even though I was carrying a child by then, too. I explained to her that there were various ways she could do this—but she said what I suggested was revolting! So, he should have married me. I'd have given him all the tumbling in bed he wanted!"

Mellie was disgusted at this loathsome woman, but the duchess wasn't finished with her history of Henning and his reluctant bride. "Isabella was very discreet with Carstairs. She was afraid of Henning, and well she might be, he's quite a violent man in his own quiet way—what was I saying? Drat you!" and she turned and slapped at her abigail. "Does your abigail pull your hair, my dear?"

"Sometimes, Your Grace."

"It is most annoying. And it interrupts my train of thought most dreadfully."

Unkindly, Mellie wondered if the duchess could keep any continuity to her conversations, she seemed so addled. Yet Mellie wanted to hear more about the late Countess of Henning, try to fathom why any woman would leave Ritchie by choice. It seemed unbelievable that a woman wouldn't be roused by Ritchie's ardent lovemaking.

"Where was I, my dear?"

"You were talking about the Countess of Henning."

"That's right, and the dreadful fellow, Lord Carstairs, with whom she had an affair." With one of her bird-swift movements, she whirled away from her mirror to face Mellie, much to her abigail's dismay. "I hear that Jamie looks just like Carstairs."

Mellie refused to be drawn.

"Henning was determined to have an heir. But he should never have let her raise the boy. Turned him into a mama's darling. Why ever did you marry him? Are you also peculiar, sexually, I mean? I

know there are such women, too. In fact, one of the mistresses at
the Select School . . . but that's another tale. But if you are one of
those, why would my son want to get you into bed? Oh, don't deny
it, Melusina. I may call you Melusina? Isn't that the Maypole's
name?'' She didn't wait for an answer, but plunged ahead. ''Do
drink your chocolate. And there's more toast and marmalade, if
you wish. But you didn't answer me. Do you hate men?''

''No, Your Grace. I try not to hate anyone.'' *But I could learn
to hate you as easily as I hate your son*, Mellie added silently. The
duchess was an old witch!

''Then why marry Jamie?'' the duchess persisted.

''There are many reasons for marriage, milady.''

''True, true. I certainly didn't marry for love. My father made
all the arrangements. He didn't even know I wanted Henning. This
was the usual melding of bloodlines and estates. So you don't love
your husband?''

''I didn't say that, Your Grace.''

''Actually, you don't say much of anything, Melusina.''

Mellie caught the look on the abigail's face, and had to cough
delicately to hide the sudden smile which the woman's comical
expression brought. How could anyone say anything with the
duchess gabbling on and on and on?

Fortunately, a footman interrupted them just then, or the wicked
woman might well have gone on questioning Mellie about the intimate details of her marriage. *What would the old hag say if I told
her the truth?* Mellie wondered. *Would she want her son to be a
party to Jamie's infamous scheme for producing the heir my
darling longs to see?*

The footman murmured something to the duchess, who clapped
her hands in glee. ''Show him up immediately. And bring more
chocolate. This has gotten cold. And more toast for his lordship.''
The footman left and the duchess smiled coyly at Mellie. ''Ah, to
be young and longed for. You have a visitor, my dear. When Alistair said he was sending out messengers, I thought that someone
might respond by this evening—but such devotion! Already!''

Mellie's heart missed a beat. Lord Henning was here. He'd
come. She hadn't been sure—she'd hoped against hope—but he
was here! Perhaps he'd insist on traveling to London with her; and
he'd be in a carriage, so she blissfully could ride with him in the
privacy of their coach.

Then Mellie realized that the duchess was peering avidly at her,
as if to siphon off some of her joyous emotion for herself. She truly